PRAISE FOR ALISON PICK AND *FAR TO GO*

"*Far to Go* is clean, crisp, and unencumbered. Pick never dwells for too long in an image or metaphor, and she creates small moments that are both lovely and frightening . . . It's deftly structured and the storytelling is seamless . . . *Far to Go* appears poised to gain a wide and significant readership, and deservedly so." — Steven Galloway, *Globe and Mail*

"Alison Pick brings her award-winning poetic sensibilities to a difficult historical subject . . . There are lines here perfect in their despair and desolation. The hopelessness and fear is conveyed in typical Pick style — with both a light hand and a punch to the gut. Pick successfully hinges together the complex narrative twists with historical records, letters, and fragments of history." — *The Walrus*

"There's a lot of very good fiction coming out of Canada at the moment and Alison Pick's emotionally powerful second novel is up there with the best of it . . . Pick's book is never less than psychologically convincing: it deftly conveys both the sense of gathering storm and the denial and self-deceit of those facing it. A potential classic in the making that deserves to be on every reading list." — *Financial Times*

"[A] fast-paced, suspenseful, moving, and unique tale about one Czechoslovakian family's experiences on the eve of the Holocaust and the ramifications of those experiences decades later . . . complex, multi-dimensional, and memorable." — *Winnipeg Free Press*

"[A] spare, powerful novel . . . intimate and strangely lovely . . . It is bewildered six-year-old Pepik, and his harrowing journey, that encapsulates the loss and hope and heartbreak that is the life-blood of this extraordinary story." — *Daily Mail*

"A poignant work that brims with feeling . . . compelling . . . Pick's gorgeous writing is to be savoured: her prose is enhanced by a poet's sensibility. She creates a richly imagined, sensuous world where flavours and aromas waft through the pages and every detail is vividly drawn . . . Ultimately, the aching need to belong emerges as the emotional pulse of this deeply felt novel." — *Quill & Quire*

"A nuanced and layered portrait of betrayal . . . What makes this novel special is not so much its storyline as Pick's challenging, even audacious way of recounting it . . . compelling and fully realized . . . An intriguing experiment in the art of storytelling. *Far to Go* explores the ways in which truths and facts can be assembled, reassembled, and jiggled this way and that, like so many fragments of stained glass inside a kaleidoscope." — *Montreal Gazette*

"[A] multilayered narrative, a tale of betrayals large and small . . . Pick spins a mesmerizing story, threading the personal with the political, the mysterious with the factual. It's a page-turner." — *Toronto Star*

"By delicately tilting her observer's mirror, Alison Pick glimpsed the outline of an original tale that could cast new light on old shadows — enough that even the Holocaust-saturated will admit there's room for more of these stories if their vantage point is well chosen . . . So the Holocaust persists in the literary imagination, and through the refining fire of fiction a new generation confronts its own version of what it means to be human." — *National Post*

"Alison Pick's Holocaust novel, *Far to Go*, puts a new spin on moral compromise and, especially, the experience of young children living in Jewish households where the growing terror becomes unbearable . . . takes the narrative to a new level . . . fascinating . . . Weaving Czech history with a contemporary mystery, *Far to Go* shows terrific craft and emotional intelligence. A winner." — *NOW Magazine* (NNNN)

FAR *to* GO

ALISON PICK

ANANSI

Hardcover edition first published in 2010 by House of Anansi Press Inc.

This edition published in 2011 by
House of Anansi Press Inc.
110 Spadina Avenue, Suite 801
Toronto, ON, M5V 2K4
Tel. 416-363-4343
Fax 416-363-1017
www.anansi.ca

Distributed in Canada by
HarperCollins Canada Ltd.
1995 Markham Road
Scarborough, ON, M1B 5M8
Toll free tel. 1-800-387-0117

House of Anansi Press is committed to protecting our natural environment.
As part of our efforts, the interior of this book is printed on paper that contains
100% post-consumer recycled fibres, is acid-free, and is processed chlorine-free.

14 13 12 11 10   1 2 3 4 5

Library and Archives Canada Cataloguing in Publication

Pick, Alison, 1975–
Far to go / Alison Pick.

ISBN 978-0-88784-295-5

I. Title.

PS8581.I2563F37 2011   C813'.6   C2011-901698-2

Cover design: Adapted from the Italian edition by Alysia Shewchuk
Text design and typesetting: Sari Naworynski

*We acknowledge for their financial support of our publishing program
the Canada Council for the Arts, the Ontario Arts Council, and the Government of Canada
through the Canada Book Fund.*

Printed and bound in Canada

For Ayla

Only guard yourself and guard your soul carefully, lest you forget the things your eyes saw, and lest these things depart your heart all the days of your life, and you shall make them known to your children, and to your children's children.
— Deuteronomy 4:9

Monday's child is fair of face,
Tuesday's child is full of grace,
Wednesday's child is full of woe,
Thursday's child has far to go.
— *Mother Goose*

Herman Bondy 1876 – 1942
Ella Kafka 1886 – 1944
Oskar Bauer 1880 – 1943
Marianne (Grünfeld) Bauer 1894 – 1943
Irma Pick 1904 – 1944
Mary Pick 1908 – 1942
Jan Lowenbach 1933 – 1943
Eva Lowenbach 1938 – 1943

༺ঌ৶༻

Jan Pick 1909 – 1986
Alžběta (Bauer) Pick 1917 – 2000
Michael Pick 1937 – 1987
Thomas Pick 1944 –

THE TRAIN WILL NEVER ARRIVE.

It winds into forever: shiny red cars, black cars, cattle cars, one after another. A red caboose and a Princess Elizabeth engine. The livestock cars, loosely linked, like the vertebrae of some long reptile's spine. It reaches forward into the unknowable future, destined to move perpetually ahead, but with no destination in mind.

From the sky it looks inconsequential, a worm burrowing into the ground. And all the tiny people aboard look insignificant too: the postal workers and pastry chefs. The mothers and children.

The little ones.

You.

I saw your face for the first time in a dream. It was so clear and true that meeting you in the flesh, decades later, somehow paled against it. You trembled against your own ideal. A child in both eras. Here and there. Then and now.

You loved that train. I don't know how I know, but I do. The short loop of track, how it covered the same ground again and again. The whistle singing out the same old warning: *The past is catching up. Get ready.*

You could not have been my child, but I loved you as if you were.

Not my child, no.

Someone else's.

2

PART ONE

THE SUDETENLAND

07/12/1939

Dear Mrs. Inverness,

Although I could write a whole book, a short note will say what I need to say.

Things are happening here — unimaginable things. And yet, our only child, our Tomáš, is safe in London with you.

Dear Mrs. Inverness, I cannot tell you my gratitude. And your detailed writing about our boy has moved us to tears.

As you are so extremely good as to be inclined to prepare his favourite dishes, I shall gladly tell you what Tomáš likes to eat. He is very fond of fruit, especially of bananas. His favourite soups are: vermicelli, mushroom, potato soup, lentil soup, cumin soup with vermicelli. As to the farinaceous food he ate little as well, but he mostly liked a chocolate tart minus cream. (First I should say to please excuse my English! It is a recent language for me.)

We long for Tomáš, surely. He is only four years old! But if we bring the sacrifice of parting with the child to exempt him perhaps of great suffering, and know that he is so well kept safe by you, we master our pain.

We will see him soon enough.

We thank you still many thousand times & remain,
Faithfully yours,
Lore and Misha Bauer

(FILE UNDER: Bauer, Lore. Died Birkenau, 1943)

I WISH THIS WERE A HAPPY STORY. A story to make you doubt, and despair, and then have your hopes redeemed so you could believe again, at the last minute, in the essential goodness of the world around us and the people in it. There are few things in life, though, that turn out for the best, with real happy endings.

And what am I doing, talking about endings so soon? The truth is, I don't even know where to begin. As a young academic I was taught to frame my research in clinical terms, to take the stance of a disinterested observer. That was how to court fellowships, publication, and promotion. I was told that the relationship between professor and subject was like that between courteous strangers, when in fact the thing that draws us to unwrap a story, a particular story, is personal.

If I've learned one thing over my very long career, it is this: we research what we recognize. We are looking into our own darkness.

I've lived a quiet existence, working late in my office, closed in by towers of books and periodicals. Avoiding faculty parties, the clusters of graduate students drinking pints in the lounge. I take my noon and evening meals alone at my desk. I've been lonely, yes. In that way I might have been better to leave all of this alone, to let — what is the expression? — to let sleeping dogs lie. After everything that's happened, what has this story given me? It has only aggravated my restlessness, that need to search for what isn't there. In what I've found there's been relief, true, but also disappointment. When there's nothing left to be uncovered . . . Well, that's just it. There's nothing left to be uncovered.

What I'm saying to you now is, don't get your hopes up. Don't expect some thunderclap, some burst of enlightenment. Life isn't like that — not yours, and not mine. Low expectations create the most favourable outcomes.

You'll see what I mean.

The letters, I should mention, are for your information only. They were given to me in confidence, sent over oceans, mailed long-distance and marked "PRIORITY." People deliver them to me urgently still, as though I am in possession of some kind of magical power. The ability to put what is senseless into a top hat and pull out a knotted scarf of meaning. When they press their letters into my hands, I don't have the heart to tell them that so few people care, that these stories belong to the past and will soon disappear entirely, like a puff of smoke from the little chimney on one of those old-fashioned steam trains.

Sometimes I have the sense that I too am aboard that train. I feel I'm being pulled along by its story, a passive passenger looking out as the green fields and small farms flash by. The Bohemian landscape disappears like a dream. I am being taken somewhere and I still don't know where; I wonder when I will arrive and what I will find when I get there. All my life I've learned to twist words, to make them say whatever I want them to say. And now, from here, I can tell you that the opposite is true. It might seem that I'm the one telling the story, when really, the story is telling me.

ONE

It was Friday afternoon, the end of a long week. Misha Bauer made one last telephone call; the operator told him there was a line through Berlin.

"Our calls don't go through Berlin," he said. She of all people should know that. But he didn't want to be angry — not at the start of the Sabbath. He was looking forward to getting home to his wife and his little boy, Tomáš.

"My mistake."

"Could you book me a line for Monday?" he asked.

"Next Monday?"

"Four o'clock." He paused. "No, four thirty."

"*Sicher. Ja.*"

"*Danke. Guten tag.*" Misha replaced the black horn on the side of the box on the wall. Pushed back his heavy oak chair and took the pince-nez off the bridge of his nose.

His secretary stood up as he passed her desk on his way out. "Good *Shabbos*, Mr. Bauer," she said. Which she need not say, given the times, and which he appreciated all the more because of it.

He had parked the car next to the city-square market where

9

the fresh flowers and root vegetables were sold. Nearby were two blinkered horses and a milkman's cart, the white cans ready for delivery. Misha was planning to buy Lore a bouquet. He passed the post office — in the window he saw a clerk in a blue uniform bent over a bookkeeper's ledger. Four or five young men were walking towards him on the other side of the avenue. One, a redhead, was carrying a bucket of water. They were, he knew, going to offer to wash his car. Even the least expensive Opel was a novelty, and an American Studebaker like his — well, people wanted to get close to it. Misha nodded at the redhead, smiling to show that the young man was welcome to take a look. The next thing he felt was a blow to his gut. His back smacked against the cobblestones and his teeth clamped down on his tongue.

Misha lay there for several minutes, the sky a dirty rag above him, the metallic bite of blood in his mouth. When he managed to turn his head sideways, he saw the redhead's shins, the long white woollen knee socks. What exactly was about to happen remained obscure, but the socks meant it would not be good.

The boy with the sideburns used a saw to cut the tailpipe off his car. Misha heard him shouting, and then the severing of the metal. One by one, the windows of his car were smashed in. Then they kicked Misha onto his hands and knees and made him scrub the sidewalk. The redhead stood above him, brandishing the tailpipe like a club. *"Augen unten, Schwein,"* he said. Misha could not see if anyone had noticed what was happening; if they did, nobody stopped to help. He was at it for an hour, the hoodlums standing guard. When he asked for a drink of water —

Here Pavel stopped talking. Marta was sitting next to him in front of the large parlour window, trying not to meet his eye. She watched a splatter of starlings swoop out from under the eaves, ten or twelve black blips on the radar of evening.

"When he asked for some water," Pavel continued, "they made him drink the soapy slop from the pail."

Marta's gaze was fixed on the middle distance. "They made him *drink* it?" she asked, hoping she'd misheard him.

"It was full of shards of glass."

"And then?"

"They beat him with the tailpipe."

Marta didn't answer. She felt as though his words were coming from very far away or from a long ago time. There was a blankness in her head that reminded her of when she was young, and she had to force herself to focus in order to hear what he was saying.

Pavel straightened his tie. He paused, as though he too was having difficulty believing what he was about to tell her. "And then?" he said finally. "They knocked him unconscious and left him. For dead."

Marta turned towards Pavel finally, looking to her trusted employer to explain how this was possible, but he was a quiet man and seemed to have said all he was prepared to say. She opened her mouth and closed it again. The day was losing shape, like a worn-out undergarment. Time coming loose, a thread at the cuff. Marta twirled a strand of hair around her forefinger. "I'm so sorry," she whispered, but the blanket of fog in her mind had now closed in, and something inside her dismissed the threat entirely. Mr. Bauer clearly had his details confused. Even if — even *if* this unthinkable thing had actually happened to his brother — well, that was Vienna. *"Ein Volk, ein Reich, ein Führer"* — Hitler had made clear his intent to annex Austria, and then he'd done it. Whereas Pavel and Marta's native Czechoslovakia was still free.

A final starling dived down through the September dark, descending at the exact speed of a clock's second hand. Its body compact, black as a bullet. And then, as though it had reached its target, there was a loud explosion close by.

She straightened. "What was that?"

"A gun," Pavel said.

"Mr. Bauer?"

Marta crossed the room to the window. Sure enough, a row of soldiers was firing a dummy round into the late afternoon sky. Pavel had a Winchester and a Steyr that he took on hunting expeditions to Hungary, so it wasn't that Marta was unfamiliar with rifles. But this was different. Another kind of fight altogether. She was twenty-three years old. Born during the Great War but too young to remember it. All she'd really known her whole life was peace.

"Do we actually need gas masks?" She found herself wanting to giggle — the whole thing was so absurd — and she cleared her throat and brought a hand to her face to conceal her expression. Why was she behaving like this? It must be nerves. She removed her hand and said, straight-faced, "The gas masks remind me of Pepik's *Botanisierbuchse.*"

Pavel smiled at the reference to his son's botanical specimen can, but now he was staring off into the distance. "The Germans want us next," he said. "But the Wehrmacht tanks are built for the plains." He squinted as if he could see into the future. "When they move into the Šumava mountain pass, we'll get them. We've got thirty-five divisions, and forts all along the border of the Sudetenland."

Marta still couldn't reconcile the rallying gunfire with their sleepy Bohemian town. It could claim the tallest church spire in the region — fifty-five feet precisely — but there was nothing else remarkable about it. A Gentile butcher, a Jewish tailor, two hundred families grouped together on the east bank of a river with nowhere in particular to go. It was quiet and safe; she knew that's why Pavel loved it. He loved a week in London, a month on the Adriatic coast in the summer, but beneath it he was a *vlastenecký*, a Czech nationalist. The thing he loved best was coming home.

Marta could see her reflection in the parlour window. Her hair was dark and curly; she had a dimple in the middle of her left cheek that seemed to drive her innocence home. Pavel got up from his chair, and he stood next to her for a moment, looking down at the town square. There was a woman trying to cram an enormous valise into the boot of a Tatra, and several more detachments of Czech soldiers. A young girl cried openly as she watched a uniformed back retreat across the square. Her man going off to fight. She held a single rose in her hand, the petals pointed towards the ground like a magic wand that had lost its power. And Marta felt suddenly the same helpless dread. The fog inside her lifted and the old familiar feeling came back. Things were about to happen, she knew. Things she would be powerless to stop.

That night she snuck out of the Bauer house. Crossed the cobbled square, passed the grocer's and the tailor's shop, her bare feet cold in her sandals. Mist lifted off the river in wisps. Little plumes of anticipation rose inside her as well. An hour ago she'd been soundly asleep, but now she felt alert, wide awake. She heard the quiet burble of water over rocks and, somewhere not far off, the sound of a window being opened. The keys to Mr. Bauer's factory were clutched in her palm. He always left them hanging from a loop of leather on a hook by the back door; she had learned to pick them up by their long metal ends to avoid the sound of them jingling together.

There was a half-moon edging out from a length of grey cloud. *Mr. Goldstein's beard*, she thought.

The moon rubbed the river's back. She crossed the foot-bridge, her sandals clacking on the wood, taking the same path she'd taken for several weeks now. Her body moved unthinkingly. The factory was enclosed by heavy iron bars but the gate had been left open an inch. Ernst had arrived before her; he'd be waiting inside.

The rusted latch fell shut behind her like the end of a morality tale.

She went in through the front hall. The secretary's desk had been cleared for the day, the typewriter covered with a thick canvas sheath. There was a framed swatch of lace on the wall from the textile factory's first day of production. She had a brief uneasy feeling, remembering Pavel's story: What had become of his brother Misha's factory? And what of brother Misha himself? She pushed the thought away, anticipating instead what awaited her. Crossed the foyer and stood next to the elevator, a wooden platform that was operated by pulling a rope. Her nipples were stiff under her sweater. She moved towards the door to the factory floor and slowly twisted the handle.

Inside, everything was dark. An industrial-sized broom had been leaned up against the wall. The giant machines were like sleeping mammals, their silvery flanks fallen still.

She didn't hear Ernst's approach. He had her from behind before she saw his face. She laughed, trying to turn in his arms to see him, but he held her firmly, pulling her against his chest. A hand held loosely over her mouth.

"You're my gas mask," she said.

"I'm here to protect you," Ernst whispered into her curls.

"To keep the filthy odours away?"

He hesitated; she felt his muscles tighten behind her. "Do you find . . ." he said.

"Do I find what?"

"The Jews. Do you find that they smell?"

Marta stiffened. "Of course not! What a thing to say." She tried to pull away, to look Ernst in the face, but he held her firmly.

"I'm not the only one saying it." He paused, as though suddenly aware of himself. "I'm *not* saying it," he said quickly. "I'm not saying it at all."

She could tell he was ashamed, and felt a rush of sympathy. He was only repeating what people on the streets were saying, after all. And who was she to judge whether these statements were true? The Jews she knew best — Mr. Bauer, for example — they weren't really *Jewish*, at least not in the way she knew was meant by the word. She tried to think if she knew anyone Jewish who was actually practising. There was Mr. Goldstein, of course, but he was perhaps the only one.

"Mr. Bauer says we will need a gas mask," she said.

Ernst's thumb was tracing her jawline.

"Perhaps he'll prove right."

"Do you think so?" This surprised her, and part of her started to panic. "I have no family," she said suddenly, although she'd told herself she would not, and pivoted in Ernst's arms so that her face was directly in front of his: the square jaw, the pockmarks, the faint pebbling of stubble. The thought of war terrified her, and she clung to him tightly. "What will I do? If the fighting starts in earnest?"

"Pavel will protect you," Ernst said mildly.

She lifted her chin to hold his eye. "He isn't obliged."

"But he will." She could see Ernst wanted to give Pavel the benefit of the doubt, to paint his friend in the best possible light, as though in apology for his earlier comment.

"You have your wife," Marta heard herself say in the petulant voice of a child.

Ernst's gaze softened; he ran the pad of his thumb over her bottom lip. "And you have your beauty," he said, as though that would solve anything. Marta had noticed this about the few men she interacted with on a daily basis; they thought a woman's good looks could protect her, like some kind of shield.

He drew her to him, then kissed her softly, holding her bottom lip between his teeth ever so briefly. He cupped her breast lightly, and then more firmly, his touch getting rough. The hand was back over her mouth, but she yielded, her body giving in to his command. She was not about to scream. This was part of it, part of their game, and if she was honest, it was the part she most enjoyed.

She was caught now. He would not let her go.

‿◦◦‿

From the kitchen came the sound of the cook chopping beets, the running of water followed by scrubbing, then the *thwack, thwack* of a knife against the board. It was the sound of Marta's pulse, of the ache in her temples. It had been another night without any sleep.

"Dinner is at seven, Mr. Bauer," she said.

Pavel, she saw, had moved to the hall and was pulling on a green wool cloak, the one he usually wore mushrooming. He held his pipe away from his face. "Off to enlist," he grinned.

She squeezed her eyes closed for a moment; she could actually feel the tired pouches of flesh beneath them. "You can finally take action," she said.

All summer Pavel had been enraged by the *Völkischer Beobachter*'s headlines: "Czech Police Burn Sudeten Farms"; "German Peddler Killed by Czech Mob." Lies, he said, every word. For months Sudeten Germans had been under orders to provoke Czechs, and the Czechs were under orders not to be provoked. But now, finally, Pavel would have the chance to stand up for what he believed.

Marta paused and shut her eyes again briefly. She took a half-step towards Pavel and inhaled deeply. Did he smell? Like tobacco, certainly, but beneath that?

"What about the factory?" she asked. "If you enlist?" It was a bold question on her part, but Pavel didn't seem to notice.

"We need men to fight," Pavel said. "We need men, and we need boys!" He punctuated with his pipe, jabbing at the air with its stem. Pleased, she thought, to have her as an audience.

"And your workers?"

"The workers will fight."

"Even Ernst?" She tasted the plant manager's name.

"I'm halting production tomorrow," Pavel said, not answering her question.

"Really? Are you certain?"

But who was she to ask? Mr. Bauer obviously had a vision: it had pulled him out of the depths of himself. She'd heard him speak more in the past day than in the thirty days before that combined.

"If Germany takes us, there will be nothing left for the workers at all," Pavel said.

There was a sharp knock at the door. It was Ernst — she'd known it would be. He'd shaved since the night before, she saw, and his sweater had been replaced with an Austrian cloak like Pavel's. An ostrich feather stuck out from the side of his cap. He seemed a different man from the one she'd just been with, remote and apart from her. To think of the intimacies they had so recently shared made her flush.

"We were just talking about you," Pavel smiled, and clapped his friend on the shoulder.

"Good things?" Ernst looked at Marta.

"Of course!" Pavel said. "I was telling Marta how the whole factory will enlist . . ."

Ernst made a noise in the back of his throat that seemed, to Marta, noncommittal. But Pavel didn't appear to notice. "We're late," he said. Then, "See you shortly, Marta."

She lowered her eyes and fiddled with the string of her apron, then slipped out of the hallway. "It's a great day," she heard Pavel announce to Ernst. "A great day for us. A bad day for the Germans!"

Ernst's voice was muffled; Marta couldn't hear his reply.

When the men were gone, Marta walked slowly around the parlour, running a palm over the polished oak table, touching the throne-like wooden chairs with the hunting scenes carved into their backs. A crystal candy dish held a bag of Pepik's chocolate-covered cherries.

Upstairs, the door to the master bedroom was open. There was an ornate Victorian sofa in the corner, the kind that would stay in the room forever because it was too heavy and awkward to move, and French doors that gave way to a little balcony with a wrought-iron table where nobody ever sat. Books were stacked up on Pavel's side of the bed: *Talks with Tomáš Masaryk* by Karel Čapek, his favourite Czech author, a boy from his hometown of Hronov who had made good. And *Das Unbehagen in der Kultur* by Sigmund Freud, the famous doctor who had just died of cancer.

Marta went over to the bed and fluffed up the goose-down pillows. There was a silver boar's-hair brush on the vanity, and the watch was beside it, left there casually, as though it was not worth a small fortune. Its case made a sound like a door that needed oil. She held the watch tentatively to her wrist; she imagined herself in a silk dress and elbow-length gloves, being twirled by Ernst across a glimmering ballroom floor. How glamorous she'd appear, how worldly. Pavel had brought the watch back from Paris; the band was made completely of diamonds, with a thin blue line of sapphires down the centre. He was trying, she knew, to convert his wealth into solid assets. If war broke out the currency would be useless.

Engraved on the underside of the band was a woman's name: Anneliese.

Marta shut the watch case. She closed the bedroom door behind her.

∼⊚∼

Downstairs Pepik was on his stomach, splayed out in front of his train with his buckled shoes crossed behind him. Two clothespin people clutched in his fists. "All aboard!" she heard him whisper forcefully. A shy boy usually, but in charge of this domain.

She got down on her hands and knees and whispered in his ear: "*Pepik. Kolik je hodin?*"

He started as though waking from a long and feverish dream. The blush of pleasure on his face at seeing her never ceased to amaze her. That she gave someone such comfort. That she could be so needed. He squinted up at the grandfather clock in the corner of the room, taller than him by half, with its regal stature and chimes.

"Two o'clock." He tugged at his suspender.

"Two o'clock minus . . . ?"

"Where's my little man?" Pepik asked.

She passed him the clothespin doll. "Minus?"

"Some minutes!"

Marta laughed. "Minus *ten* minutes," she said. "Look at the long hand."

Pepik wiggled his fist, causing the tiny man to run away and hide behind the caboose.

"Would you like one of your chocolates?" she asked.

She knew he would say no: he was saving them to share with his friends. It was a magnanimous approach for such a small child, but she also knew where it came from — Pavel was equally generous.

Marta suddenly remembered Pepik's first weeks home from the hospital, how hard he had cried in the evenings, and the thrill she felt as the cloudy newborn eyes slowly clarified to the same bright blue as hers. A stranger might see them together and remark on how the child took after his mother.

Was this what every governess secretly hoped for?

A sharp gust of wind squealed down the chimney. In the silence that followed another shot rang out; the soldiers across the square were hard at work at target practice. Pepik didn't seem to notice but Marta shivered involuntarily; she kept expecting the whole situation would blow over, but instead it seemed to be escalating. She got back down beside Pepik and crossed her legs and looked at him closely. *"Miláčku,"* she said. "Did you hear that gun? Do you remember the big trucks yesterday?"

He looked at her blankly. Blinked his long lashes.

"That was the Czech army. They're here to protect us."

Pepik turned back to the train, focused on his goal. "All aboard," he muttered again. But Marta took his face by the chin and turned it towards her. This was important.

"Your *tata*," she said, "and all of his workers — everyone is ready to fight."

She paused, wondering if this was really true.

Would Ernst fight? On which side?

And which side was she herself on?

"Come here, Pepik," she whispered. She wanted, suddenly, to hold him. But Pepik seemed to have forgotten her entirely. He turned back to the scene in front of him, the Princess

Elizabeth engine, the livestock cars loosely linked like the vertebrae of some long reptile's spine.

Pepik flicked the switch.

The electric train seemed to hesitate for a moment. Then it sighed on its tracks, a traveller hoisting very heavy bags.

∽◉∾

Pavel wasn't home until eight o'clock that evening. Marta heard him say thank you to Sophie the cook as he passed her his felt hat. He came into the parlour, his jacket thrown over his shoulder and a copy of *Lidové noviny* tucked under his arm. Whistling. He was off-key but she recognized the first few notes of Smetana's patriotic "Má Vlast."

"Where is your train headed?" he asked his son. "Is it off to fight the Germans?"

Pepik was in his blue flannel nightcap. He nodded mutely, pleased with his father's attention and suspicious of it at the same time. Marta could tell he knew something strange was astir. He sensed his environment, she thought, in the same way an animal could sense rain. She remembered the farm where she had grown up, how the chickens would fuss on a hot July evening. As the air thickened there was an increasing sense of panic. Or maybe that was just how she'd felt; hot weather meant her father would be restless.

"How's the Crown Prince?" Pavel asked his son, trying again to engage him. But Pepik was allowed only a few more minutes of play before bed, and he ignored his father, focused on his train. He was fiddling with the little piece on the front — what was it called? — the fan shape that stuck out like a dustpan. It reminded Marta of Hitler's moustache.

Vermin, Hitler had called the Jews. But he spoke with compelling confidence.

Pavel gave up on his son and turned away and opened his leather briefcase on the oak table. He was wearing not his usual business suit and tie but informal soldier's clothes: corduroy pants and a sweater with leather patches on the elbows. He pulled several manila dossiers out of the case, each neatly labelled, and smiled at Marta. "I'll have a cup of coffee, please," he said. He considered for a moment, then slid the files back into the case, snapping the clasps shut. "No," he said. "I'll have a whiskey."

The decanter was chiselled crystal with a stopper shaped like the Eiffel Tower. Pavel placed two small glasses close together on a round silver platter.

"Care to join me?"

"Me?"

But there was nobody else in the room. "To what occasion?" asked Marta.

"To victory!" Pavel responded with gusto, but didn't yet raise his glass. He looked at her, challenging, his jaw square. For a moment she saw what he must have been like as a child: stubborn, impulsive. Something else he'd passed on to Pepik.

"To beating the bastards down," Pavel said, gesturing with his drink to the window and the implied enemy beyond it. "The Russians are on their way with support . . ." He railed on about fortifications, about the Maginot Line. Marta had never heard him so energized about anything. She wondered vaguely whether he knew that tomorrow was the first day of

Rosh Hashanah. How did she herself know this? Someone must have told her — Mr. Goldstein? Yes. Who else could it have been? There was no Judaism in her family, of course — none as far as she knew — but she found the religion's customs curious, the candles and skullcaps, the prohibitions against various foods. Marta thought about the Jewish New Year, and Yom Kippur, which would follow — the Day of Atonement, Goldstein had said, the day of repenting for sins.

Could she ask forgiveness for her own sins? If only, she thought, it was that simple.

"Either Hitler gives in," Pavel was saying, "or there will be a war." He paused, and Marta was suddenly aware that he had asked something of her, that he was soliciting her opinion. She blurted out the first thing she thought of. "Those white woollen knee socks," she said. "Are they worn by Nazis?"

She was remembering Pavel's story about his brother Misha, how he'd been knocked to the ground by the gang of boys and had seen their socks and *known*.

But Pavel ignored her. "Even if the government yields," he said, "the army would never listen." And the truth of this seemed confirmed for him in the act of speaking it aloud. "You," he said to Marta, "have no idea how lucky we are now. Compared to the way it was before."

Before, she knew, meant before Tomáš Masaryk, before 1918, when Czechoslovakia did not exist. He was right, she thought; it was hard for her to imagine. She told him as much.

"That's the peril of youth," Pavel said. "The lack of experience against which to compare."

He was thirty. There were only seven years between them, but he chose to assert them now.

"You old man," Marta said, smiling.

"And you are a lovely young lady." Pavel raised his glass. "To beating those Germans," he said, holding her eye, just as they heard his wife coming up the stairs.

Anneliese Bauer's fingernails were painted a deep shade of scarlet. She was carrying a flat white box tied with a blue ribbon, the signature of the Hruska patisserie. What she was doing buying the *medovnik* herself Marta couldn't imagine, and for a moment she felt guilty, or neglectful, as though this somehow reflected on her own job as hired help. There was something wrong about it, something out of order. Then again, Marta thought, everything was topsy-turvy these days. And Anneliese, she reminded herself, was not one to do anything she didn't want to do.

"Am I to be included in cocktails?" Anneliese asked now, stepping into the parlour and fanning her face with an open hand, as though her nail polish were not quite dry. Her brown hair was set in a finger wave, the wide curls clinging to the sides of her head. She looked like a model from an ad for the alpine spas where Pavel's mother went to convalesce in the summers. Marta imagined herself sashaying across the Persian carpets, mingling with the men with gold-tipped walking sticks and women in hats with veils. The European elite gossiping over their wineglasses, shifting effortlessly between languages to get across the exact nuance of what they meant.

She curtsied, and Anneliese turned and acknowledged her, passing her the cake. "Put this in the icebox, please?"

"Of course," Marta answered, part of her relieved that the natural order of things had not been eclipsed by the mobilization after all. Anneliese would still make requests and Marta would still carry them out.

Pavel had gone to the sideboard and was bringing down a third glass. "To what do we owe the pleasure?" Anneliese asked her husband.

"To war," he said. He could barely keep the smile off his face.

From the corner of the room came the *tick-tick-tick* of Pepik's electric train rounding its track.

Anneliese grasped her earlobes and pulled off her clip-on earrings one at a time. She snapped open her small Chanel purse and deposited them inside. "Let's hope it's over fast." She dug around for her silver cigarette case. "The Fischls are leaving," she announced to her husband.

Pavel was being generous with the whiskey; he did not turn to face her. "Bon voyage to the Fischls." Now he turned and passed the glass to his wife. "Just goes to show. One bit of trouble and they're out of here as fast as Jesse Owens." He paused, pleased with his comparison.

"They're leaving tomorrow. Hanna Fischl got an international phone call — from her mother in England," Anneliese said.

Marta remembered the box of cake in her hand. She put down her whiskey and went to the kitchen, wondering if she'd understood correctly. An international phone call — but England was an ocean away. How was it possible to speak across such a distance? She pictured a thin wire high above the clouds, and then she pictured tiny men running back and forth through the hollowed-out centre of the wire to deliver their messages into the waiting ears of their listeners.

She put the cake in the icebox, just as Mrs. Bauer had asked.

"They're all going," she heard Anneliese say to Pavel. "Even Dagmar and Erna."

"The nieces?"

"Oskar's daughters."

"And Oskar?"

"All of them, Pavel." Anneliese's voice revealed frustration. She was a gorgeous young woman, intelligent and sassy, who'd married a mild-mannered, average-looking industrialist. Marta loved both of the Bauers, but the match still sometimes confounded her. Anneliese needed someone with more . . . what? More *flourish*. Pavel was wealthy, well-bred, intelligent, but Anneliese was diminished by him somehow. She loved him, Marta thought, but part of her had been squandered.

"We did the right thing buying those defence bonds," Pavel was saying as Marta returned to the parlour. Anneliese gave him a sharp look that meant *not in front of the help*. "To beating the Germans quickly," she said, to change the subject. The Bauers raised their glasses.

Marta lifted her own glass, pleased to be included, and then waited for a natural pause in the conversation. "Would you like me to make the coffee now, Mr. Bauer?" Sophie was the cook and Marta the governess but Marta had been there longer. She knew exactly how Pavel liked it, the tiniest bit of sugar stirred in.

Pavel lifted a forefinger to show he'd like another whiskey instead.

Marta moved to get the decanter but saw that Anneliese

was eyeing her, looking her up and down as though trying to make up her mind about something.

"Shall I?" Marta asked, suddenly uncertain, and gestured in the direction of the alcohol.

Anneliese nodded to show she should proceed, but she was still looking at Marta, evaluating. "Ernst seems to be around a lot these days," she said finally.

Marta swallowed. "Would you like a *boží milosti* as well?"

Anneliese ignored the question. "He keeps stopping by."

"Let me bring in a plate of cookies."

But Anneliese wouldn't let her get away so easily. "Why might that be? Any idea?"

"Perhaps because of what's going on." Marta paused, flushing. "The mobilization, I mean."

She lowered her face and hurried into the kitchen. Reached up to the top shelf, flustered, and the tin crashed down, bits of cookies spilling across the floor. Marta cursed under her breath and knelt down to brush up the mess, replaying Anneliese's words. What exactly did she know? And had she told Pavel? It wasn't likely, Marta reassured herself. Anneliese had a secret of her own, something she wanted her husband never to find out. Marta had stumbled on it, in a matter of speaking. They were tied to each other, Marta and her mistress. Like runners in a three-legged race. If one went down the other would go down with her.

❧

The next afternoon, Marta held Pepik's small hand on the way to the train station. They passed Mr. Goldstein crossing the square, a piece of fringed material draped over his arm. *"Shana tova,"* he said to Pepik.

Pepik kicked at the toe of one shoe with the heel of the other. "Fine-thank-you-and-how-are-you?"

Mr. Goldstein laughed. "Have a good year," he translated. "Remember I told you? About Rosh Hashanah?"

Marta held Pepik against her leg, her fingers combing through his curls. "I was just thinking about it yesterday," she said.

"So my teaching has not been for nothing!" There were crinkles in the corners of Mr. Goldstein's eyes. "And what about you, the little *lamed vovnik?*" He looked down at Pepik, but no answer was forthcoming.

Marta prompted her charge. "Do you remember, *miláčku?* About the Jewish New Year?" Of course he wouldn't remember — the Bauers' home was completely secular — but what was the harm? Marta had always liked the old tailor, and he was so kind to Pepik.

"The minute hand is longer," Pepik declared solemnly, confirming her hypothesis that he had no idea what they were talking about. "Would you like a chocolate?" He held out his precious bag.

"How kind of you. But no, thank you. I have to get back."

"Are you working?" Marta asked politely. Wasn't work forbidden on the holiday?

Mr. Goldstein shook his head. "Not working. Praying." And he held up his arm with the length of material — which she now saw was a prayer shawl — folded over it. He rolled his eyes, pretending to bend under the weight of the holiday's rigorous requirements, but Marta knew how devoted he truly was.

She laughed. "Happy praying!" She squinted, trying to recall the correct salutation. "*Shana tova?*"

"To you too," he smiled. He looked down at the boy. "*Shana tova*, Pepik."

Pepik reached up to twist the tip of the tailor's long beard. This was a joke that they shared. Mr. Goldstein's beard held the cone shape as he hurried across the town square.

The train station's platform was crammed with soldiers and housewives and young girls pushing prams and crying. A man with mutton chop sideburns wore a ribbon on his jacket, gold and black, the colours of the old Austro-Hungarian Empire. Marta held Pepik's little shoulders, guided him around two women in wide-brimmed hats. She heard one of them say, "It makes sense to create one big country out of two German-speaking ones."

"You mean Germany and Austria?"

"I mean Germany and the Sudetenland!"

Through the crowd she thought she saw the back of Ernst's head. She checked herself; lately she saw the back of Ernst's head everywhere. And what would he be doing here at the station?

Still, she craned her neck. She couldn't help it.

Pepik was tugging at her dress. He wanted to be carried. "You're a big boy," she said, absently. "You've started school now." She stood on tiptoe. The man with the mutton-chops moved and she got a clear view of Ernst's profile, the pocked cheeks and high forehead — it was him after all.

"School is over," Pepik said, triumphant. He was pleased with his reasoning.

Marta scanned the platform, looking for Ernst's wife, but didn't see her anywhere. He must be alone. She lifted a hand to the side of her face, trying to get Ernst's attention, but discreetly.

"School is over," Pepik repeated.

"It's not over. It will start again soon. The soldiers are just using it as a base." Her eyes were on Ernst, willing him to meet her gaze.

"Will they learn to tell time?"

Marta finally looked down at Pepik, a rush of affection rising through her. "Yes," she said gravely. "Just like you."

That was all he'd needed, she saw, a little bit of attention. He was emboldened. He ran across the platform with his bag of chocolate cherries clutched in his hand, shouting something at a blond boy he must have recognized from his class.

Marta watched him disappear into a wall of bodies. She turned back; Ernst was moving purposefully towards her. She hastily smoothed down her curls with the palms of her hands. When he was a few metres away, he motioned with his head towards a nook beside the ticket counter.

She ducked into the small space behind him.

They didn't speak. The desire to lie together was palpable, a carpet of heat laid out beneath them. "Tonight?" Marta said, before she could stop herself. It was wrong, what they were doing; she should be able to extricate herself. But part of her was lonely all the time, a young, hungry part, and it got the better of her. Something in her was starving to be noticed, truly *seen*.

Ernst looked down at her; he was taller than her by a head.

"Not tonight," he said. "Unfortunately." He didn't need to explain; it would be some kind of obligation with his wife. "Tomorrow?" he asked.

She smiled. "You have something . . ." She reached over and picked an eyelash off his cheek.

"Thank you," he said. "I'll try for tomorrow."

"You're busy?"

He shook his head, to show that, yes, he was busy but did not want to waste their time telling her about it. He leaned towards her, his lips an inch from hers. She wanted to push her own weight into the bulk of his, to fuse herself with the feeling he lit in her chest. Instead she tried to say something that she knew would please him.

"We just saw Mr. Goldstein. You were right. He did smell a little."

Ernst pulled back, raised an eyebrow.

"Remember? You said —"

"I said what?"

"About the Jews."

"What about them?"

"How they smell," she said finally. But Ernst's face registered nothing, and she swallowed, wishing she hadn't brought it up. The slur tasted wrong in her mouth, like cookies made with salt instead of sugar.

"I said nothing of the sort," Ernst said, a bemused expression on his face. "I might have thought it, but I certainly would never have voiced it. Nor should you. It doesn't become you."

Marta flushed. "It was just a joke." How had he managed to make her seem the fool when it had been his idea in the first place?

She tried again. "Remember? You said . . . the other night . . . ?"
But she could see he would admit to nothing. Which was to be
expected. If their secret was discovered it would be, she knew,
the same — he would save himself at her expense.

She wound a curl around her forefinger and tugged at
it. A sliver of anger was rising within her, and she groped
around for some way to correct the imbalance, for some way
she could hurt him back. "Anneliese suspects," she heard herself saying.

She had a flash of a bathtub full of blood.

Ernst's expression immediately went slack. He took a large
step back. "About us? How?"

There was the roar of the train arriving in the station.
Marta didn't answer his question; he deserved to sweat, to feel
the same fear she felt. She looked away from him, nonchalant,
and leaned for a moment out of the nook where they were
hidden. She saw Pepik standing next to a group of boys: Hanka
Guttman's son Ralphie and one of those very blond Acker-
mans, with eyes like blue ice — what was his name? They all
looked so identical, and so much like their father.

"Marta," Ernst said urgently. "Are you sure? How does she
know?" He was a married man, Pavel's right hand at the factory, and close friends with both of the Bauers. It would not
do to be caught sneaking around with their governess. But she
still didn't answer: her eyes were on Pepik now. He was standing with his back to her; she saw him hold out his chocolates
to the Ackerman boy. The boy grabbed the sack out of Pepik's
hand. A fat man in a conductor's uniform blocked her view,
and the next thing she saw was Pepik's shocked face and the
bag of chocolates spilled across the pavement.

Ernst grasped her elbow. "*Marta*," he said. But she jerked away and pushed past a woman carrying a violin case, a group of young girls who were playing marbles. Pepik was behind them, standing still. Bewildered. She could not get to him fast enough. A stone hit the side of his face. He brought his hand to the back of his head and rubbed it. Another stone hit his forehead and he flinched and covered his head with his hands.

Marta finally reached him and scooped him up and pulled him close to her. The relief at having him safe in her arms.

The Ackerman boy had stopped throwing stones and was now making a show of stepping on Pepik's chocolate-covered cherries. They broke on the pavement, Marta thought, like blood vessels.

"Crybaby!" the boy said to Pepik. "*Sehen Sie sich die Heulsuse an!*"

Marta turned her back to the boys, Pepik in her arms. He'd been cut by one of the pebbles — the cut was small, but quite deep. She licked her thumb to rub the blood off his cheek. "You should be ashamed of yourself," she said, turning again to face the Ackerman boy, surprised by the fierceness in her voice. "Wait until I tell your mother."

But the boy wasn't chastened. "My mother will be pleased," he said, and folded his sturdy arms across his chest, defiant. There was a scab, Marta saw, large and infected, on his elbow. And behind his shoulder, hanging from the station rafters, was a banner depicting the German coat of arms, the black eagle with a wreath in its talons, a stylized swastika at its centre.

~ひ~

On the walk back home Pepik was quiet. He didn't want to be lifted onto the stone ledge at the edge of the square to balance with his arms out as he usually did. He declined Marta's offer of a piggyback. When they entered the house, Anneliese was standing by the big window, wearing ruby high heels and a skirt cut on the bias, smoking a cigarette. Pepik dropped his satchel on the leather ottoman and ran into the dining room to lose himself in his empire.

His mother inhaled from her cigarette and pitched her voice in his direction. "Pepik," she said. "Come back and take off your shoes." She touched her bottom lip with her forefinger.

"It's a lovely day," said Marta, trying to keep her voice cheerful. She could see that Anneliese was in a mood, and wanted to shield Pepik after what had just happened at the station. But Anneliese would not be distracted.

"Pepik. Tomáš. Bauer," she said (the *Tomáš*, Marta remembered, was in honour of former president Masaryk. Many little boys had the name). "Come back here this moment and do as I say."

Pepik hesitated, weighing his options.

"Pepik," Marta said softly. "Listen to Mamenka."

The boy turned towards them, and Marta thought he was going to obey, but instead he ran towards her, burying his face in her skirt.

Anneliese's jaw clenched. She took another sharp drag on her cigarette. "Why isn't he at school?" she asked, smoke coming out of her nostrils.

"My cheek hurts," Pepik mumbled into Marta's leg.

But Marta kept her eyes on Anneliese. "The school has been occupied by the young Czech reserves, Mrs. Bauer." She tried to relay this information as though for the first time, although she had already told Anneliese, the previous evening as they fiddled with the radio dial waiting for the BBC broadcast to come on. The opening notes of the program's theme, Beethoven's Fifth "Fate" Symphony, always brought the whole house to silence and turned their ears to the radio. Pavel was the only one who understood English, though. It fell to him to translate.

"So where have you been?"

"We went down to the station to watch the trains."

Anneliese held her cigarette over her shoulder between two polished red fingernails. "Let's have him doing something school-related, shall we? Not taking him somewhere that's overrun with hooligans and indulging his every whim?"

And then, in a ploy to win back her son's affection, she softened her voice. "Did you see the trains, *miláčku*?"

Marta knelt down in front of her young charge. She wrenched open the small hands. His chubby cheeks were flushed and the skin around the small wound was puffy and pink. She pulled him close and whispered in his ear, "Go and give Mamenka a big kiss."

It was a gamble. If Pepik didn't obey she would appear willful, telling him secrets in front of Anneliese. Pepik was frozen, his doe eyes moving back and forth between the two women.

"Go on," Marta said. She raised her eyebrows to show she meant it.

Pepik pulled from her grip and ran across the room to his mother, where he assumed the same position, burying his face between her legs. Anneliese crushed out her cigarette and ran her slender fingers through the boy's curls. "There," she said to Marta. "Poor thing, he just wanted his mother."

The comment took Marta by surprise, and she flushed with indignation. Two words flashed through her mind: *dirty Jew*. She flushed more, surprised at herself for thinking them, but she let the words hover behind her eyes, testing out their weight. She had just been the one to encourage the child to go to his mother; where did Anneliese get the nerve to make such a jab?

But Marta took a deep breath, steeling herself. She reminded herself that she was the one who had really raised Pepik. She knew how much chocolate to sprinkle on his kashi and how long to warm his milk at night. She was generous too, sharing the child with his mother. And, although she would never admit it, deep down she felt that Pepik loved her more.

Anneliese bent down in front of her son. She looked up at Marta sharply. "What happened to his face?"

Marta hesitated. "He fell, Mrs. Bauer," she said.

The lie gave her a little thrill, a tiny moment of retribution. Besides, to explain about the Ackerman boy would mean explaining that she hadn't been properly supervising Pepik. Anneliese was already suspicious about Ernst; Marta did not want her to guess she'd been paying attention to him instead of Pepik.

Marta told herself that she shouldn't bother Anneliese with the truth. Anneliese was still upset by Hitler's speech the previous night: he was asking for the surrender of the Sudetenland. The Bauers had stood over the radio, fuming. Hitler had said that after the last war Germany had given up all sorts of places — Alsace-Lorraine and the Polish Corridor — and now it was Czechoslovakia's turn. Pavel had translated rapidly, almost under his breath.

"He doesn't mention that Germany was *forced* to give those places up," Anneliese had said to her husband, her fists clenched by her sides.

No, now was not the time to further upset Mrs. Bauer with this new injustice against her son. It was for Marta to know, who already knew everything about the boy. She kept the secret, along with all the others. She told herself it was for Anneliese's own good. And that Anneliese deserved to be deceived.

In the early evening Marta glanced out of Pepik's window to see Ernst looking up at her from the street. He held her eye for a moment, gave a little nod. Almost indiscernible, but there it was.

She pulled Pepik's nightcap down over his ears and kissed his forehead, inhaling the scent of soap from his bath. "Sweet dreams, *miláčku*." His breathing softened to sleep almost before she could extinguish the lamp. The Bauers were sitting beside the radio in the parlour; she bid them goodnight and went into her own narrow room. Took off her sturdy shoes and lay down on top of the blankets, fully clothed. The voices from below rose like woodsmoke, a warm, unintelligible murmur. She drifted off but woke to the sound of Pavel climbing the stairs and the Bauers' bedroom door closing down the hall.

She waited another hour, just to be certain.

The factory keys were cold in her hand, and she wished she

had thought to bring gloves. The nights were getting cooler, she thought. Winter, like a bad premonition. She crossed the footbridge, let the heavy iron gates fall closed behind her. The factory foyer was dark; the shadow of a black trench coat hung on a hook by the door. Ernst's face made her think of the train station, of the little boys throwing stones at Pepik, but there was nothing she could do about it now, and she pushed the thought out of her mind.

Flax dust coated the floor like snow. Ernst got her up against the chilly wall, pressing his weight into hers. The rough cement grabbed at her stockings. He leaned in to kiss her; Marta turned her head coyly. "Aren't you even going to say hello?"

He laughed. "Hello, lovely." He brushed his hands lightly over her bottom. "What's new in your world?"

She tried to think of something of interest, something notable, but her days were all the same. "The Bauers are getting nervous," she said.

"About?"

"About Hitler."

She said nothing about her earlier comment at the train station — that Anneliese suspected their liaison — and Ernst didn't ask. His mind seemed to be elsewhere. "I think he might succeed after all," he said.

Marta moved his hand off her rear end. "Hitler? At what?"

Ernst moved his hand back, smiling. "At liberating us. From the Czechs." He gave her backside a little squeeze.

"From the Czechs? Aren't you one of them?" She paused. "One of us?"

"I'm German," he said quickly.

Well, of course he was — along with a huge portion of the Sudetenland's population. This was why, Marta knew, Hitler was so popular in the territory.

"The Sudetenland polled eighty-five percent Nazi in the last election," Ernst said officiously.

"So you're pro-German," Marta clarified, "but not anti-Jew?"

Ernst made a noise from the back of his throat that she couldn't interpret.

Marta leaned back so she could see his face. She wanted to touch his cheek, but her arm was pinned behind her, caught between her back and the cement wall. "Hitler is just a bullying schoolboy," she said. But even as she said this, she wondered if it was what she really thought. Her own true feelings — about Hitler, about anything at all — were locked inside her chest, the key long lost. Her contents as much a mystery to her as to anyone else. And what did she really know, about Hitler or anyone else? She was probably just repeating something she'd heard Anneliese say.

At the thought of Anneliese, Marta felt a flash of indignation. *Poor thing, he just wanted his mother.*

Ernst looked at her closely, seeing the flush of anger on her face. "Hitler might be a bullying schoolboy. Or, he might be the man of the century," he said mildly. "Either way, it doesn't bode well for the Bauers."

"Why not?"

Marta worked to free her arm, but Ernst's body against her own was too heavy.

"They aren't Jewish," she protested. "At least, they're not *Jewish*. You know that."

Ernst had his hands in her hair; he made a knot with his fist and tugged lightly. "People are saying that it's not just a religion." He paused. "They're saying it's a race."

"Do you really —"

He nodded. "I'm beginning to think so. An inferior race. I've joined a group that . . ." But his voice trailed off, leaving Marta to surmise exactly what kind of group Ernst was now part of. Could he be right? she wondered. It seemed a ridiculous idea — anyone could see the Bauers were just the same as everyone else — yet something about the statement rang true for Marta too.

Ernst coughed into the back of his hand. "You, at least," he said, "you're one hundred percent pure."

She raised her eyebrows.

"A beauty like you," he said.

Marta squirmed again and he saw her discomfort, her arm bent back so she couldn't move it. "I'm sorry," he said, and leaned back so she could change position. He looked at her tenderly, then shifted his gaze, his eyes focused on the wall several inches above her head. He spoke suddenly, the softness gone: "The Jews are the cause of so many of Germany's problems," he said. "You can't separate the two issues."

"How —" she started, but Ernst seemed to have forgotten she was there. He seemed to be speaking to himself now, as though cementing the answer to a question he'd been wrestling with in his mind.

"Germany — and Czechoslovakia too — would be better off with no Jews at all."

Marta raised her face to speak — to object — but he covered her open mouth with his own.

❧

Something woke Marta early on the last day of September. Usually she heard Sophie bumping into things in the kitchen, but it was 5:00 a.m., too early even for that. She put on her slippers and went out into the hall, where there was a row of photographs of Pepik, one for each birthday. Five in total; the sixth was still at the framers. It amazed her, really, how he'd grown. The everyday miracle of it. She went quietly into his bedroom; he was on his back with his arms above his head and his fat cheeks flushed like the belly of the coal stove. Since the incident at the train station he had taken to sleeping with one of his lead soldiers clutched in his hand. He clung to it like a vial of magic potion that had rendered him unconscious and would now be required to bring him back to the world of the living.

It was almost, she thought, as though the whole country had fallen into slumber. September 28 — the feast day of Saint Wenceslas, patron saint of the Czechs — had passed with none of the usual fanfare. Like the flare of a match, she thought: a brief light, the fall back to darkness.

Marta pulled the covers up under Pepik's chin, kissed him, and left him to sleep. She went downstairs to grind the Bauers' coffee beans; it was Sophie's job, but Marta didn't mind doing it. When she came into the parlour, though, the radio was on, and Pavel was standing with his back to her, facing the big window. He was wearing only his thin white cotton nightshirt, through which she could see the muscled contours of his behind.

She couldn't think what he was doing up so early, and she began to back slowly up the stairs. He heard her move, though, and turned towards her.

He said her name, just once. "Marta."

On his face was a look that Marta had never seen before. The word that popped into her mind was *stricken*.

"Mr. Bauer? I was just going to —" But Pavel cleared his throat loudly. He seemed not to notice that she was barely decent herself, wearing only her thin robe and slippers, her curls still messy with sleep.

"He's betrayed us," Pavel said.

Marta pulled her robe tight around her. "Who has?"

She had a sudden sinking feeling that Pavel had found out about Ernst — what had she been thinking, taking his factory keys right out from under his nose? — but Pavel said instead, "Good old *J'aime Berlin*."

"Pardon me?"

"*J'aime Berlin*," he repeated. He waited, but Marta didn't understand the French pun. "*Cham-berlain*," he said finally. "Chamberlain. Britain. And France."

She blinked. "I was just going to make your coffee," she said.

"We had a pact. And now they have gone to meet with Hitler and have given us up to Germany. The entire Sudetenland. As if we were theirs to give up!" Pavel took a slow, deep breath. "They didn't even ask us to the table," he said. "They peeled us off Czechoslovakia like so much nothing."

Marta pictured the thick peel of a Christmas orange.

The Bauers celebrated Christmas along with almost everyone else, as a kind of folk holiday, the chance to gather with family. She would have to remind Ernst of this.

Pavel was looking at her directly for the first time since she'd come into the room, and she saw now that this was serious — he had tears in his eyes. "Hitler convinced them.

Daladier, Mussolini. Chamberlain is saying it will be 'peace in our time.'"

He touched his face, as though to make sure he was still there.

Marta cast around, wondering what she should say. Perhaps Ernst could help? But that was a silly idea, considering his recent comments; she snorted. Pavel looked up sharply. "What?"

"Nothing," Marta said. "I just can't believe this has happened."

And it was true, she couldn't. There had been so much talk of Austria and the *Anschluss*; months and months of Hitler on the radio, singing the praises of his Nuremberg Laws. The thought that the Sudetenland would belong to him, that he would now come here, seemed impossible. Life happened in the big cities, in Frankfurt and Milan, in Prague, where the Bauers attended symphonies and business meetings. Nothing would ever happen here in their small town. Not now, not ever.

The radio was babbling on like a kettle on low boil. Pavel nodded in its direction. "It's an actor from the National Theatre reading a script. President Beneš didn't have the guts to tell us the news himself. Nobody from the government did."

He was standing a foot away from her in his nightclothes. But Marta realized she could forget about what she was wearing, about what he was wearing; he was not going to notice.

"Cowards," he said, and she could not tell if he was referring to their own Czech government or to the British and French who had betrayed them.

The room was slowly gathering light as a small child gathers cornflowers in a field. It would be another warm day. Marta and Pavel stood looking down at the square. Marta had never been to the cinema but she had heard about the big screen, and this was how she thought of the window looking over the town: as a screen on which the events of the world played out. A sound was moving towards them now, rumbling over the cobblestones. Pavel swore under his breath and held his face in his hands. He looked up again, then lowered his face quickly, as though to make what he had seen disappear.

Trucks were entering the square. Large trucks, with guns protruding from them, and tanks that bore the Wehrmacht insignia. The morning light crept up behind them, a rosy pink that was almost flattering to their shiny metal. Pavel squared his shoulders in defiance. He lifted a finger and put it on her elbow, as if he could not face this alone.

Marta shifted away automatically — it was not right to touch her employer. She had a flash again, of Ernst saying, "Dirty . . ." But Mr. Bauer smelled of soap or shaving lotion, and beneath that of warm blankets and skin. He smelled as she did: human. Besides, something dramatic was happening, something extraordinary, and extraordinary events called for extraordinary measures. It was the kind thing to do, to reassure someone in distress. She knew nothing about politics, but the Bauers were her family. What had she been thinking? They were the same as they'd always been, and she was on their side. On Mr. Bauer's side. Ernst could believe what he wanted.

Marta shifted back towards Pavel and their two arms touched again. They stood as a team, next to each other, as the German tanks filled their town square.

～๑～

By mid-morning, when Marta came back downstairs, Pavel had taken the car to the factory. He could afford a chauffeur, like everyone who had an automobile, but he chose not to employ one. Why, he liked to ask, would he pay for someone else to have the pleasure of driving?

Marta spent the bulk of the day tidying Pepik's room. She swept beneath the bed, where she found two lost lead soldiers and a pair of brown knickerbockers crushed up into a ball. She shook them out; there was a round hole in the fabric, the exact size of a ten-koruna coin, and she set to work darning it, all the while trying not to think about the arrival of the Germans. The occupation would be short-lived, she told herself; it had to be.

In the late afternoon she went down to the kitchen to make herself a cup of linden tea. Sophie was standing over a bowl of peeled apples, the peels' perfect corkscrews like the ones on Sophie's head. Of course, thought Marta, Sophie slept with strings tied in her hair.

Sophie was in her late teens, and would have been almost beautiful if not for her harelip. It was not a severe one — just a spot beneath her nose where the skin looked shiny and flat. Still, Marta found it hard to look past.

"You're making strudel," she said.

"What about it?"

"Isn't it too . . . German? On today of all days?"

Sophie picked up an apple. "Pass me the knife."

"Mr. Bauer's mother is coming for dinner. It's Friday."

"What do you mean, too German?"

"With what's going on." Marta raised her eyebrows but Sophie only shrugged.

"Isn't it wonderful?" She did not bother to lower her voice

and Marta worried Anneliese would hear her, but from above came the sound of floorboards squeaking and then the scrape of the stove door being opened and the thud of a charcoal brick being tossed in.

"Is it?" Marta asked. "Wonderful?"

"Of course it is. He's rooting them out."

Sophie held the paring knife still, turning the fruit under the blade.

"The Jews?" Marta asked dumbly. Why did everyone care so much about Jews all of a sudden? First Ernst, and now Sophie. It was tiresome. And worrying.

Sophie nodded. "If you have one grandparent who is *Juden*," she said, "then you are *Juden* too. You must have four pure grandparents to get an *Ariernachweis*."

"To get a what?"

"Here." Sophie passed Marta the peeled apple.

"What's a —"

"Here." She passed Marta the knife.

"Ouch! *Careful.*"

"Sorry," Sophie said.

Marta put her finger in her mouth. "Soph, to get a what?"

"*Ariernachweis*. An Aryan certificate."

Marta spoke Czech. The only German she knew came from *Der Struwwelpeter*; Pepik could recite its stories by heart, about a boy who sucked his thumb and had it cut off by a tailor with big shears, a boy who refused to eat his soup and died of starvation, et cetera. An ominous book, to be certain.

"If you don't have an *Ariernachweis*, you'll need one," Sophie said. "Soon." She spread her fingers and began to lick the juice from them, one by one.

Marta moved the bowl of peeled fruit aside, covering it first with a chipped porcelain plate. She had never known her mother, let alone her mother's parents. There could be any number of secrets in that part of her past.

Her father she remembered, despite the desire not to — but the Bauers were her family now. They had never said so, not in so many words, but she felt they had an understanding.

"Chamberlain says there will be peace in our time," Marta said.

Sophie dumped the apple peels in the bin under the sink. She filled the empty mixing bowl with water and scrubbed.

"Peace in our time," she said. "We'll see about that." She leaned out the window to pour the dirty contents down the outdoor drain.

"We'll see about that? What do you —"

But there was the sound of Pavel entering the house, the clinking as he hung his factory keys on the hook by the door. Through the archway between the rooms Marta saw his business suit and cufflinks. She thought of him just that morning in his thin nightshirt, and of the moment of closeness they'd shared. But he was changing guises so frequently these days. Now he seemed a different person entirely.

Marta heard Pavel shout upstairs for his wife, and then she heard Anneliese's footsteps descending the stairs. There was no small talk, no kiss hello. "I want to leave for Prague," Anneliese said.

There was a silence, and Marta looked up from the *chlebíčky* she was making. Pavel was lighting his pipe, teasing out the strands of tobacco, holding a match to the bowl and sucking on the stem to make it catch. His cheeks working like bellows.

"I am buying new bobbins," he said.

"New what?" Anneliese asked.

"New bobbins. For the flax-spinning frames."

"Pavel. Did you hear what I said?" Anneliese was unused to her wishes being challenged. There was the click of her own lighter; from where Marta stood in the kitchen she could see the parlour filling up with smoke, the grey of Anneliese's cigarette rising to meet the sweeter blue of Pavel's pipe.

"Two types of bobbins are possible," Pavel said. "Ernst recommended the more expensive type."

"What an ass," Anneliese said, forcefully. "To be thinking of bobbins at a time like this."

Marta wondered if she meant that Ernst was an ass, or her own husband, standing in front of her.

There was another silence and Marta turned back to her task, laying slices of cheese against the dark, dense bread. Pepik liked onions too, and she cut him a sliver — the smell was sour and made her eyes water. When Anneliese finally spoke again there was a waver in her voice. "Hitler has arrived, Pavel," she said. "Don't you see what is happening all around us?"

Beyond the window a stream of people was moving towards the train station. They were carrying baskets and hat boxes and birdcages, their winter coats pulled on top of sweaters despite the fact that it was a gorgeous fall day. But Pavel did not indulge his young wife. "We have invested in our country, and we shall continue to do so," he said, testing out his new-found certainty. "The only way to function here is to base our actions on a belief in permanence."

"Prague is part of our country."

"The factory is here."

"But your mother — she wants to go."

Pavel scoffed. "Like Jesus rose to heaven she does!"

"She's too old to stay if things continue this way."

"My mother would not leave here if —"

"Then what about Pepik?"

Marta had heard a rumour that the Jewish children from Cheb had been rounded up and shot. It was only a rumour though, and nothing she could be sure of. She wiped it from her mind like a schoolgirl wiping a sponge across her slate.

Pavel was saying something Marta could not discern; she cocked her ear towards the parlour but made out only the words "bonds" and "infrastructure." She could see him sweeping his wife into his arms, stroking her dark, curly hair. When he spoke again his voice was clear and calm. "My mother will be fine," he said. "She wouldn't leave here if you put a gun to her head. And Pepik will be fine. I'll make sure of it." He paused. "We can't run away, Liesel," he said. "We must stay and live what we believe in. Otherwise Hitler has won without even firing a shot."

"Hasn't he already won without firing a shot?"

Marta realized that Anneliese was right. But Pavel would not be baited.

"We'll stay," he said. "You have to trust me. Everything will be fine."

Three days later Marta carried a telegram over to Pavel to open. The Bauer factory would be occupied by the Nazis.

Český Krumlov, 1 March 1939

My dear son Pavel,

Where are you? Have you arrived?

I posted a letter to you via Ernst Anselm, but as yet have heard nothing. I also asked him to send a telegram on my behalf.

Did you not receive it?

I hope that Anneliese is happy to be in the city of her birth. Have you settled into Max and Alžběta's flat? And how is your new job? Is the factory continuing to run despite ██████ *?*

██*. I am very eager to discuss this. I fear I made a grave mistake by staying behind. I have tried to contact you, but to no avail. I wonder why I've received no response and I wonder if* ██████████████████*.*

██████████████ *Please, send a letter or a cable as quickly as possible.* ██████ ████████ ████████████ *phone lines, so it is better to write. I look forward to hearing from you and trust you will help me join you and that we will all be happily reunited.*

Please give my love to Anneliese and little Pepik.

Your forever loving,
Mother

(FILE UNDER: Bauer, Rosa. Died Birkenau, 1943)

S OMETIMES I'LL BE WALKING.

Say it's dusk, and the end of October. The buses leaving the university are lit up like bright aquariums, the buses themselves swimming through the dark element of the evening. The ducks have forgotten to fly south, and huddle dimly together at the edge of the pond. Say there's a chill in the air; I've been resisting my winter jacket, and now the wind slips a cool hand down my back, the first touch I've felt in . . . forever. It comes over me then. I've had a good day at my desk but still I get the sense that I'm missing, or that something within me is missing, some crucial piece of me that used to make my whole self run. I've been taken apart one too many times, and the little cog at the centre of my chest has slipped into the gutter and been lost.

It's hard to imagine anyone ever finding it.

It's too hidden, too covered in leaves.

It would take a small person, someone curious, someone low to the ground.

It would take a child — and of course it's far too late for that.

The children suffered the most. This is what my research has led me to believe. Some would say otherwise, but the children *did* know. Even the little ones — perhaps the little ones especially — soaked it all up. They absorbed it directly, a straight hit to the bloodstream. All of the stress, the incredible tension, the relentless, insidious day-to-day: encroaching hunger, restricted living quarters, the edicts marching forward, a row of shiny boots and polished guns. They took in their parents' fear like black milk — that's Celan, of course — from the breast. They were raised on it, fed on fear, until fear itself was in their bones, in their visible skeletons, where baby fat should have been. When the children at Auschwitz were sent towards the gas chambers, on the most basic level they knew what was coming.

Tell me, how should I have faith in the world when I know the things that I know?

The children I've dedicated my life's work to — they got out. But it wasn't easy for them either. They were sent away from their families, from houses full of fighting they could not understand, and they blamed themselves. They were given away as Chamberlain gave away the Sudetenland. They thought they had done something terrible to merit this. Even when they were reassured otherwise.

Sometimes, walking in the evening, a toque pulled low over my thin white hair, I try to summon up the child I myself must have been. All I get are flashes: shoes with brass buckles, a curl against my forehead, a sliver of female laughter and a back that turns and disappears.

There is a feeling that I could have done something. Shame that I couldn't save her.

Beneath the shame: fear. Beneath the fear: grief. Alone in my small rooms, so late in life, the knocking from the centre of my ribs. Someone is locked inside there. Has been for years. I roll onto my side, pull the pillow over my ears. And still the little voice, the pleading. *Mama*.

I've lived almost my whole life without her. There is no reason I should expect to be walking late in November, my hands in my pockets, and turn a corner and see her, her thin coat, no scarf. Her cheeks hollow, the way I last remember her, in the winter of 1945. There is no reason I should still hope to find her, to take her home to my apartment and heap blankets over her, to spoon hot soup into her mouth and whisper her to sleep.

I will never sing to her — some old Yiddish folk song — while the snow sifts silently down.

It's shameful really, the weakness of my longing. And yet the heart continues. There's the fluttering in the ribs. The hope that all the loss might somehow be redeemed.

Ach — that's the phone. Probably the new department secretary. Mara? Marsha? Excuse me for a minute. No, don't. I'll just let it ring.

What was I saying? Yes, the children. There were, of course, among the children whom I study, situations that worked out well. There were the people we now call "righteous Gentiles," Christians who risked their lives. There were families in England who gave up everything they had, and often what they did not have, to offer a tiny traveller some kind of home. There are stories of love and heartbreaking humanity — but these are not the bulk of the stories.

What I have found far more frequently are cases of trauma and upset. The Kindertransport children who were sent out of Czechoslovakia often spoke no English. They arrived in a country with no desire for war, battling tensions about its own role in the conflict brewing across the Channel. The children arrived in homes where money was scarce, to foster parents who had been shamed into taking them. At what we would now call a "critical developmental stage," everything solid was pulled out from under them. Children do not forget that. It stays with them, a wall that goes up at the first hint of intimacy.

We academics are told to frame the world in objective terms, but I am speaking now, as you've guessed, from my particular experience.

There are things I remember about my mother.

The growling of her stomach late at night.

Her fingers combing gently through my hair.

The first notes of — what? — a lullaby? No. Something less certain, less solid.

I remember a dim street, late fall, and my mother at the end of it, a kerchief knotted under her chin. She was looking back at me already then, as though across a great gulf of time. I tried to move towards her but the street was so long, and there were people blocking my path. When I caught another glimpse, she had taken off her scarf. It was crumpled in a ball in her hand, which she held against her chest. A bit of wind played with the hair around her face. She held my gaze — there was something she was telling me, something she needed me to know. The whole history of our family was contained in that look. Then she turned a corner and was gone.

I've spent years going back to this memory. It is so clear, so real. And yet. What was she doing leaving such a very young child alone in the street? The first flakes were already falling.

Time is a snow globe; you shake it and everything changes. A thin coat of white and the world disappears. This memory I have of the look on her face: it must be something I made up.

The mind plays tricks, inventing what wasn't there.

Of my father, I remember absolutely nothing.

TWO

PAVEL BAUER WAS ON HIS WAY OUT when the telegram arrived. He read it. He read it a second time. He slipped it inside his coat pocket.

"I'm off."

"Where to?" Anneliese asked.

"Where do you think?"

He spoke as though the answer should be obvious to his wife, but Marta had no idea where he might be going either. He was now forbidden by the Nazis to set foot in his own factory. Although she did not want to admit it, this unnerved Marta. That someone else had this authority over Pavel — Pavel, whom she had only ever seen as being in charge. She found herself uncertain about exactly how to speak to him now. She couldn't help but feel that some sort of imposter had snuck in and taken his place.

Anneliese was acting oddly too, Marta thought, although perhaps this was more to be expected. The town square was overrun with Hitlerjugend and Wehrmacht, after all; with rifles and polished boots and tanks. The Goldstein Tailor Shop was still closed. There was no question of Pepik's going outside to play. All the good citizens were cooped up like rabbits in holes, Anneliese told Marta, and all the hooligans were parading about like they owned the town. Still, this didn't stop Anneliese from leaving in the middle of the morning — once she was sure Pavel was gone — with her large Greta Garbo sunglasses and fresh red lipstick. She whispered to Marta that she was going to look in on the Hoffmans. She said she'd be gone several hours, but she returned twenty minutes later. The unpasteurized milk was boiling over on the stove; Sophie was on the patio playing with her Ouija board. The pointer made sweeping sounds, whooshing across the cardboard.

"Sophie!" Marta called. "Mrs. Bauer is back."

"And?"

Marta winced at the teenager's insolence; she was finding Sophie harder to bear these days. In light of everything that was going on, though, in light of the occupation, Marta's earlier grudge against Anneliese was forgotten. It was like that with Anneliese — one minute Marta resented her, the next she adored her. Well, that's the way it went with family, she supposed. It was the way a daughter might feel about her mother, or a mother about her child. And it was true, she felt almost protective now as she watched Anneliese trying to undo the knot on her kerchief. Anneliese's fingers were trembling, and it took her several attempts. Finally she succeeded, smoothing down the triangle of bright silk, only to crumple it up again and shove it back in her purse.

"The Hoffmans are gone," she announced to Marta. She dug around for her silver cigarette case, which she laid on top of the glass-topped cigar box. She dug through her purse some more.

Marta saw a thin film of perspiration on Anneliese's brow. She offered her the tortoiseshell lighter off the mantel, shielding the flame with her cupped hand. "Mrs. Bauer?"

Anneliese looked up, her cigarette dangling from her lower lip, like a heroine in a romance novel. "Oh, yes, thank you, Marta." She leaned over and sucked until the tip of the cigarette glowed red. Then she leaned back and let out a long, slow exhale. Her fingers fluttered at her throat. "They left the door unlocked," she said. "But everything is gone. That beautiful chandelier."

"*Hanna* Hoffman?"

Marta had thought that Anneliese was going to look in on Gerta Hoffman. Hanna was lower down on her priority list. She was someone Mrs. Bauer thought of when all the most important dinner guests had already been invited.

"The breakfront is still there, and the armoire, but the side-board is gone and the Persian carpet. I looked in her wardrobe. In both of them. Empty."

Anneliese seemed hesitant to convey this last bit of information — that she had gone upstairs and looked through her friend's closets — but Marta nodded encouragingly to show she understood the circumstance. That Anneliese was acting in accordance with the dire times.

"I suppose they left the door unlocked to prevent the windows from being smashed. They must have figured the hooligans would get in one way or another if they wanted to." Anneliese shrugged. "There was a steamer trunk left behind too. Several dresses hung on the wardrobe side. As though they left in a hurry."

Marta heard Sophie slip back into the kitchen and begin banging pots and pans together loudly. It sounded like she was making the noise on purpose, like a child's imitation of cooking. Marta wished Mrs. Bauer would scold Sophie, show her that, despite the chaos of the occupation, the Bauer household

would continue to run unchanged. But Anneliese only grimaced in the direction of the kitchen and said she was going
to go take something for her nerves and lie down and should
not be disturbed.

She paused, though, before climbing the stairs. "Hanna
isn't even Jewish!" she said. "But Francek is enough for them,
it seems." She hesitated again. "And who knows about Hanka.
Maybe she has an illegal grandfather in her past."

At the word *past* a silence rose up between the two women.
Marta liked to pretend that nobody knew the depravity she
came from, but that of course was not the case. Anneliese
knew. Maybe not everything, but she knew enough. And was
kind enough to pretend she did not. What if things were otherwise? What if she weren't so gracious? Anneliese exhaled
cigarette smoke and fanned above her head as though trying
to clear the air of what had suddenly materialized. The ghosts
seemed to respect what Mrs. Bauer wished; the moment
passed and Anneliese crushed out her cigarette, climbing the
stairs to her room.

Pavel was gone for hours, returning only in the middle of the
afternoon, with Ernst. They came in the door mid-conversation.
"It might be wise," Ernst was saying.

"All the accounts?"

"Just as a precautionary measure. To have them in a Gentile's name."

Marta looked up. What was Ernst up to? She tried to catch
his eye, but the men took the stairs to the study without even

removing their overcoats. She heard the heavy door closing behind them. By the time they came downstairs again the sun had slunk from the square like an old stray tabby. Anneliese had still not reappeared, and Marta was feeding Pepik an early meal of *knedlíky* cut into bite-sized pieces.

The men had obviously concluded whatever business they'd been discussing. The conversation had moved on to lighter things. In the front hall she saw Pavel pass Ernst his hat. "What's the definition of the perfect Aryan?" Ernst asked.

Pavel made a face to show he didn't know.

"Number one," Ernst said, raising his forefinger, "he's as slim as the fatso Goering. Number two, he's eagle-eyed as the bespectacled Himmler." He paused. "Number three? Swift and stealthy as the club-footed Goebbels. And number four, he's as blond as the dark-haired Hitler!"

Pavel laughed, then the two men lowered their voices, speaking for several minutes in hushed tones. "There's something else," she heard Ernst say to Pavel.

"What's this?"

"Put it on your lapel."

"But they must know I'm —"

Marta peeked into the hall and saw the small flash of the swastika Ernst was pinning to Pavel's breast. He looked up as he did it, catching and holding Marta's eye. He winked. She felt, for a brief moment, like she was going to be sick.

"It can't hurt," Ernst said to Pavel.

"Are you sure?" Pavel asked.

"Just don't forget to take it off if you cross into France!"

Pavel clapped Ernst on the back. "Good man," he said. "Thank you."

Marta turned back to give Pepik another bite. She heard the sound of the door opening and closing, of Pavel turning the lock.

Pavel Bauer was a thin man; Marta would even use the word *small*. And now as he sat at the table, he seemed, she thought, like a lost little boy. His shoulders were narrow and the skin at the back of his neck where the barber had shaved looked as pink and exposed as a newborn's. She could barely stand to look at him, so vulnerable, so unaware of his friend Ernst's shifting allegiances.

Pavel Bauer sat for along time with his hands folded in front of him.

He slowly lowered his head into his hands.

❧

Now that the factory had been occupied, there was nowhere for Pavel to go during the days. He took Pepik across town to visit his Baba and brought him back home in time for dinner.

"I feel all cooped up," Anneliese said at the table. "Like a rabbit in a hole." She held her silver cutlery to her head like long ears. It was an analogy she had grown fond of in the past several days, an analogy she thought was particularly apt. But Pavel said, "Things will change. I just need to make myself indispensable."

He tucked his linen napkin into his shirt. "Pepik," he said. "Stop that."

Pepik had massed his mashed potatoes like mountain ranges and was — with his fingers — placing individual peas in a row behind them. The peas were soldiers taking refuge behind the potato peaks. "Those are the bad guys," Marta whispered in his ear. "You'd better eat them all up!"

Sophie had left the house earlier that afternoon and was still not home by five o'clock, so Marta had taken it upon herself to braise a small red cabbage from the root cellar. Cooking was not her job, nor her strength, but she was willing, these days, to help in whatever way possible. Pavel was distracted and Anneliese kept repeating that her nerves were shot; Marta felt that it fell to her to preserve some semblance of normalcy. Along with the cabbage she'd prepared chicken with butter and seasoning salt, the way she knew Mrs. Bauer liked it. It was now 7:05 and there was still no sign of the young cook. Marta hoped there was still some strudel left over from last night that she could serve for dessert. She leaned over and moved Pepik's hands away from his plate, showing him again how to properly hold his cutlery.

"But darling," Anneliese was saying to her husband, "there's no way for you to be indispensable." She cleared her throat. "To the Germans," she clarified. "Of course you're indispensable — to me!" She laughed. "But there's no way they will see that."

"You're right," Pavel said. "Why can't they see it? They need flax. They need cloth. If they convert the factory . . . *Think* of the area we supply. Think of all the smaller factories that will grind to a halt. Lipna and Trebelice and Marsponova and . . ."

He stabbed at a piece of chicken with his fork. "Pepik, I said *stop*."

"Not to mention Krumlov," added Anneliese.

"But what should I do? Am I supposed to just walk away? From what it took my father fifty years to build?"

Anneliese nodded her chin at her son. "There are more important things to worry about now than money."

Pavel Bauer sighed. "I didn't say it was about money." He paused. "Well," he said, "of *course* it's about money. You have no idea — thank God Ernst suggested —" Then he said, forcefully, "It isn't about money. It's about family."

The implication was that Pavel would teach his son about the business in the same way his own father had done with him, that to give it up would be to forsake not only the factory but Pepik's own future.

"Pepik is a child," Anneliese said.

"Children grow up."

Marta considered how hard it was, at the moment, to imagine. She had resorted to spoon-feeding Pepik his peas, a hand cupped under his chin as if he were an infant. She agreed with Anneliese. It was difficult to picture him at the helm of such an industry. He was too sensitive, too introverted. It would only mean disappointment for everyone.

Anneliese said, "There was a telegram from —"

But Pavel knew about the telegram and interrupted. "Liesel, we are not leaving. Give me some time!" He began to speak rapidly in German — it was Anneliese's mother tongue and the language the Bauers reverted to when they fought. Marta did not understand the words, but she understood the way Pavel jabbed his fork in the air, the chicken dangling precariously.

Pepik had left the battle between potatoes and peas to wage on his plate. His eyes were now moving from one parent to the other, as though watching strikes being exchanged between the famous Italian fencer Aldo Nadi and his brother Nedo.

Marta tried to remove herself from the Bauer's argument by focusing on their son. *"Miláčku,"* she said, hunching over him, "try one more bite," but Pepik was saved by a knock at the front door.

The family fell silent and waited one heartbeat for Sophie to answer it, before remembering that Sophie was not there. Marta jumped up and smoothed down her apron.

"Shall I, Mrs. Bauer?"

Pavel straightened his tie and put down his fork. He was working to rearrange his facial features, to hide his frustration.

At the door, Ernst handed Marta his coat. He looked over her shoulder to make sure they were alone, then reached forward and pinched her nipple.

Marta winced, and then giggled. "What are you doing here?" she whispered. Up close, Ernst's pockmarks appeared even deeper than usual, but there was something about them that she considered vaguely handsome.

"What do you mean?" he asked.

"You're here all the time," she said.

"And so?"

"I thought you felt . . . Mr. Bauer is —"

She had been about to remind Ernst of Pavel's religion, but Ernst interrupted her. "Pavel is my dear old friend." He looked at her intently, as though this should explain things, but Marta was still perplexed. It must have shown on her face, because Ernst spoke again. "My dear old *wealthy* friend." He held his earlobe briefly between thumb and forefinger.

So Marta's suspicion was confirmed: Ernst was taking advantage of the occupation to try to get hold of Pavel's money. A wave rose within her — guilt, and shame, and something even darker she couldn't name. Part of her wanted to extricate herself; another part wouldn't allow it. She moved to press herself against Ernst, trying to blot out her feelings, to forget what he'd said. She turned her face up to his, waiting to be kissed. The Bauers were right there in the next room, but something in her suddenly wished to get caught, wished to have the whole thing out in the open. The liaison was exhausting, not to mention the secrecy — and this new information about Ernst's motivation. But Ernst raised his eyebrows to show a kiss was too risky.

"I'm sorry," he whispered.

Marta shrugged, pretending indifference.

"Don't be like that," he said. "I need you on my side. Don't you know that?"

Marta didn't answer but she saw all at once that he meant it. He was more uncertain than he was letting on, about his feelings towards the Jews and how his old friend Pavel might fit in with them. He wanted to be bolstered, reassured. Ernst too, Marta realized, felt guilty. Even if he himself was unaware of it.

He winked at her but moved away towards the parlour, towards the sound of the Bauers' voices. Partway across the hall, though, he turned back to her. She thought he was going to kiss her after all, but he only drew her close, rather roughly, and pressed his mouth to her ear. "Did you hear me?" he whispered. "I need you on my side. You'd better decide whose side you're on."

∼◎∼

In the dining room Pavel and Anneliese had successfully trans-
formed into a tableau of a happy couple. Ernst said, "No, no,
don't get up," but Pavel stood anyway, the embodiment of perfect manners. He leaned across the table and shook his friend's
hand.

"What's going on at the factory?" he asked, as quickly as it
was polite to do so. Pavel had been let go because of his religion, but Ernst, his Gentile plant manager, still had to report
to work each day. "What's Herrick doing down there? Any
news?"

"Would you like some chicken?" Anneliese asked.

Ernst took Pavel's cue to sit. "Herrick is bumbling around
like the idiot that he is. He wants to know about the jute
cartel. He wants to know about the accounting system, and
the American Fraser investment. I told him he'll have to ask
you, that if they would only bring you back in . . ."

Ernst paused and shook his head again. "No," he said. "No
news."

But he had removed a piece of folded paper from his
pocket, which he now pushed across the table in Pavel's direction.

Marta wondered at the extent of the deception. First the
joke making fun of the Nazis, and now this. Ernst was presenting his usual face to Pavel — a kind one, the face of a friend.
He seemed willing to go to extraordinary lengths to present
himself as other than he really was.

It was, she realized, a trait she recognized in herself.

Anneliese was fussing with the silver pepper mill. "We
are living in a very historic time," she said, laying her cutlery
down to peer up into its mechanics. "When has it happened

— I mean, when in the history of the world has it happened —
that a state has voluntarily given up part of its territory?"

She looked at her husband enquiringly. Then she turned
to Marta. "I think this needs refilling," she said, holding up the
pepper mill like a hammer.

Marta nodded and moved to stand.

"After dinner will be fine," Anneliese said.

"You're right," Pavel answered his wife. "But we have a
good army. We have —" He stopped and swiped at the edge
of his mouth with his linen napkin. "We *had* the Skoda works
and the munitions. Think what we've given up. What they've
taken. The industry."

"The industry, yes, and seventy percent of our steel,"
agreed Anneliese. She turned to Ernst. "Did you know we've
lost seventy percent of our steel? And seventy percent of our
electrical power? And three and a half million citizens!"

"Well," said Pavel, "they mightn't see it that way." He was
referring, Marta knew, to the many German Czechs who saw
Hitler's arrival as something that would reunite them finally
with their *Vaterland*.

"It was President Beneš who was betrayed," Pavel continued. "But he'll come through for us. How, exactly, I don't
know. But I believe —"

"You believe what?" challenged Anneliese.

"Pepik, *please*."

"Beneš couldn't help if —"

"Masaryk would not have let this happen, it's true. But
mark my words, there'll be hell to pay from Beneš when it is
all over."

Ernst had been sitting silent, with his elbows on his knees

and his fingers pressed against each other in front of his face.
Now he straightened. He touched his necktie and said, "I don't
know that Beneš . . ."

Pavel looked at his friend. "You don't know that Beneš
what?"

But Ernst, Marta thought, seemed to realize that respond-
ing might expose his allegiance. "No," he said quickly. "Never
mind." He cleared his throat; the edges of his mouth turned
up in the faintest of smiles. "What does Marta think of all
this?" he asked.

Anneliese lifted her head sharply, looking from one to
the other. Marta cursed Ernst internally, and her desire to be
discovered completely vanished. It was all well and good for
Ernst to make fun — he had a family to go home to. She felt
Anneliese's eyes on her and didn't speak, her own eyes lowered
and her hands in her lap. Eventually the moment passed and
the Bauers kept talking.

"You understand," said Anneliese to her husband, "that if
we lived in Germany right now we would not be allowed to
attend the theatre. We would not be allowed to attend a con-
cert. Or the cinema." She paused, tapping the polished table-
top with a perfectly filed red nail. "We would not be allowed to
sit on a public bench!"

She gave a little chuckle. "What we would be doing sitting
on a public bench I have no idea — but you get my drift."

"That's just in Germany," Pavel said, stubborn.

Anneliese spread her hands open in front of her. "Welcome
to Germany," she said.

∽◉∾

School resumed a few days later, on October 5 — Marta knew better than to mention the fact that it was Yom Kippur, the Day of Atonement. Mr. Goldstein had told her so. She also didn't say anything to the Bauers about the note she'd found from Sophie, tucked under her pillow: Sophie was leaving for good; she refused to demean herself by working for Jews. Marta thought that Sophie must have left a similar note for Pavel and Anneliese, but they didn't bring it up, and neither did she. They were all, Marta knew, trying to pretend that nothing had changed.

It was clear, though, when she went to pick up Pepik at the end of his first day back at school, that things were indeed very different. Classes had resumed, but under German control. Pepik was waiting for her outside his classroom, clutching his slate, the sponge dangling from its string. He looked so helpless, so vulnerable, she thought, in his cap and short pants with his little knees exposed.

"I had to sit at the back of the room," he told her.

"In your usual seat?"

He shook his head. "Facing backwards. With Fiertig."

Fiertig, she knew, was the only other Jewish child in the class.

Marta rushed towards Pepik and knelt in front of him, kissing his cheeks, right and left, back and forth at length, but she didn't ask for more details. She couldn't stand to hear them. As they were leaving the schoolhouse she saw that a large swastika had appeared in the front hall, along with three new photographs outside the principal's office. The first showed Hitler, with his little moustache that reminded Marta of the snout on Pepik's electric train. The second was of Heinlein, the leader of the Sudeten Nazi party. The third photo showed a man Marta didn't recognize — there were round glasses perched on the bridge of his nose. Maybe it was the bespectacled Himmler from Ernst's joke about the perfect Aryan.

When they got home, Pepik ran upstairs to play with his train. Marta heard the sound of someone moving around in the pantry, a grunt as something heavy was lifted, and then the squeak of a chair being pushed across linoleum.

"Sophie?" she called. She fully expected Sophie to have changed her mind and returned — she was like that. Unreliable. Easily influenced. Marta took off her coat, wondering where the girl had been. Maybe serving strudel at the "soup kitchen" the Germans had set up for their poor starving countrymen who had been living so long under Czech rule. Talk about *Greuelpropaganda*! If Sophie wanted to discuss the spreading of false rumours of atrocities . . .

"Sophie?" she called again.

But it was a slimmer rear end that met Marta's gaze when she stuck her head into the pantry, and narrower hips. Where Anneliese's skirt had risen up at the back of her knees a creamy fringe of lace from her slip was visible. She twisted around, almost losing her balance. "Oh, Marta, for God's sake. Don't *do* that."

Anneliese laid her palm over her heart and closed her eyes. "I'm sorry. You scared me. I thought I was alone in the house."

It was close and warm in the pantry. Marta undid the top two buttons of her cardigan. She looked around and saw several large crates of groceries and an oversized sack of potatoes. "Did *you* buy all of this?" she asked Mrs. Bauer.

Yom Kippur, Mr. Goldstein had told her, was supposed to

be a day of fasting, and here they were surrounded by food. There was a huge stack of tinned sardines, piled on top of each other like Pepik's wooden building blocks. An enormous piece of lard that Marta knew would never keep. There were fifteen or twenty jars of preserves — lindenberry, it looked like, and plum. The deep bluish purple was the same colour as the sapphires in the watch from Paris, the one she'd imagined herself wearing as she waltzed across a glamorous dance floor. The one, she saw now, that Anneliese was wearing.

Anneliese followed Marta's gaze, then extended her arm to give Marta a better view. "It's lovely, isn't it?" She nodded to show Marta could touch it. The diamonds were cool and neatly symmetrical, like a child's milk teeth.

Marta wished for a moment that she was the one who owned it, the one with the privilege to show it off. But she had to pretend she'd never even seen it before. "Beautiful," she said, her jaw tight. And then she thought how odd it was for Anneliese to be wearing the watch in the middle of the day, when it was clearly meant for dinners or balls. She looked at Anneliese closely — her complexion seemed suddenly pale. And she kept craning her neck to look over Marta's shoulder, as though she suspected they were being watched.

"Is everything okay, Mrs. Bauer?" Marta asked.

Anneliese bristled. "Of course it's not okay. Look at what's happening all around us! The Germans are now claiming places that are purely Czech. They use some technical or strategic reason, like the railway line. They're swallowing up everything other than —"

Marta cleared her throat. "What I'm asking is . . ." She cast around in her mind, trying to put it delicately. "Are *you* okay, Mrs. Bauer?"

Anneliese got out her compact and rouged her cheeks, looking at Marta slantwise. "I'm sure I don't know what you mean." She snapped the compact closed and reached for her cigarettes.

Marta passed her the silver Zippo, flipping back the catch with her thumb. "I was worried you might . . . I was thinking of the time . . ."

"What time?"

There was reproach in Anneliese's voice, a kind of warning, and Marta knew she should drop it. Instead she said, "I was remembering when you —"

Anneliese flicked the lighter closed before Marta could finish the sentence. "I know what you're thinking, Marta. And I've asked you not to bring up the subject."

Marta felt herself flush. "Certainly, Mrs. Bauer. It was only out of concern for your well-being." As she said this, though, she knew it was only partially true. She didn't want what had happened to ever be repeated, but also — if she was honest — part of her enjoyed the fact that she could either keep or tell Anneliese's secret. The power she held in this one single arena. She was, she realized, still upset about the other day, when Anneliese had diminished her role as Pepik's governess. She hadn't forgotten about the jab after all; she hadn't forgotten about any of the jabs, but rather had let them build up inside her like a big pile of *palacinky*. And now, to top it off, she found herself jealous of the watch. Which, she realized, was ridiculous. What had she ever done to deserve something so beautiful? Not to mention that she'd have nowhere to wear it . . .

"As I've said to you before," Anneliese said, "those were special circumstances." She inhaled, holding the smoke in her lungs for a long moment. Then she exhaled. "The baby," she said.

Marta saw Anneliese's hands were trembling, and realized she had really unnerved her. And for no reason at all. "Of course, Mrs. Bauer. I understand. I'm sorry." But Anneliese still looked pale, and Marta knew she was now thinking of the lost baby girl, was slowly being sucked into the tide pool of grief. Now look what she'd done! Anneliese already had enough to worry about without being reminded of the greatest tragedy of her life. Marta had the sudden thought of repenting even further, to distract Anneliese by letting her in on another secret. "I know someone else who tried to kill herself," she said. As soon as she'd spoken, though, Anneliese's face fell, and Marta cursed herself for her bad judgement. Why didn't she just stop talking already?

"Who?" Anneliese asked, a weariness in her voice. She didn't really want to know, Marta saw, but she had no choice now but to pursue the conversation. "Hella Anselm," she said.

Anneliese looked up sharply. "Ernst's wife? When?"

"A long time ago."

"She didn't succeed?" Anneliese laughed at her own question. "Obviously not!"

"I don't think she wanted to."

"Most people don't."

"She's not the most stable person," Marta said, cautious.

"I won't ask how you know that."

The silences lined up between them, a row of children with blank faces.

"How did she —" Anneliese started, but she stopped herself mid-sentence. "No, don't tell me."

Marta exhaled, relieved. They could finally drop it. "Here, Mrs. Bauer," she said eagerly. "Let me help you unpack this." She reached out to lift the sack of potatoes, but Anneliese blocked her path. "I'll do it," she said. "I need to be doing something." She hoisted the burlap bag onto the shelf, clearly as relieved as Marta to have something else to focus on.

"I apologize again," Marta said under her breath. But Anneliese didn't hear her or else chose to ignore the comment. "I'm going crazy inside all day," she said instead. "Like a little scared rabbit in its hole."

She looked up and saw Marta smiling. "What?"

"Nothing. I understand what you mean."

Anneliese held her cigarette away from her face in her left hand and swabbed at her eyes with her right. "Do you?" she asked. She touched her eye again. "I simply can't keep living like this. And I don't know why Pavel can't see it. It's dangerous to stay, because you get used to it. You accommodate. You think, well, it isn't so bad if the Herrings don't want to associate with us. And it isn't so bad if the Reichstag Company won't sell to us. It isn't so bad if —" Here she looked up at Marta. "But it is bad, isn't it. We should leave, don't you think?"

Marta paused with her hand on a jar of preserves. "I don't know," she said slowly. "I suppose that I . . ."

"Shouldn't we leave?" Anneliese asked. "Doesn't it make sense for us to get out 'as fast as our little feet will carry us'?"

This was a line from *Der Struwwelpeter*, a line Pepik especially liked to repeat. Marta smiled nervously but she could see Anneliese was frustrated, that she would have to produce an opinion or risk displeasing her benefactor for a second time. Did she think they should leave?

It was a question that had so many other questions attached to it, one linked to the next like the butcher's strings of sausages.

Where would they go?

What would happen to the house?

What about Ernst?

And at the end of this string, the final question, the one that for Marta gave all the others weight: if the Bauers left, what would happen to her?

She opened her mouth to speak, and as she did there was a loud crash above their heads. It was followed by a moment of silence, and then a slow wail that gained in momentum until it filled the air around them like a siren.

The two women looked at each other.

Pepik.

"I'll go," said Anneliese, but she didn't move. Marta took her cue. "No, I'll go," she said, grateful to finally be of some use. "Mrs. Bauer, leave it to me."

Marta went upstairs and soothed Pepik and taped a piece of gauze over the almost invisible cut he had incurred; he'd overturned the lamp on his mother's bedside table reaching for her peppermints. For such a small injury he was making a big fuss. He seemed, she thought, to be weeping for the crumbling order of the world around him. Marta held him and patted his back until the crying subsided, and then gave him a half-hearted talking-to about not going into his parents' bedroom in their absence. She got him into his pajamas, settled him in his green bed with the painted yellow feet, and placed *Der Stru-wwelpeter* in front of him. It was like setting a needle down on a gramophone. Anyone who didn't know better would think Pepik was actually reading.

Marta moved around the room, tidying up. She gathered the lead soldiers together and put them in the playroom across the hall, the room that had been meant for the baby girl. It had been painted a beautiful buttercup yellow in the fifth month of Anneliese's pregnancy, and curtains made with lace from the Weil factory in Nachod had been purchased. Marta remembered the earnestness with which Pavel and Anneliese had debated where to place the change table. Next to the door? Or beneath the window, so the little angel could look up at the clear blue sky from whence she'd come?

The baby died at three weeks of age. The doctors couldn't say what had happened; Anneliese had gone in to see if she needed a new diaper and discovered her face down in her crib. That was all. There was no need to repaint the room, but the frilly drapes were removed. Pavel must have done it himself in the middle of the night. They were there one evening and the next morning they were gone. So was the change table and the linen diapers with their safety pins and the butter-fly mobile made of hand-carved ivory from Pavel's safari in Kenya. Anneliese herself did not reappear for days. Dasha, the cook at the time, would leave a breakfast tray with an egg cup and toast outside the bedroom door and retrieve it when it reappeared several hours later, untouched. Pavel dealt with the death as if it were just another business deal gone bad. "We've lost Eliza," was all he said to Marta, and Marta had nodded to show she understood.

Marta's memories of the baby were vivid. The knot of the umbilical cord turning black against her tiny belly. The cry that sounded so much like a kitten. And, just after her birth, a family photograph in which Marta had been included: the thrill of posing for the camera standing behind Pepik, and Pavel with the bundle in his arms. Pepik, though, had been too young to remember. As far as Marta could tell, he had no idea he'd once had a sister.

There hadn't even been a funeral, no sitting shiva. Marta hadn't even seen the body.

When Pepik was done reciting his story, she helped him wash his face and brush his teeth. "Measure me!" he said, and pressed his back against the tape on the inside of his closet door. "Am I bigger?"

He was obsessed, after just one day back at school, with being a great big grown-up boy. Marta knew he thought that if he grew tall enough he could once again sit with his friend Villem, up near the front, instead of in the back corner next to Fiertig Goldberg.

Marta couldn't bear to tell him otherwise.

"You're bigger," she said.

"How much?"

He was drawing himself up to his full height, chin tucked in, cheeks puffed out.

"Almost half an inch."

She made a mark with the lead pencil and showed him. "Time for bed, *miláčku*." She patted his bottom.

He pouted for a moment. "My cut hurts," he said, pointing to the gauze on his elbow.

Marta raised her eyebrows to show that she meant it.

"Okay," he said, relenting. "Time for bed." And he nuzzled his face into her arm.

Marta tucked Pepik in and went downstairs. Anneliese had abandoned the unpacking of the potatoes. There was a note in her deep blue fountain pen ink that said *I've gone up to bed, would you mind unpacking the rest of the food?* It was signed with a large flourish of an A. Marta was slightly insulted. Of course she would unpack the food; she had expected to.

The thick of the heat had gone out of the day and left a cool that was both pleasurable and ominous. A little taste of the colder evenings to come. The window had been left open an inch and Marta could hear the clip-clop of a horse's hoofs over cobblestones. Somewhere far away a young girl laughed. Marta's arms were bare in her short-sleeved dress and she shivered. She was so seldom alone, and she was suddenly aware of herself in a different way, as though the self she thought of as solid was instead a million little fragments. As though all of the pieces could fall off their string at any moment and scatter across the pantry floor.

It was odd, really, the way humans went about their days so boldly, ordering coffee, weighing out exactly half a pound of potatoes on the greengrocer's scale, as though their lives were something that could be controlled, portioned out as desired. When really, all it took was one little upset to reveal the . . . imbalance of things. Marta thought of how unnerved Anneliese had become earlier, and she wondered about other people's inner lives; if, despite their polished exteriors, people's insides were as full of holes as a piece of Swiss cheese. She shivered again — she didn't like to think of it. If the politicians, the councilmen, Ernst, even the Bauers were as uncertain as she herself was —

She had a sudden sensation of being watched and she turned around to see Pavel. His necktie was undone and his shirtsleeves pushed up. His arms crossed in front of him. Marta flushed, ashamed to have been caught daydreaming. "I'm sorry," she said. "I'm almost finished." She gestured at Anneliese's stockpile, the potatoes and the soup cubes she was arranging on top of the preserves.

Pavel took a step into the pantry. He was close enough that she could see a spot on his chin he had missed shaving. "There's nothing to apologize for, Marta."

He said her name as though testing the water at the edge of a lake, dipping his big toe in to get a feel for the temperature.

"I wanted to tell you myself," Pavel said.

"Mr. Bauer?"

He hesitated, as if he wished to protect her from what it was he had to say.

"It's President Beneš."

Marta held her breath, her uncertainty rushing back. Had the president been shot? But Pavel said instead, "He's resigned."

Marta exhaled. This was better by far than an assassination. Still, her face fell along with her breath. She knew what this would mean to the Bauers: their last hopes to save their home-land swept away like flax dust from the factory floor. Pavel saw her dismay and mistook it for something different. He reached over and touched her bare wrist.

Marta looked down at Pavel's hand. His fingernails were neatly clipped and clean. Fine dark hair on the back of the knuckles. It was hair that must also travel, she thought, up the backs of his forearms and onto his chest. She flushed more intensely. She tried to focus on something else — the pile of potatoes, dirt still caked on their skins — but she couldn't make herself stop; she must look as if she were standing next to a bonfire at the Burning of the Witches.

"I'm so sorry to hear it," she managed finally.

"On the Day of Atonement," Pavel said.

So he knew about the High Holidays after all. "What's he repenting for?" she asked.

"He's gone into exile."

"He's repenting for what the Allies have done to *him*."

Pavel smiled at the irony. He circled her forearm with his hand and gave it a little squeeze, and when he backed away he seemed reluctant, or defeated, as though he, not Beneš, was the one who'd been forced to step down.

Through the kitchen doorway she saw him pause in front of the large window. She heard the swish of the curtains being opened; Pavel stayed there for a moment, looking down at the town square, before he turned to climb the stairs to his wife.

It took Marta several minutes to move from the pantry. She was exhausted, suddenly, every last ounce of energy wrung out of her, as though she were a bedsheet that had just emerged from the communal mangle.

She stood there, leaning against the pantry door, looking down at her arm. She half expected to see a mark where he'd touched her, a blister or a burn. Some kind of scar. Pavel's squeeze had left its opposite: an emptiness, an intensely felt absence. She felt cavernous and echoey. There was a great *whoosh* in the middle of her chest; it was the sound of the curtains being pulled open, revealing a town square in the centre of herself that was completely unpopulated. The wind blew through it, pushing the dry fallen leaves.

date?

My dear Pavel,

I do not know where you are. I am sending this to your mother's house in the hopes that it might reach you. In truth, however, it has been months since your mother's disappearance, and so I am writing into a void. Of absence. Of so many kinds.

I want only to tell you I am sorry. Sorry for our misunderstandings, for my actions that have come between us, sorry for Axmann, for everything. I cannot help but feel that if I had acted differently we would still be together right now. I hope you are safe, wherever you are. Protected. I hope you feel my love.

The way things transpired might lead you to doubt me. You must believe this: I was trying to save us. You can't imagine how I miss you now. You have known me since I was a child. You have fathered my children. Come back to me, darling. From wherever you are.

Anneliese

(FILE UNDER: Bauer, Anneliese. See Bauer, Pavel, for details.)

I HAVE LOVED, SURE.

It was years ago — years — but contrary to common wisdom, time does not diminish loss.

I myself would say that the opposite is true.

But goodness, my hip is sore today.

What was I saying? Something about hope. For a while it existed, that's all. In the face of everything: the pogroms, Kristallnacht, the acts of violence and betrayal both small and enormous. The Jews kept planning, trying to get out. What is it they say? That hope dies hard? True enough. If I think of her orange sweater.

I have had a good career: publication, promotion. Things I know other people long for. I'm almost inclined to say my success has come easily, although that would be discrediting much time and effort. As I said, I lived at my desk, cluttered as it was with old Chinese take-out cartons and memos I ignored. Still, there were years when I felt myself swept along, when study came as naturally for me as love seems to come for others. It was hard to be alone.

Of course, I'd never complain.

You'd think I could forget, though, since so much time has passed. Memory bleeds out, or gets covered in snow. We have

databases — who escaped and who wasn't so lucky — lists of
the dates they were moved to the ghettos or sent from Theresienstadt to Auschwitz. There are whole libraries full of books
on the subject. It is even possible to construct little narratives,
to attempt to give the whole thing order. But it's all just memory's attempt to make order from chaos. It is a trick of the
mind, to keep it from boggling. The enormity of the loss can
be too much to handle.

I never travelled with my lover. We never slept in an Irish
country inn in a single bed under the eaves. We never walked
down a gravel road holding hands as the crickets started singing. And all the things we didn't do come back now as though
they really happened. This is the nature of longing. I wish to
wake to the sound of her shovel, to hear the door open and to
pull back the covers. To watch her peel off her snowy clothes
and crawl in beside me. And stay.

People disappear. Despite all the information available to
us, there are cases that are never solved. We can guess what
happened but we cannot say for certain. And there is nothing
to be done about it now anyway, so late in time. Even in the
instances where there are surviving cables and telegrams, they
tell only a fraction of the story. For my part, among all the letters I have read, there is one that I always keep with me. "Your
mamenka and I send you a hug and a snuggle . . ." I could probably recite that letter by heart. And yet, I'm aware of its failure,
of all the white space surrounding its words.

Sometimes I have the sense, when I'm meeting somebody
to record their testimony, that I'm opening a worn paperback
three-quarters of the way through and trying to piece together
a very complex plot. To glean even a fraction of what came

before. People's lives, their infinitely tangled histories, are almost impenetrable — to themselves, let alone to an outsider. My students, of course, would cringe to hear me say this, so full of optimism are they about the historical method. Some still believe in the idea of truth; some, even, that they will find it.

I'll admit there is something shared between the stories I hear, though, something common to those who survived. The gnawing longing, the desire to keep searching, even when your rational mind knows everyone involved is gone. That particular ache at the core of human memory. I have to say I am familiar with it myself.

The vows we never took have their own particular bittersweetness. I can only imagine her coming in from the snow, slipping a cold hand under my sweater. I imagine that pain, the opposite of pleasure. The other side of being alive.

Precisely because my lover went, there is something to wait for. And this is the history of the people I study as well. The presence of loss makes a longing for arrival. The other side of leaving is return.

The last time I heard her was on my machine. When she said my name, there was a catch in her voice. It was winter; she had a cold. She was clearing her throat. It was probably nothing.

Still, I lay in bed by the flashing red light and listened.

To my name. To my pain. To that breaking.

It seems so long ago it might never have happened. It could be that I made it up, the orange sweater, a fragment to keep me warm. It's possible, I guess, that my lover never existed.

It's possible I've spent my whole life alone.

THREE

MARTA'S FACE WAS PRESSED INTO the cold concrete wall, her underpants down around her ankles. Ernst fumbled with the buckle on his belt; she wasn't ready, but he didn't seem to notice. He spat on his fingers and touched her briefly, then grunted, pushing himself inside her. She inhaled sharply, surprised by the pain. "Wait —" she started, but her back was to him and she knew he couldn't hear, or was choosing not to. With each thrust her cheekbone dug into the rough wall; she braced herself with her palms, pushing back against his weight, but Ernst was stronger.

"Stay still," he panted.

She felt a dribble on the inside of her leg. He was already close, she could tell. The head of his penis swelling. For a moment she thought of Pavel — a brief flash of his hand gripping her wrist — Ernst gave a final shove and moaned, emptying himself inside her.

He pulled out right away. Tucked in his shirttails and zipped up his fly, taking his time to adjust himself inside his pants. She turned to face him, leaning weakly back against the wall. Her knees were shaking. Ernst glanced at her, then looked again. "You're bleeding," he said.

She brought a hand to her face. He was right.

"You'd better watch it," he said.

"The bleeding?"

"You'd better watch yourself."

Marta's underpants were still around her ankles; she bent to pull them up, followed by her stockings. Her body felt numb, as if it were made of rubber. She was suddenly shivering with cold.

"What do you mean, watch myself?" she asked, but she knew exactly what he meant. It was dangerous for her to be aligned with the Bauers — Ernst had been saying it for days now. That uncertainty she'd noticed in him, the need to be reassured, was gone. All at once it was like he'd never had any doubts, like he'd been dedicated to National Socialism all along.

Ernst was pulling on his jacket. He looked at his reflection in the shine of the flax-spinning mill and smoothed back his hair with the palms of his hands.

"Jews have taken over everything," he said, gesturing around at the other machines on the floor, the industry Pavel and his father had worked so hard to build. "It's time for it to stop."

But Marta could hardly hear what he was saying; his voice seemed to come from very far away. Ernst was buttoning his jacket. He leaned in towards her, suddenly an inch from her face. "Clean yourself up," he said, then turned to leave.

She touched her cheek again. Her fingers came away stained with blood.

The next night Marta lay in her single bed, breathing. Her palm on her stomach, the slight rise and fall under her ribs. Like the surface of the sea, she thought. She had never seen the sea, but she imagined its shimmer in late afternoon, the way the light would sparkle over the waves.

Cold black shapes slipped through her depths.

She shifted in her sheets, let her eyes slowly close. She tried to forget what had happened with Ernst the night before. His fingers digging into her flesh, the little row of bruises he'd left along her forearm. She tried to forget altogether that he existed. It had seemed so simple at first; not love, of course, but attention, something to relieve the monotony of her day-to-day. And for a time it had worked. But now the bubble had popped and the darkness was rushing back in. She should have known it would happen like this. The weight of Ernst's body on hers was suddenly the same as her father's; his hands were not a distraction but a terrible reminder. She worked always to forget what her father had done to her, the nights he would slink into her room, get in beside her, put a hand over her mouth. Her sister frozen with fear on the other side of the bed, the heat on her own face the following morning, not being able to look her sister in the eye. And now the old shame came back, newly disguised.

The Jews were dirty, Ernst had clearly said. But Jews were all that she had.

Ernst had explained his plan. The Bauers' assets would be taken; it was unavoidable. If Pavel was going to loose his money anyway, Ernst could certainly use it. Pavel had always under-paid him, Ernst had told her. Marta knew this to be untrue, but Ernst seemed adamant. And now, he said, by keeping up the pretense of their friendship, he would get his due. He'd already convinced Pavel to transfer a portion of his investments into his name, "for safekeeping," he'd told him. There was more, though. It would take time, and patience.

Marta wondered if Ernst's motivations weren't more complex; if, deep down, he didn't still love his friend and feel more ambivalent than he realized. Regardless, she knew she needed to end their relationship — something had turned inside her. The filthy feeling, the repulsion, had come back stronger than ever. She could no more continue with him than she could willingly return to the country of her childhood. But Ernst would be angry. He could reveal their secret to Pavel, who would then have no choice but to fire her. Ernst was the one who was married, but she, the hired help, would be blamed. The same thing had happened with the Maršíkov maid, Helga: there'd been a brief affair with Mr. Maršíkov, and Helga was gone so quickly Marta had not even had a chance to say goodbye.

She pushed the sickness of her situation down into her stomach, but the images kept asserting themselves, rising to the surface like debris after a storm. A branch, a torn stocking. A silver key — to what? She reached out for it and it slipped through her fingers; she plugged her nose and dived down after it. There was the sound of the key turning in a lock; she sat up in bed with a start.

She must have been asleep.

She struck a match, touched it to the candle's wick, and squinted at the clock on the wall: 12:15. She lay back down.

Pavel said, "Here, give me that." The Bauers were standing directly under the stove vent; Pavel's voice was so clear that Marta thought for a moment he was speaking to her.

But Anneliese said, "The slivovitz?"

"The absinthe." Pavel paused. "You won't embarrass me like that again."

"Wouldn't you say that this whole situation is a little — what did you call it? — embarrassing? Not being allowed out after ten o'clock and having to come home for a curfew like children?"

Marta heard the delicate snap of Mrs. Bauer's earrings coming off and then the louder snap of her purse opening and closing. "Mathilde says we can stay with her and Vaclav in Prague if need be."

Pavel snorted. "Will we bunk in with Clara and baby Magda?"

"She was just trying to be helpful. What's happened to you? You've become so . . . contrary."

"We're not leaving."

"All the more reason to consider my idea," Anneliese said.

There was the barely perceptible click of her lighter.

Marta blew her candle out. She pulled her quilt up over her shoulders and willed herself to fall back to sleep. It was late, and she was beyond exhausted. And Pepik had recently taken to waking with the sunrise. But the longer she squeezed her eyes shut and focused on her desire to sleep, the more awake she became and the closer the Bauers' voices seemed.

"That pork was undercooked," Anneliese said, and Marta felt she personally was being accused.

"Listen to me, Liesel," Pavel answered. "My grandfather was an elder of his synagogue. My earliest memory is of seeing him there on the High Holy Days, in his place of honour."

"It doesn't mean anything. To us. To you. When was the last time you set foot in a synagogue?"

"But this is my point. I am realizing it actually does."

Anneliese scoffed. "You've chosen a perfect time to realize."

"Do you know how long ago the Jews in Bohemia were granted equal rights?" The floorboards squeaked as Pavel started pacing.

Anneliese said, "I don't know. And do you know something? I don't care."

"Which is odd, seeing as you are a Jew of Bohemia."

"Hush, Pavel," Anneliese said. But her voice was rising too. "I don't feel Jewish," she said forcibly. "No more than I feel . . . I don't know . . ." Marta pictured her waving her hand through the cigarette smoke above her head. ". . . Catholic."

"Yes, Liesel, I understand," Pavel said. His voice revealed a sincere attempt at patience. "It's not the religion I'm talking about. It's the culture."

"The culture?"

"The Jewish culture."

"It's not a culture, it's a religion."

Both of them were quiet then. Marta pulled her blankets higher, under her chin. She could tell from the silence that the Bauers were surprised to have stumbled on this difference of opinion about their faith. They had obviously never discussed it before, at least not from this particular angle; they had each assumed the other felt the way they themselves did. She had noticed this tendency in people who were married — the tendency to forget that the spouse was a separate person with a separate past, and secrets you would never guess at.

"My stomach hurts," Anneliese said quietly.

Pavel cleared his throat. "It was 1848 when the Jews of Bohemia were granted equal rights. Less than a century ago."

"That has nothing to do with our situation."

"It has *everything* to do with our situation. My grandfather was the mayor of the Jewish City of Prague."

"You said it didn't mean anything. You said it was a charity that gave money to soup kitchens."

"It meant something to him," Pavel said fiercely. "All he wanted on his tombstone — the only thing he wanted — was *Adolf Bauer, former Mayor of the Jewish City of Prague*."

"His poor wife," Anneliese said. "And what about his children? I see you come from a long line of men unconcerned with the well-being of their children."

Pavel now began to shout in earnest. "Don't you dare speak to me about the well-being of my children!" There was a thump, as though he had thrown a heavy object to the floor, and the sound of the pacing resumed. "That's *exactly* what this is about. I do not want Pepik to see his father shamed like a dog by a bunch of schoolyard bullies! He deserves a better example."

"My sister had her girls baptized."

"Alžběta? She has no more principles than you have!"

"It's a good idea. It could save Pepik's life."

"Listen to me, Liesel. This is important. I want you to hear what I say now." Pavel paused. "I would not convert to Christianity if I were the last Jew on earth. The very last Jew on earth!"

"That's fine. Because nobody is asking you to convert."

There was a note of desperation in Anneliese's voice that had not been there before. Perhaps, Marta thought, she knew something that the rest of them didn't.

"It's the opposite of what you think, Pavel. I'm thinking of the big picture. Please," Anneliese said. She was begging now. On the verge of tears. "Just in case. He's my only child . . ."

The cloaked reference to the dead baby worked in Anneliese's favour. The voices from downstairs quieted. "I know," Pavel said softly. "I know he is."

What would Pavel have been like if the other child had lived? As the father of a little girl.

Pavel's voice was now just a murmur, the sharp edges of his words smoothed out. Marta rolled over and put the pillow over her head. The fights always ended this way, she thought, in a kind of mutual stalemate. They weren't willing to give in, nor were they willing to go to bed angry. They needed each other too much. They would be moving towards each other now, she knew, reconciling, Pavel wrapping his arms around his wife.

Marta loathed them for this with a ferocity she did not understand.

It wasn't that she was jealous because she had nobody to hold her after a quarrel; she had nobody to quarrel with in the first place. What she resented was the Bauers' softness. She needed them to be strong, to be above mortal failings. Instead they were human, after all.

The boy with the wine-stain birthmark showed up to deliver the coal. He was wearing the national colours in his button-hole, and a peaked cap of the kind popularized by Pavel's hero Tomáš Masaryk. Only on seeing the delivery boy did it occur to Marta to wonder about the date. Was it? Yes, it must be.

October 28, Czechoslovak National Day. Pavel had been acting remote and preoccupied, and she wondered if the boy's blatant show of nationalism would buoy his spirits. He seemed not to notice though, and when Ernst arrived at the house after lunch, Pavel didn't mention the holiday at all. "Shall we go?" was all he said.

"Ready when you are," Ernst answered, without catching Marta's eye.

They rushed off without saying goodbye.

Marta gathered up the soup bowls and wrapped the cheese in its cloth. In the parlour Anneliese was holding her compact in front of her face, her lips pursed, putting on lipstick. "Don't worry about cleaning up right now," she called in to Marta.

Marta paused, confused. "Pardon me, Mrs. Bauer?"

"You can do it when we're back. We're going out."

Marta hesitated, a ladle in her hand. "Are you sure? I could just . . ."

But Anneliese wasn't listening; she was looking out the window to make sure her husband was gone. Then she called to Pepik, "Come here and put your sweater on." He was big enough to do this himself — it had taken Marta some weeks to teach him how — but Anneliese didn't have the patience. She guided his arms briskly into the little sleeves. The zipper nicked his chin: "Ouch!" Pepik said.

"I'm sorry, *miláčku*."

But Anneliese didn't seem sorry — she seemed distracted, preoccupied, her eyes moving repeatedly towards the window. Marta wondered why she was putting Pepik in a sweater at all when the afternoon was so warm, the sun shining. It had continued to be a striking fall, the colours more vivid than she remembered from previous years: the dazzling golds, and the red leaves like so many bloodied hands.

"Where are you off to?"

"I told you, you're coming with us."

Marta knew better than to ask any more questions.

They went down into the street, the three of them, Pepik sullen but his mother determined. She led them out through the gate and along the path by the river, towards the edge of town. She was wearing an Elsa Schiaparelli tailored suit, with big shoulder pads like Marlene Dietrich's. Large dark glasses shielded her eyes, as if she were a movie star trying to conceal her identity.

They walked for several minutes in silence, passing the milkman's cart, the containers on the back of the wagon empty.

"Can I pat the horsies?" Pepik asked.

But Anneliese ignored her son, hurrying them past Sanger and Sons, where a Victrola was displayed prominently in the window, and Mr. Goldstein's shop, which had a CLOSED sign on the door. Even Marta had to work to keep up. Down a cobblestone alley they went and across the footbridge over the river. Pavel's factory loomed in the distance, like something from an earlier life. Marta thought perhaps they were taking Pepik to feed the ducks, but Anneliese stopped in front of the Catholic church. It dawned on Marta all at once what was happening: Anneliese was taking action despite Pavel's wishes to the contrary.

The church was the largest structure in town, grey stone with a cone-shaped spire that reminded her of the tip of Mr.

Goldstein's beard. Anneliese led them up the side staircase and into the dimly lit nave. It was cold inside, and they squinted around, trying to get a feel for the layout of the room. The priest who stepped out of the darkness must have been waiting for them; he appeared before them like a ghost.

"I'm sorry. Did I scare you?" He was a thin man with a long face and drooping eyelids. "Father Wilhelm."

He extended his hand, but it was a small town: everyone knew who everyone else was.

When the priest turned around Marta saw that he had a bald patch on the back of his head the exact size and shape of a yarmulke.

Marta had been in this church only once before, but she remembered the heavy oak pews, the stained glass windows showing the Stations of the Cross. The priest ushered the three of them through a side door into a much smaller and more functional room. There was a leather-covered desk with an ink-pot on top of it. In the corner a statue of the Virgin Mary with her eyes rolled up towards heaven.

Marta crossed herself instinctively, like someone flinching before a raised fist.

Now that they could all see each other clearly, Father Wilhelm addressed Pepik directly. *"Hallo, mein Kind."* Pepik's face was buried in Marta's pinafore. Anneliese moved forward. "Pepik, come here," she said, firmly. "Say hello to Father Wilhelm."

Pepik stepped forward and extended his hand. "I didn't touch the horses," he said.

The priest smiled and took Pepik's hand in his own. He was wearing a gold ring, Marta saw, with a cross on it. "Let's begin."

The priest's Czech was rusty as an old knife — he kept switching tenses — but when Anneliese said, in German, *"Denken Sie dass das sonderbar ist?"* Father Wilhelm only shrugged and answered, "The Lord works in mysterious ways."

The priest busied himself with a folder on top of the desk, removing several sheets of carbon paper and spreading them out one next to the other. He dug in the desk drawer and came out with a quill. Then he turned to Anneliese and said, matter of factly, "If you'd like I can just sign the papers."

There was a moment of confusion, and Anneliese and Marta looked at each other. They understood at the same time: he would baptize Pepik out of kindness. It was his small act of defiance against the Nazis. The priest knew this was not a religious decision.

Anneliese clarified, "You mean without the water?" She nodded at the font in the corner of the room.

Father Wilhelm nodded back and said, "I am happy to be of assistance in whatever way I can." For the first time, though, he looked over his shoulder nervously, as though making sure nobody had slipped in the side door and was watching from the shadows. It was clear that he would prefer to get this over as quickly as possible. The whole thing had the feel of a shady transaction, Marta thought. Like a body being disposed of.

She thought of Anneliese in the tub, the water crimson red.

"Water or papers?" the priest asked, looking at the watch he wore on a gold chain around his neck. Anneliese was eyeing the font warily. Marta could tell she was worried that without the water the ceremony wouldn't take. Not the actual baptism, but whatever protection it was supposed to eventually summon.

"Let's do it properly." Anneliese's tone implied that she knew she was being superstitious but was willing to take the risk.

"*Ganz richtig,*" the priest said. "Come here, Pepik."

Pepik stepped forward gravely, a young Isaac about to be forsaken.

Marta was half expecting something elaborate: a choir of angels emerging from on high, complete with white robes and tarnished halos. Or maybe Father Wilhelm would pull back a velvet curtain to reveal a galvanized tub in which the naked Pepik would be entirely submerged — even held down for a minute or two, just until he began to struggle. But Father Wilhelm only took Pepik by his shoulders and said, "Close your eyes," as though he was going to give him a surprise for his birthday.

He dipped his fingers in the font and touched Pepik's forehead and mumbled some words that Marta could not catch. Pepik's eyes were clenched shut as though he were steeling himself against a terrible vision. Father Wilhelm had to give him a little shake. "It's okay. It's all over!"

Pepik opened his eyes and wiped the drops of water from his forehead with the back of his sleeve. He looked around tentatively, as though expecting to see something marvellous — his mother turned into Saint Nicholas, or the priest turned into a frog. Pepik lifted his arm and looked at it closely, inspecting the sleeve of his shirt. The priest laughed. "You're just the same, *mein Kind,*" he said. "You're just as before." And he shook his head — in satisfaction or in regret, it was hard to say.

Father Wilhelm brought his hands to his chest and folded them, his long, bony fingers interlaced. Marta thought he was about to start praying, but instead he said to Anneliese, "I'll see you out now, Mrs. Bauer." He paused, as though he might have forgotten something, and looked at the font slantwise. "Unless you'd like . . ." He made a sound in the back of his throat.

"I'm sorry?"

"Unless you'd like the same for yourself."

Anneliese opened her mouth and then closed it again. Did she want to be baptized as well? It was obvious to Marta that the thought hadn't occurred to her. "I see we're not the only ones . . . ," Anneliese started, but her words trailed off. She looked at the font intently, as though an answer might somehow bubble to the surface, like a dumpling in the *hovězí polévka*. Then she looked back at Marta. "Do you think . . . ?"

Marta paused; she wanted to help, but the situation was beyond her. She knew how Pavel felt. Then again, look at what was happening all around them. "I don't —" she started. "I'm not —"

But her fumbling had settled it. "No thank you, Father," Anneliese said, smiling briskly. And she turned away, looking anxiously for Pepik as though he might have been spirited away by some evil demon.

The day was bright as they stood outside on the church steps, blinking. "I can't see!" Pepik giggled. "I'm blind!"

He took one of his mother's hands and one of Marta's, letting them guide him down the steep stone stairs. He walked between them as if he belonged to both, and Marta felt for a moment as though it was possible to share him after all.

Anneliese led them home the roundabout way, sticking to the edges of town. She'd put her dark glasses back on to shield her eyes from the sun, but from the side Marta could see her glancing back and forth nervously. Anneliese looked perplexed, as if she was wondering what to say about what had just happened. "It's how my sister Alžběta and her daughters got out," she said finally. "They managed to leave the country. With passports saying they're Catholic. And the papers to back them up just in case."

She glanced over at Marta.

"Even the baby?" Marta asked.

"Yes." Anneliese pushed her dark glasses up on her forehead to look Marta in the face. "Even Eva."

"How did they get their *Uebertrittschein*?"

"I don't know. They must have bribed someone."

Pepik had broken away from them, run ahead and climbed up onto the stone wall. He was balancing along it with his arms outstretched; he looked like he was about to take off into flight.

"You know something?" Anneliese said. "I feel better. I'm glad to have done it. If it doesn't help — well, it hasn't hurt him." She paused and brought a cupped hand to her forehead. "You're not to tell Mr. Bauer about this," she said. There was a pained expression on her face, as though she wished she did not have to be so explicit but wasn't sure if she could trust Marta otherwise. It was, Marta knew, an indirect reference to their earlier conversation about the suicide attempt, another topic she'd been instructed to ignore and that she'd stirred up nonetheless.

It had happened after the baby died. Not immediately, but several months later. It wasn't that Anneliese's hope had withered or that she felt a large of part of herself had died along with her child, although those things were certainly true, she'd told Marta. It was that someone had taken an axe and hacked a hole in the centre of Anneliese's chest. Only nobody could see it; the hole was invisible, as was the pain, the excruciating near-physical pain she was in. By comparison, she'd told Marta, the birth had been nothing, a tickle between her legs, a trickle of blood. Whereas after the baby died she could not turn over in bed or her severed heart would fall out of her chest cavity. She lay on her back with her breast ripped open while the wolves bloodied their snouts in her grieving.

Dasha brought her toast. Marta kept Pepik away. Pavel tried to carry on as if nothing were wrong. Anneliese was alone with the weight of her baby's death, and it was simply too much. She couldn't bear it.

It was Marta who'd found Anneliese unconscious in the tub. Marta still shuddered to think of it, Anneliese's skin sallow, as though she was made of wax, her small breasts loose and exposed. Her neck had lolled back at a terrible angle that Marta had trouble forgetting. And there, on her wrist . . .

Marta had been the one who'd turned the spigot off, who'd stopped the bleeding, wrapped the gash in gauze. She'd been the one who'd stayed with Anneliese, nursing her back to health, telling Pavel that his wife was sick with influenza. This was when the bond between the women had formed.

Put another way, Anneliese owed Marta her life. The two of them never mentioned this but Marta felt it was always there between them, asserting itself, as the unspoken tends to. And it would change things in ways neither one could imagine.

Pepik had run back towards them and was leaping about like a little leprechaun, making whirring and clicking noises and flapping his arms. Then he stood still on one foot, his arm aloft holding an imaginary bayonet, pretending to be the statue at the centre of the town square. He said to Marta, gravely, "I got baptized. But it's a secret from Tata. We made a pact." And he made a motion of tying his top lip to his bottom, as he had recently learned to do with his shoelaces.

Marta saluted. "Yes, sir!" she said. "I will eat the secret and swallow the key, *sir*." This was as much for Anneliese's benefit as it was for Pepik's, but she pretended all her attention was on the boy. She took her house key from the folds of her skirt and tipped her head back as though to swallow it, sliding the key at the last moment down her sleeve.

"Where did it go?" Pepik gaped at her, wide-eyed.

Anneliese kneaded her own shoulder and said to herself absently, "I had no idea how tense I was in there. I'm exhausted!"

"I gobbled it up," Marta told Pepik. She patted her belly.

Pepik said, "Yum."

The afternoon was waning, the long light lending every-thing a hint of heaven. They turned the corner and saw Mr. Goldstein coming out of his tailor's shop. He smiled at Pepik. "How's the *lamed vovnik*?"

"Fine-thank-you-and-how-are-you?"

Mr. Goldstein laughed. "Remember? A *lamed vovnik* is someone very important to the world. Someone on whom the world depends." He cupped Pepik's head with his palm, rocked it gently back and forth. "Remember I told you?"

Mr. Goldstein crinkled the corners of his eyes, but Marta thought he seemed tired, worn down. Despite his sunny nature the occupation must be getting to him. He raised his hand to show he was in a hurry, but before he rushed off he let Pepik twist the point of his long beard.

Marta looked at Pepik's face, the flush of pure gladness. This was the gift of childhood, she thought. To be thoroughly delighted by small things. He was throwing himself into the air, making birdlike chirping noises, happy for the first time in weeks. It was like something in that bit of holy water had actually bought him time, had worked to hold some demon at bay. He looked as though he really had been saved.

❧

Now that Sophie was gone, the shopping and cooking fell to Marta. Anneliese said they would hire someone new as soon as things were back to normal. Marta didn't mind helping out, but coupled with her duties with Pepik, it meant she had twice as much work and often fell behind schedule. So it was that on November 9 it was late afternoon by the time she returned from the grocer. Dusk was already falling. She cooked hurriedly — *česneková polévka* using leftover garlic, *vepřové* for Anneliese — and ate alongside the Bauers, but she got up from the table before they did to start the dishes. The Bauers finished their cutlets leisurely and laid their knives and forks parallel on their plates. Then Pavel, who understood that no families would let their children play with the Jewish boy anymore, rolled up his sleeves and crawled under the table with his son.

Marta came back into the dining room to remove the serving dish from the marble-topped credenza. "What are you building under there?" she asked. Pepik's train track snaked between the legs of the chairs; the clothespin people were grouped together at one end of the carpet and the lead soldiers at the other, protecting them.

"Only a kingdom," Pavel said lightly. "We've already got the Crown Prince." He gave Pepik's bottom a little slap. "We're looking for a princess. Do you know anyone?"

She moved the silver salt and pepper shakers back to the credenza.

"I don't believe I do."

"Are you certain? I think you yourself might —"

"What about me?" Anneliese called from the parlour, where she was leafing through the pages of a fashion magazine. She was warm towards her husband again now that her son was taken care of.

Pavel looked up, surprised and pleased by her tone. "Why, darling," he said, "you're already the Queen!"

Pepik was dinging the silver bell on the train's engine over and over. He looked up and said, "Where's that key?"

Marta paused, serving dish in hand. "What key, *miláčku*?" But right away she remembered the baptism and said, "Oh, that key. I swallowed it, of course." She brought a finger to her lips to remind Pepik he was not to tell his father. Then she said quickly, "Your train has become so long! How did you make it so long?"

But Pepik was not diverted. "She swallowed the key," he said to his father. He cupped a hand around his mouth and said, in a stage whisper, "The key to our secret."

Pavel peered up at Marta from under the table, his eyebrows raised. "Secret? What's the secret?"

Marta pretended she hadn't heard his question; she

squinted at the credenza, frowning, then picked an invisible bit of food off its surface with her fingernail. She heard Anneliese come into the room behind her.

"I'd like some port," she said.

"Liesel? What secret?"

"Never mind. Don't be foolish."

"Liesel . . ." Pavel said, half warning, half teasing.

Anneliese crouched down so she was eye-level with her husband under the table; Marta saw her instep and the shine of her silk stocking where her heel lifted out of the back of her shoe. "It wouldn't be a secret if we told you now, would it?"

Pavel paused. "I suppose not." He smiled at his wife. "A queen has her secrets."

"Now you've got it, darling."

"You get a lot past me?"

"I'm sneaky with my king."

"You're sly."

"I don't deny it."

She winked and Pavel blushed. Marta thought the moment had passed, that Anneliese had been successful in diverting Pavel's attention. She picked up the serving dish in one hand and the salt and pepper shakers in the other, moving towards the kitchen, but she paused in the doorway when she heard Pavel ask, "What do you think about your mother's secrets, buster?"

She turned in time to see Pepik make the motion of tying his lips together. He looked at his father meaningfully. "I can't tell you."

Pavel lunged and tickled his son again. "Tell me!"

Anneliese stood up, unsteady on her heel. "Careful with

him," she said lightly. There was a hint of panic in her voice. Marta knew this would egg Pavel on.

"Mamenka knows!" Pepik shrieked, gleeful. He was trying to squirm away from his father's grasp.

"Does she?"

"Yes! Mamenka! And Nanny! And Pepik!" he shouted. He began to act out the baptismal scene, putting two fingers to his forehead and closing his eyes and muttering something unintelligible that nevertheless sounded to Marta quite a bit like Latin.

Anneliese was frozen in place; someone had to do something. "Pepik!" Marta shouted, as though about to scold him for some unspeakable transgression. He looked up, startled — she never, ever yelled. She couldn't think what to say next, but before she was forced to speak a loud crash came from outside. Pavel jerked his head up, banging it on the bottom of the table. "*Hovno*," he swore, rubbing his temple.

He crawled out from beneath the table, his son forgotten, went to the window and pulled back the drapes. It was as if he'd opened the curtain on a play, mid-act. They could all see, across the square, a group of Hitlerjugend crowded around the entrance to the Goldstein Tailor Shop. Night was falling but Marta could make out the armbands, the tall lace-up boots. The boys were shoving each other, a knot of pent-up anger, or perhaps, she thought, they were just drunk. One of them, the tallest, had a bat in his hands. He pushed the others aside and stood in front of the storefront, the bat held straight above his head as if reaching up to strike a piñata.

Pavel was transfixed. "Liesel," he said, without moving his eyes from the scene. Anneliese crossed the room to her husband in time to watch the young man bring the bat down, just once, into the window.

Marta could not see this — the distance across the square was too great — but she imagined lines spreading out across the glass of Mr. Goldstein's storefront like a map of Adolf Hitler's ever expanding *Lebensraum*.

A chunk of glass fell to the cobblestones. Then a second chunk. The boy with the bat kicked at what was left with his steel-toed boot, and it too fell out of the frame. Where before there had been a surface that looked like nothing, now nothing itself took its place. Anneliese gasped. "What —?" she said. "What are they —?"

She leaned her chest into Pavel's back for protection, resting her chin on his shoulder.

The Hitlerjugend entered Mr. Goldstein's shop via the now windowless storefront. Six or eight of them, eighteen or nineteen years old. The last of the light was draining from the day like dirty water down a drain. Marta squinted hard but the young men had all disappeared into the shop. Several minutes passed before they emerged again, their facial features now completely blurred by the November night. The Bauers stood at the window together, not speaking. There was a lick of flame. Perhaps Mr. Goldstein had seen what was coming and kindled a small fire in his hearth. A small blot of light against the darkness.

Except the flame was getting higher in the night.

The storefront was again crowded with the gang of *Jugend*; there was more pushing and shoving amongst them. The light from the fire reflecting across the shards of broken glass made it easier to see now. The tallest boy appeared dragging

Mr. Goldstein by his ear. Until now it had seemed to Marta
that she was watching some kind of macabre spectacle put
on as entertainment, but now, seeing the old man, it was suddenly real. She panicked, wanting to protect Mr. Goldstein
and knowing there was nothing she could do, that to attempt
to intervene would be to risk her own life. The tailor looked
small in his nightshirt, his beard reaching almost down to his
waist. He was doing a kind of sideways crab-walk, leading
with the earlobe that was pinched firmly between the gang
leader's fingers. If it hadn't been so terrifying there might
have been something comical about the sight, the old man's
eyes darting in confusion, his nightcap slipping off the side
of his head. The next thing Marta saw was Mr. Goldstein on
his knees surrounded by the ring of young people. The fire
was roaring now, eating up the store, making long shadows
of the scene.

She was caught behind her own pane of glass; it was like
watching a film, she imagined, with the volume turned all the
way down.

For the second time Marta saw the bat rising and falling.

She put a hand over one eye, as if she were reading an eye
chart.

She covered both eyes, disbelieving.

When she looked again, the street was clear. Except for a
single person — a body — crumpled on the cobblestones.

～⊚～

The following night at supper, nobody spoke. Pepik was free
to mass his *knedlíky* into mountain ranges as he desired. He

seemed to think he had done something to provoke the silence at the table and began guessing what he was supposed to apologize for. "I'm sorry for playing with my food like a baby?"

The Bauers kept eating.

"I'm sorry I wet my bed last night?"

Anneliese looked at Marta with raised eyebrows, and Marta nodded to show this was true. Pavel got up and kissed the crown of his wife's head. He turned on the Telefunken. They heard static, and then a voice flared like a struck match. Pavel lowered the volume. He fiddled with the dial until a different voice, with a British accent, came through. "I don't doubt that the orders came from above," it said.

"How can you be so certain?" another man asked. Marta didn't understand the words but his voice was slightly different; she had heard that in England you could place a person within twenty miles of their birthplace based on speech. Here there were only four or five accents. A slightly different pitch if one came from Brno. And the singsongy lilt adrift on the voices of Prague.

Marta wondered what was being said, but it wasn't her place to ask. She waited patiently until Anneliese said, "Can you help us out, darling?" She was holding her husband's wrist loosely in her hand.

Pavel translated the first man's answer: "Because of the coordination. The timing was so precise, with the shops being vandalized not just in one town but all across Germany." He paused, working to catch up. "And indeed across Austria, and the Sudetenland. Both of which, of course, now belong to Hitler's Reich. The — what's that word? coordinated? — No, the *synchronized* nature of the pogroms leaves little doubt — I myself would say that it leaves no doubt — that they were planned by a central body."

The first voice interrupted and Pavel looked at the ceiling, concentrating. "He's asking if it could just have been a series of lootings by thugs," he summarized. "And now the other man is answering." Pavel resumed the direct translation: "Certainly the so-called thugs and low-lifes may have jumped on board without any urging. But the timing of the attacks, in so many different towns and cities, leads us to believe — leads us to *conclude* that they were coordinated. Also, the violent nature of so many of the . . ." The man speaking searched for the words, and Pavel paused along with him. ". . . of so many of the bodily attacks."

Pavel snapped the radio off. He tipped his head back so his chin was pointed directly at the copper Art Deco chandelier; he took a deep breath, which he let out slowly. He crossed the room to his rack of pipes, chose one, and began to tap tobacco down into the bowl. The match he took off the mantelpiece was long, meant to reach into the back of the massive stone fireplace, and he misjudged its reach and nearly singed his eyebrows.

Pepik was mashing his dumplings with the back of his spoon.

"Goldstein," Pavel said, his pipe clamped between his teeth. "They're talking about what happened to Mr. Goldstein." He held the pipe away from his face. "It could have been us, darling," he said to Anneliese.

Marta looked to Mrs. Bauer, but her face was blank, unreadable. "Of course it couldn't have been us," she scoffed. "We're different. He was . . ." She did not need to finish her sentence.

Mr. Goldstein had been Orthodox, practising. The Bauers were assimilated, secular.

Pavel shook his head. "Those distinctions don't matter any more," he said.

"What do you mean 'don't matter anymore'?"

Pavel drew on his pipe; Marta found the smell familiar, comforting. There was something almost sweet about it, like cookies ready to come out of the oven.

"I mean just what I say," said Pavel. "Things have changed. The Germans care only if you're Jewish. It's black and white. In their minds."

"Really?" Anneliese asked. "How is that possible? We couldn't be more different if . . ."

But Pavel didn't answer. He'd been looking at the silver candlesticks in the middle of the table; he now lifted his face towards his wife. "I'm proud to be a Jew," he declared. Marta shrunk back, waiting for Anneliese's answer, but she was silent. "I didn't realize it," Pavel said, "until now. Until all of this." He moved his eyes in the direction of the window. The drapes were closed tightly. Behind them someone had taken the old tailor's body away.

"Proud, darling?"

Marta could see Pavel searching around for what he was feeling, discovering it himself as he spoke it aloud. "It makes me . . . I've always been so proud to be Czech, to be a *vlastenecký*. It's like I'd forgotten this other . . ." He cleared his throat. "This thing that has happened to Goldstein," he said. "It's changed me."

"I hope it's not you next."

"What I mean is, I'm starting to know our own value. As a people."

"I hope I won't have to sit shiva and tear my clothes into rags!" Anneliese's laugh was shrill. "And cover . . . the windows?"

"The mirrors," Pavel said quietly. Then he added, "I finally understand what's important."

"Being *Jewish*?"

"Teaching Pepik who he is."

Marta locked eyes with Anneliese. She knew the baptism was fresh in both their minds.

"You see what happened to Mr. Goldstein?" Anneliese started. "You see *why* it happened? Because of his religion."

But Pavel took his wife's words not as dissent but as agreement. "Yes," he said. "Exactly! We're lucky, Liesel. There's still time for our son to grow up knowing the worth of his people. With a fierce sense —" He was smiling now, wryly, aware of the irony of the timing. "With a fierce sense of Jewish identity!" He put his hands on his wife's shoulders, shaking his head. "Who would have thought," he said.

Marta was frozen in her chair, her mind racing, as though she, not Anneliese, was going to have to answer for the baptism. And wasn't she equally responsible? Hadn't she gone along with it willingly? She could have resisted, could have stood up for what she knew Pavel felt. Part of her wanted to leave the room, to find something that needed washing or mending and escape the consequence of her actions. Another part, though, longed to be held accountable. Something of great magnitude had happened, something she'd been involved in, and the feeling of importance was hard for her to deny. Although, of course, she'd have to defer to Mrs. Bauer.

Marta looked up at Anneliese; she was holding a knuckle

on her right hand between the thumb and index finger of her left. "Pavel," she said.

"My darling?"

"I should tell you."

"You should tell me what?"

Marta thought for a moment that Anneliese was about to confess. But she only paused and looked up from her hands.

"I should tell you that I love you," she said.

Pavel hatched a new plan. He would negotiate with the government — with the Czech government, in Prague — to be sent on a goodwill mission to South America. He would go as a sort of ambassador for the Czech textile manufacturers, to try to persuade the business community there that Czechoslovakia, even in its reduced form, would continue to be a reliable trading partner.

Anneliese agreed with Pavel's new idea but wasn't sure how they'd pull it off. "Who are you, to represent the whole Czech textile community?" she asked one evening as she and Pavel relaxed in the parlour. Marta was ironing quietly in the corner. She could see a copy of the new Henry Miller book, *Tropic of Capricorn*, and a Czech-English dictionary open in Anneliese's lap. "I'm playing devil's advocate," Anneliese clarified.

"That's a racy book," Pavel said.

"And do you like my reading glasses?" She batted her eyelashes at her husband from behind the thick frames. Marta knew that Anneliese would wear them only in the privacy of their own home.

"Okay," Anneliese said, "let's figure this out." She clapped her hands together like a schoolteacher. "How can we convince them that you're the one to represent the industry if your factory has been occupied by Heinlein?"

"My reputation precedes me," Pavel said. "Perhaps I am the man for the job precisely because the factory has been occupied."

"How so?" Anneliese asked.

Pavel paused, and Marta could tell he was grasping, that he couldn't make it make sense. "Now that Hácha has been elected . . ." he said, referring to Beneš's replacement.

"Hácha will be of no help," Anneliese said. "He's a Catholic with no political background. A lawyer. A *translator*." She snapped her Czech-English dictionary closed in disgust. "I have faith in you though, *miláčku*," she said to her husband. "I know you'll think of something."

Pavel had pulled his grandfather's Star of David out of his pocket. He touched it now, as if it might help.

There was a knock at the door, three short raps. Marta set her iron down; it let out a hiss, a steam engine departing. She went into the front hall and undid the deadbolt. Ernst was standing there, two inches from her face. Her hands rose of their own accord to smooth down her hair.

"Hello, Mr. Anselm," she said.

Ernst mouthed something Marta could not make out. She looked over her shoulder to make sure nobody was watching, and leaned in to better hear him.

"Tonight," he whispered. Then: "May I give you my coat?" he said loudly.

"Certainly."

Marta reached out for the boiled wool cloak and summoned her courage. She shook her head. *No, not tonight.*

Ernst raised his eyebrows, not angry so much as concerned. He took a step in towards her. "Marta," he whispered, "what's wrong?"

The Bauers were still in the next room, Pavel saying English words and Anneliese repeating them back to him. Marta shrugged, her arms crossed over her chest. She bit her bottom lip, afraid that if she spoke she'd start to cry.

"Has something happened?" Ernst whispered. It was as though he'd forgotten the other night entirely, how rough he'd been with her, how cruel. His gaze was soft, genuinely worried, and part of her wanted to relax, to lean her head against his torso and have him stroke her back like a child. But she touched her upper arm and felt the bruised skin, the place where he'd gripped her so tightly. She remembered Mr. Goldstein, the terrible tumble of his body to the street. "Pavel trusts you," she whispered back.

A flush rose to Ernst's face. "And what does that have to do with you and me?" His voice hardened and she felt suddenly young, afraid of standing up to him and losing everything. Who else did she have?

Pepik, she told herself. She had Pepik — and he depended on her. It could have been him, Pavel had said.

Ernst looked over Marta's shoulder at the doorway beyond. They only had another second or two before the Bauers would wonder about her absence. He lifted his hand in the air. Marta had a sudden, unmistakeable feeling that he was about to strike her — her father's memory evoked yet again — and she flinched, her arms lifting automatically to shield herself from the blow. But Ernst only laid his palm against her cheek. "Don't be silly, darling," he whispered. "I'll see you tonight."

He'd never called her darling before, but she braced herself against the endearment. She thought again of old Mr. Goldstein, the way the boys had dragged him by his earlobe, and how helpless he'd looked in the light from the flames. His death had clarified things. She could no longer deny what Ernst stood for. Not to others. Not to herself.

"It's settled," he said.

But she shook her head: *No.*

"I'll hang your coat behind the door," she said. And she turned on her heel before she could lose her nerve, and left him standing in the hallway without her.

The following morning Anneliese's brother-in-law Max showed up at the house. He was a barrel-chested man with a moustache and white hair, and Marta had always liked him. He didn't ignore her as some of the Bauers' other friends did, treating her like she was just another piece of furniture that happened to have legs and a face; instead he asked after her, remembering little details like the needlepoint she'd been working on when he'd last seen her several months ago. Maybe this difference in attitude came from not taking his good fortune for granted; he'd met Anneliese's sister Alžběta late in life, Marta knew, at a charity ball given for the volunteer firemen of his father's factory. His life with her and their two young daughters were gifts he would never stop being grateful for.

"I've fired Kurt Hofstader," Max said now, coming into the front hall. He smiled at Marta as he passed her his hat.

"Your foreman?" Pavel asked.

Max paused. "Thank you, Marta." He looked to Pavel: "Yes, please. Half a glass."

"It's a vintage '29."

"Not foreman. Plant manager."

"A Nazi?"

"You know I wouldn't let politics get in the way of business." Max lowered his voice. "But I think he was informing."

Anneliese came into the room. "Informing about what?" she said darkly, from the corner of her mouth, pretending to be Sam Spade. She laughed at her poor imitation and threw her arms around her brother-in-law. "Hello, Max!"

Marta made her way into the small sewing room off the parlour. Several pairs of Pepik's stockings needed mending; things had been so chaotic lately that she'd let them pile up. From the other room came the sounds of a cork being pulled and of liquid being poured. Chairs squeaked across the floorboards. Marta licked the tip of her thread — it had split a little — and squinted, guiding it through the eye of the needle. She had to make several attempts; the light wasn't good, she thought, or perhaps her eyes were getting weaker. She heard the click of Pavel's steel Adler — he was jotting something down on a pad of legal paper. Then Max said, "I was wondering if you'd come and replace him."

Marta paused, the threaded needle pressed between her lips. Max wanted *Pavel* to replace his plant manager? Did he mean they should go to Prague? She shifted her chair so she could see around the door frame and into the parlour.

Pavel cleared his throat; there was a long silence before he asked the same question. "In Prague?"

Max laughed. "You make it sound like the moon."

Pavel cleared his throat again. "I'm flattered you'd ask," he said. He lifted a hand and touched the chandelier directly over his head, as though to steady it, or himself. "I will certainly consider it," he said finally.

Anneliese said, "I've been wanting to go to Prague all along."

Pavel turned to his wife. "And now, my darling, we'd have a reason to go."

"A job?"

"Employment."

But Marta knew Anneliese wouldn't let herself get excited too quickly. "What about the factory?"

He shrugged. "You know as well as I do."

"And your mother?"

"She wouldn't come."

Max interjected. "I could send someone down to keep an eye on her."

"Won't a Jewish plant manager be as much trouble as a Nazi?" asked Anneliese.

Pavel smiled at his wife. "Prague is not under Nazi rule. And Max is your brother-in-law!" He grasped Max's shoulder and shook it.

"You could stay in our flat," Max said. "I'll be leaving the country for a while to visit Alžběta and our girls."

Anneliese straightened at the mention of her sister and nieces, but Max had made it clear he could tell nobody where they'd gone.

"Yes," Anneliese said. "Yes, that sounds . . ." She was quiet again. And then she said, all at once, "I'm thrilled!"

Pavel threw an arm around his wife's shoulders and gave her a squeeze. "We'll leave in the morning." He was wearing his overcoat; he looked as if he planned to rush out the door that very minute.

Marta was still, her sewing needle poised. Was this really happening? After all her years of service to the Bauers she was about to be abandoned after all. They were acting in their own best interest and forgetting about her entirely. And why shouldn't they, she asked herself. They had never promised her anything; her position in their family was as hired help, nothing more. Still, she felt a panic rising in her chest. She tried to reassure herself that things would work out somehow, but another part of her couldn't see how; she would starve to death all on her own. And part of her thought she deserved to.

"We'll need some time to pack," Anneliese was saying in the other room. "To wash the linen and cover the furniture and thaw the icebox and . . ." She gestured around the parlour.

Max cleared his throat. "I'm sorry, Anneliese, but I'll need him as quickly as possible. Hofstader has already been let go. And I have a business to run."

He smiled at Pavel as though to say that the world of commerce was beyond a woman's comprehension. Marta thought perhaps he was not as kind as she'd imagined him to be. She felt tears rising and blinked in rapid succession, trying to clear her eyes. Be patient, she told herself; there's time to figure something out. But clearly there wasn't. The decision made, the Bauers had moved immediately into planning mode. "Your mother could look in on the house," Anneliese said.

"Or Ernst. I'll meet with him to tell him the plan."

"And the school?"

Pavel grimaced. "They're not teaching Pepik anything worthwhile down there anyway. They've got him facing the back of the class. Did you know?"

Anneliese coughed; there was the furtive sound of her raising a hand to her mouth and lowering her voice. "What about . . . ?" Marta looked up to see Anneliese tip her head towards the sewing room.

"Pepik can't be without a nanny," Pavel said loudly. "Marta will come with us."

"But Sophie's already run off. Maybe Marta is about to do the same."

"You want to look after him yourself?" Pavel teased his wife. "You want to . . . you want to . . ." He was clearly searching his memory for what it was Marta actually did. "You want to cook his dinner? You want to give him a bath? Every night? And dry him, and dress him, and —" But Anneliese smiled and waved her hand to show he could stop. She did not want to do any of those things, and they both knew it — certainly not in Prague, where there were opera houses and movie theatres and her old friends from her teenage years.

"Marta!" Pavel called.

Marta made a stitch and pulled the thread taut. She waited a moment before setting down her needle and standing up and entering the room.

"We are going to Prague and you will come with us," Pavel said, magnanimous.

He paused.

"If you wish."

Marta had to blink some more to clear her eyes of tears. Such fear, and now such relief. She had nobody else — especially not Ernst — and deep down she knew she wasn't capable of getting by on her own. Surely Pavel must know this? But he seemed to be waiting for a reply, so she bobbed her head quickly and said, "Of course, Mr. Bauer."

Marta knew she should get Pepik ready to go first. But she was so relieved she couldn't help herself: she hurried upstairs to pack her own belongings.

Two days later something woke Marta in the middle of the night. She lit the candle on her bedside table and lay still, straining to hear. There was the sound of someone putting a foot down at the top of the stair, then pausing, then slowly putting another foot down. An image of Ernst flashed in front of her eyes and she was overcome by the familiar feeling of being dirty, that compulsive need to wash and clean that she knew, in the back of her mind, was what made her such good hired help.

The footsteps continued on, ever so carefully, past her door.

Marta began to fear for Pepik. His room was at the end of the hall, in the direction the footsteps were headed. There had been looting reported again recently, in a Jewish home in Kyjov; a young girl had been taken by a hooded man and was still missing. Marta swung her legs over the edge of the bed and lowered herself to the floor. The wood was cold but she didn't feel for her slippers; she took her robe from the back of the door and held it to her chest like a towel. Her movements made the floor creak loudly. Whoever was outside froze. Marta summoned her courage all at once and flung the door open.

She and the intruder stood there, gaping at each other. Sophie's hair was loose and frizzy, the candlelight playing over her face.

"Soph!" Marta whispered. "What are you doing here?"

"Lovely to see you too."

"Are you here for your things? I thought you already —"

"I forgot something. I came back for it." Sophie held up her silver key to the house. It glinted like a pirate's tooth.

"What time is it?"

"I'm finished with cooking."

"But your room, it's . . ." Marta pointed in the opposite direction, towards the other end of the hall.

Sophie looked uncertain. "It's none of your business. What I'm doing is none of your business."

Marta put a finger to her lips, then wondered why she was whispering. Shouldn't she call out and wake the Bauers?

"I thought the Bauers had left," Sophie confessed.

"Shhh! Did you hear something?"

"I thought they'd gone."

"Not yet."

"Mr. Bauer is still here?" Sophie touched her heart as she said Pavel's name.

"Yes."

"But he's leaving?"

"We're just . . ."

Marta pointed to the suitcases open in the hall. She saw Pavel's boar-bristle shaving brush and the elastic of his underthings. White cotton peeked out; it looked like the strips of cloth Anneliese used during menstruation. Marta had a sudden urge to zip the suitcase shut, to shield the Bauers' personal belongings from Sophie's gaze.

"You're going with them?" Sophie asked, eyes widening.

"You think they wouldn't take me?" Marta clutched her robe to her chest.

Sophie scoffed. "I think you shouldn't take *them*," she said. "It's very . . . you could get . . ." Her voice trailed off and she seemed at a loss for words. Then: "You shouldn't go," she said. "I heard there's a man, a very important man, who is very angry because he was fired by Mr. Bauer's brother-in-law, and because Mr. Bauer — Pavel — has been hired in his place."

Sophie touched her lip unconsciously with her tongue.

Marta said, "I don't see why that —"

But Sophie cut her off. "*Sie sind dumm.*" She raised her voice, and Marta brought her finger to her lips a second time, but Sophie continued to speak loudly, disgusted. "Do what you want, Marta," she said, and turned on her heel. "I'll be seeing you. Or maybe," she added, looking back over her shoulder meaningfully, "I won't be."

Marta saw that Sophie had a large empty sack over her shoulder, like a collapsed lung. She descended the stairs the way she'd come, the sack hanging loosely down her back. Marta waited until she heard the back door close. She went back into her room and hung up her robe. She cupped the candle flame with her hand and extinguished it with a short *huff*. Her bedsheets were cool, and she rubbed her feet together to warm them. She turned on her side and pulled the pillow over her head.

Only after she had been lying there for several minutes, her breath becoming more shallow, did it occur to her to wonder what Sophie had really been doing in the house. What exactly she had come back to retrieve.

∽◎∾

Anneliese heard a rumour.

Or perhaps, she said, it was the truth. There was a young British stockbroker who was helping Czech children leave the country. On trains referred to as Kindertransports. "What do you say?" she asked her husband. "Could we consider sending Pepik?" On December 2 the Führer had spoken on the radio, announcing his intent to take Prague. But Pavel was firm. He had a job in Prague, and he wanted his son with him. Hitler or no Hitler, he said.

The departure for the capital was delayed, though, by a last-minute call from Herrick, the German in charge at Pavel's factory. Pavel was summoned; he had no choice under Nazi rule but to go down and answer the man's questions. When he returned home, Pavel said he could guess, based on the machinery that had been removed and on the industrial-size grey metal tubes stacked in the foyer, that the place was being converted into a munitions factory. Perhaps to supply the Skoda works. They had wanted to ask him about the book-keeping, which was a complex system he had started in order to accommodate the jute cartel. His presence was required over the course of several days. The sixth of December, Saint Nicholas Day, found the Bauers eating their last supper in the house before their move.

They were in the middle of the *varenyky*, Marta's first attempt at dumplings stuffed with beef and herbs — they had turned out rather poorly, she thought — when the doorbell rang. Pavel put down his silver cutlery. He cleared his throat and said, "Pepik, why don't you get that?"

Pepik looked to Marta for confirmation. She nodded to show he should go.

He went into the hall and they could hear him struggling with the heavy handle. Pavel and Anneliese were looking at each other, little smiles of anticipation on their faces.

"Do you need some help?" Marta called. But the door was pushed in from the outside and Pepik gave a little squeal.

"Who is it?" Anneliese called out innocently.

A booming voice: "It's Saint Nicholas!"

Pepik leapt into the dining room. He made a face like Henry in the comic book his great-uncle had sent from America: mouth wide open, hands on his cheeks but no sound. Then he stuck his head back out into the hall to make sure Saint Nick had not disappeared.

There was more rustling and Pavel Bauer shouted, "No need to take your boots off! Just come around here so we can get a good look at you."

It was Ernst Anselm who came around the corner. He was dressed in a bishop's tall hat, a fake beard, and his wife Hella's foxtail fur coat. Marta flushed and averted her eyes. She was having trouble catching her breath, her heart was beating so fast. She braced herself, waiting for him to address her, but he only said to everyone, "I've brought the Devil with me." There was a slur in his voice — he'd been drinking. He looked around the table at each of them in turn and then tugged on a chain. Sure enough, a little man in a red suit came around the corner.

"See? The Devil." Anneliese pointed to show Pepik.

Pavel threw his head back and hooted. "Look at you both!" he said. "A regular Pat and Patachon."

"What a clever comparison," Saint Nicholas said.

Pavel raised an eyebrow at his friend.

"You're lucky I showed up," Ernst said. "I mean, you're lucky Saint Nick came."

"But Saint Nick, you come every year. Why should this year be different?" Pavel was cheerful for the benefit of his son, but Marta could see he was confused by Ernst's comment.

"Saint Nicholas," Anneliese said, "would you like a drink?"

"He seems to have had enough to —" Pavel started, but the Devil interrupted. "Yes, he surely would." He leaned back on his heels.

Marta recognized the Devil but she wasn't sure from where.

Saint Nicholas tried to elbow Pavel, but missed and stumbled before regaining his balance. "Mr. Bauer, I'll trade the drink for your Parker investment," he said. Then he looked at Marta; his face registered surprise, as though he was just now remembering their last conversation, when she'd left him standing in the hall. He opened his mouth to speak. "And who do we —" he started, but Pavel grasped his shoulder. "Don't you have some business to attend to?"

Ernst belched quietly into the back of his hand. "Ah, yes," he agreed sagely. "I have some very important business." He motioned for Pepik to come over, forehead furrowed, focused all at once on the task at hand. He had played the role of Saint

Nicholas for Pepik since the boy was born. Every year the same charade. He was good at it, Marta had to admit.

He was good at all sorts of charades.

"Are you . . ." Ernst consulted a piece of paper in front of him, "Angus Bengali?"

Pepik was eyeing the Devil warily and clinging to Marta's skirt. He shook his head no.

Ernst feigned confusion, crumpling his forehead again. "Oh," he said, "I thought . . ."

He peered more closely at his list, which Marta could see was a newspaper article clipped out of *Lidové noviny*. "Herman von Winkledom?"

"No," said Pepik, a smile starting to show.

"Ludwig von Twicky-Twacky?"

"No!"

"It says here . . ." Ernst said, bringing the paper close to his face. "I left my spectacles with Krampusse." He ran his forefinger down the fake list. "You're not . . . I don't suppose you're . . . Pepik Bauer?"

"I am!" shouted Pepik, who had now completely forgotten about the Devil. "I've been good!"

"Have you?"

Pepik nodded enthusiastically and then, unable to contain himself, he made a lunge for the sack of gifts. Ernst held it above his head. He paused, his eyes far away. "Have you *really* been good?" he asked.

A shadow crossed Pepik's face. He drew back and crossed his small arms in front of his chest. He said, "No."

"No?"

"I've been bad."

The Devil gave a little laugh. "Finally I get some action!"

Ernst laughed too, but Marta could see he was unprepared for this. He was struggling just to keep his balance, swaying unsteadily on his heels. "Well," he said, eyeing Marta slyly, "everybody is naughty sometimes. It's never too late to correct one's mistakes."

She felt the heat rise straight to her face.

"Hear, hear." Pavel raised his glass, unaware of what he was toasting.

"What I meant to ask," Ernst continued, "is have you been good most of the time?"

But it was too late. Pepik shook his head gravely. "*Ne.*"

The whole thing had taken on the air of some kind of religious ritual, something akin to the confessions Marta remembered from her youth, and so she was not surprised when Pepik said, "I was bad. I let the water man put his water on my forehead." He looked up at the Saint. "To make me not Jewish," he clarified.

The room fell silent. The Devil and Saint Nicholas looked at each other. Anneliese lowered her head. It was Pavel who spoke first. "You were —" he glanced at his wife, whose face was in her hands, and back to his son. "You were *baptized?*"

Marta heard Ernst mutter something that sounded a little like *amen.*

"*Miláčku?* The priest put water on your forehead?"

Pepik nodded, hesitant, his eyes moving between his parents.

Pavel stood up. "I can't . . . I don't . . ." He looked at Anneliese, who would not meet his gaze. He opened his mouth and closed it again. He looked at his son and at the

Devil and the Saint, and said, without expression, "If you'll excuse me."

The parlour fell silent. Only the teenaged Lucifer seemed oblivious to the implications of what had just taken place. "Who baptized you?" he asked Pepik. Marta saw that the Devil's face was thin and there were two large boils on the side of his neck. It was Ernst's nephew, she remembered — Armin? Irwin?

Pepik was fighting back tears. "Father Wilhelm," he said.

Marta was astonished that Pepik had remembered the priest's name — he could barely remember the letters she was teaching him. Then again, perhaps he knew what the important things were, where to place his attention. Perhaps he remembered more than they gave him credit for.

There was more strained silence, the remaining adults looking nervously at each other. Saint Nicholas inserted his fingers under his fake beard and scratched vigorously at his face, suddenly desperate to get the whole thing over with. "Pepik," he said. "I see here now, on my list" — he peered at it again "— it says you've been good. So I've brought you a present."

He shoved the box at Pepik, who held it uncertainly, as if it were a bomb about to go off.

"Go on, open it," Saint Nicholas said. "I've got lots of other children left on my list." He lifted his sack, which was clearly empty.

Pepik set his gift on the table. He sat down in front of it. He peeled back a piece of tape carefully.

"Go on!" Saint Nicholas repeated.

It was a terrible present in light of what had happened. Pavel had given his son his own grandfather's prayer shawl. The tallit was nestled between two pieces of ivory tissue paper.

Pepik unfolded it and held it in his hands, out from his body as though it was an offering. The adults looked at each other; nobody knew what to do.

Pepik too had clearly been expecting a new caboose, or a toy helmet with the insignia of the Masaryk government. A tallit was inappropriate for a boy his age. But he seemed to understand instinctually the symbolic weight of the gift. He unfolded his great-grandfather's prayer shawl and draped it over his shoulders. The edges hung down, the tzitziot touching the floor.

"I don't know if —" the Devil started, but Ernst jerked his chain to silence him.

Pepik looked up at the adults, one by one, defiant.

This is who I am, his look said.

The Bauer family left for Prague the following morning. The automobile was loaded up to the roof with trunks, boxes, Pepik's *Botanisierbuchse* and butterfly net. The old town fell behind them like discarded skin.

There was stony silence in the front seat. Pavel's jaw was clenched tight and his eyes glued to the windshield. His knuckles were white on the steering wheel. As they pulled out into the lane that ran around the perimeter of the town square, Marta saw that there was a rally going on, a pack of Hitlerjugend crowded together wearing armbands and lace-up boots. There were maybe forty of them. A man in front of the crowd yelled something into a megaphone. The crowd responded, shouting *"Sieg Heil! Sieg Heil!"* and shaking their fists in the air.

She had a flash of Mr. Goldstein lying dead on the cobble-stones.

"Goodbye, old town," Pepik said morosely.

Anneliese was dealing with her husband's rage about the baptism by pretending he wasn't there. She chatted brightly to Pepik and Marta about where they were headed. "Wait until you see Václavské náměstí. And all the spires, and Charles Bridge with the statues of the saints all along it." She looked over her shoulder at her son in the back seat. "In the summer we can go on a steamboat and go to Kampě Island and have an ice cream and go swimming in the river! Wouldn't you like that?"

"I forgot my pennywhistle," Pepik said, forlorn.

But his mother persisted. "As soon as we've arrived we'll go and see the astronomical clock. Every hour a trapdoor opens and Christ marches out with his Apostles. The skeleton of death tolls his bell as the hour turns."

Pavel said wryly, "As though we need to be reminded."

But Marta suspected he was relieved to be going as well, to be fleeing the German-occupied territory. Part of him too, even if he would not admit it, was afraid of what was happening all around them, a part of him that was eager to retreat into the fantasy of a picnic on the island with cold chicken wings and lemonade, and Hitler just a bad dream.

They had circumnavigated the area and were now pulling out onto the cobbled road. Marta turned back for one last look at her home. The crowd of *Jugend* looked larger from this angle, filling half of the town square. Boys, mostly, in thin winter jackets, Nazi insignia sewn onto their sleeves. They chanted along with the man at the megaphone. Marta saw one girl, a girl with frizzy hair: it took her a minute to realize it was Sophie. Her curls were tied back from her face and her mouth was wide open, screaming. There was a thin boy pushed up next to her. Marta knew him too.

It was Ernst Anselm's nephew. Armin? Irwin?

The last thing Marta saw, her last memory of the old town, was Sophie holding the Devil's hand.

PART TWO

PRAGUE

19 January 1939

Dear Pavel and Anneliese,

I am sorry to have been out of contact for so long. All is well. Business continues apace.

I trust you enjoy your books as usual. The one before The Castle *is excellent.*

Please give my love to Alžběta if you see her. And to the little girls.

Best regards,
Max

(FILE UNDER: Stein, Max. Died Auschwitz, 1943)

I'VE LIVED A LONG TIME.

"May I ask your age?" you said when we first met.

"You may not!" I smiled, feigning offence. It was the kind of teasing that usually passes between people who have known each other all their lives. Which I felt, in a particular way, I had.

I'd been looking for you for years, Joseph. Even when I didn't know I was looking.

In Hitler's Czechoslovakia, degrees of Judaism didn't matter. There were families in Eastern Europe who were completely assimilated — ugly word, but that's what they called it — families who'd had their children baptized, who celebrated Christmas. Even they had very little hope. All that mattered was whether there had been a single Jewish grandparent. People who were estranged from their families, who'd never known their parents . . . all it took was a little detective work on the part of the authorities and they were condemned. And, of course, the practising Jews, the ones rooted deeply in the richness and beauty of tradition, who lit the Sabbath candles and awaited the coming of the Messiah — I don't have to tell you what happened to them.

They tried so hard, but it was almost always too little, too late. After the *Anschluss* in Austria they emigrated, but only as far as Amsterdam, say, or Prague. After Hitler made clear his designs on Czechoslovakia, they emigrated again, but this time perhaps only as far as France. In some cases people had exit visas but chose not to use them. While the bulk of European Jewry were begging and bribing, there were those who clung to their homes and their futures, even as those things were disappearing out from under them.

When I was working on my second book, I interviewed the granddaughter of a survivor whose own parents were murdered in Birkenau. "They had exit visas," this woman kept repeating, as though trying to make it make sense. "Why didn't they use them?" I tried to explain how her great-grandparents could not have anticipated the death camps, how the Czech Jews especially had enjoyed decades of peace and prosperity, how they thought they were doing what was best for their families and for the country they loved. I could see she didn't understand, was thinking only of her mother's suffering and her own terrible childhood as a result.

They can come off as selfish, the survivors and their children. As closed and cramped, dark knots of grievance. That too is Hitler's legacy: the poison never fully flushed out.

After the war, nobody wanted to talk about what had happened. Things were still difficult by the time I did my doctorate: I remember how hard it was to find willing interview subjects. It wasn't until much later that the stories started to come out. The survivors were ageing, and it was suddenly understood that if we didn't hear from them now there would be nothing left to hear. A few of the Kindertransport children started talking then as well, but they were still considered the lucky ones, the ones who had escaped. In comparison to the others, the thinking went, they had nothing worth talking about.

Not that anyone said that directly to my face.

It was later, as the older survivors of Auschwitz and Bergen-Belsen began to die, that these now-adult children started coming out of the woodwork. The first Kindertransport reunion sparked an incredible reaction. The participants came to understand that they had been part of something larger, pawns in a story for which they had not been to blame. They had been caught inside the giant train of time. They compared notes, and in the end they did not feel so totally alone.

Telling this to you now makes me wish I had been at that reunion. I still would have been an outsider, though. Isolated because my story is different from theirs. The truth is, it suits me being alone. Put me in a crowd and I only feel more lonely. Looking always at the shape of people's backs. For someone in an orange sweater. For a kerchief.

Could you excuse me, please? I need a moment.

Don't worry. I'm not about to cry.

It's like this: since the sixtieth anniversary reunion in London in 1999 there has been a flood of stories about the Kindertransports. The word in vogue is *testimony*, although that word doesn't sit well with me, with its implications of a justice system, the possibility of retribution. Still, the things people tell me are often remarkable. For example, two sisters. Their parents took them to the station on the date of the Winton transport and put them both on the train. But the smaller was only a baby, and she'd been sick with a flu that had been going around; at the last minute the parents pulled her off. The older girl remembers handing her infant sister out through the window, the weight of her tiny body like a warm loaf of bread. It was the last time she saw her sister. Or either of her parents, for that matter.

Another story: a boy whose parents left it too late. The Kindertransport was already full. The waiting list was three times the train's capacity, but Winton's secretary took a liking to the boy. Something about the way his ears stuck out, or how his knobby knees were wider than his thighs. He was just six years old and does not remember his father's words, but he can still describe his happiness when the secretary moved his son to the top of the list. Perhaps a bribe was exchanged, but that's not what the man remembers. He remembers seeing his father cry tears of relief; he might die — did die — but his only son would get out.

For several years — many years — I was able to lose myself in the vastness of these stories, the stories of losses and searches and discoveries. They allowed me to forget the person I was looking for. The child from the letter I carried with me. When I finally sought you out, I was surprised by how easy it was. I knew your last name: I looked you up in the phone book.

There you were, in my city. It was simple.

I gazed out the window while the telephone rang, trying to ignore the fact that I could hear my own heart. A single tennis shoe, tied by its laces, hung from the neighbour's clothesline. I heard your voice on the answering machine and was confused by the muddled accent. I stood still, blinking rapidly, taking deep breaths. Finally I realized the machine was recording my silence. I forced myself to speak before it was too late: I gave you my name and a bit about my research. Then stumbled over my telephone number and had to repeat it several times. I must have sounded like a blubbering old idiot. Which, I suppose, I was.

When I hung up the phone, I did not step away from it. It was clear to me all at once that you probably wouldn't call back. Why would you? I should have said something different.

But what should I have said?

The truth, I told myself.

Which is? I answered back.

Which is the most crucial piece of the puzzle.

I nodded. And all at once every bit of me agreed: I should have told you what only I knew. That I'm the sibling you never knew existed.

FOUR

THERE WAS A CRIB AT MAX AND Alžběta's that belonged to their little daughter Eva. Anneliese could not stand to look at it. Marta knew what she was thinking: how old would her own baby girl be now, had she lived? Marta tried to picture what she would look like. Dark curls, like Anneliese, or the slightly paler brown of her father? A kind child, or petulant? There was a phantom in the family, growing taller all the time, but never quite catching up to her brother, Pepik, to the world of living flesh and blood.

The Bauers unpacked their belongings. They waited to hear from Max, but there was no news. Maybe he was still en route to meet Alžběta and their daughters, or maybe he had other reasons to make himself scarce. Either way, the apartment was empty, and they moved into it like actors onto an empty set. Pepik chose the room that had been his Uncle Max's when he was a boy: it had a bunk bed and a stag's head mounted on the wall. Marta had a whole suite of rooms to herself — cook's, butler's, chauffeur's. It was much more space than she was used to, but she tried to act nonchalant, wandering the large urban flat as though she belonged there. At night you could see from the front window of the parlour all the way down to the heart of Praha, the streetlamps lit and glittering like debutantes coming out for a ball.

"There's the opera house," Anneliese pointed out the first night, her cheeks pink with excitement. And beyond it was the castle itself, lit up, like the largest jewel in a crown.

"Hitler's new house," Pavel said flatly. He didn't look his wife in the eye, still angry.

"I prefer the Belvedere," Anneliese said.

"I heard someone call the castle 'Hitler's new house' today," Pavel persisted. He crossed his arms over his chest. "Over my dead body," he said. But his voice sounded hollow to Marta. The new flat elevated Anneliese, but it had the opposite effect on Pavel. He seemed younger here, Marta thought, or smaller. He seemed defeated.

A night-letter arrived and Pavel left early the next morning to meet Max's foreman, Hans, at the factory. Anneliese took Pepik and Marta out to see the city. Winter was just setting in, a dusting of snow over everything like confectioner's sugar. Marta's breath made puffy clouds in front of her face. She wiggled her toes to warm them in her stiff lace-up boots, and rubbed Pepik's fingers in his mittens. They walked down Vinohradská, past Italská, Balbínova, and Španělská streets, past the Živnostenská banka and the Myslbek art gallery on Na Příkopě, which was showing an exhibition of Nazi paintings. They strolled the periphery of the broad tree-lined avenue, Marta looking around, trying to take it all in. She had never seen so many people in one place. Women in Chanel coats with silk scarves tied at their throats, groups of teenagers clustered together like grapes, old men riding bicycles. There was an Orthodox shop on a corner: through the boarded-up window she saw a calendar with a picture of a rabbi blowing a ram's horn. The blue and white Zionist collection boxes abandoned.

Anneliese pointed out the bakery, still the same as when she was a girl. They passed the butcher shop and saw carcasses, pink and bloody, hanging on hooks in the front window. They looked, Marta thought, strangely human. At the Wagons-Litz Travel Agency there was a line snaking all the way out the front door, people trying desperately to leave the country. Red trolleys criss-crossed the square like fate lines on the palm of a hand.

Marta had had a picture in her mind of Prague, a picture she hadn't even known was there and which she now realized was basically an enlarged version of their old town: two of each kind of shop instead of one. But Prague was something else altogether. "I feel like I'm in a completely different country," she said.

Anneliese shrugged and smiled. "Welcome back to Czechoslovakia," she said. A sign caught her eye over Marta's right shoulder. "Look at what's showing! *Snow White and the Seven Dwarfs*. It's that American fellow, Walt something-or-other."

Marta looked down at Pepik, his cheeks pink like apples. "Well?" She clasped her hands in front of her chest, beaming. And before she knew it she was about to see her first moving picture.

The cinema was dark, with seats ascending on an angle. It smelled stuffy, like dust and stale peppermints. They were plunged into blackness and Marta reached for Pepik's hand. There was silence, someone sneezing, someone unzipping a coat. For a moment they heard the *tick-tick-tick* of the projector and then all at once the screen lit up. A girl with creamy skin, jet-black hair, huge eyes. A princess, Marta thought. It was like entering another dimension, the vastness of the girl's face, the brightness. Marta didn't know where to look. The scene changed to a forest, and everything in front of her had life in it: the trees, the stones, the animals. Her whole field of vision teemed with colour. She wanted to glance over at Pepik to see how he was taking it but found herself unable to peel her eyes from the screen.

After the film there was a newsreel that showed Hitler spouting off about the expansion of his *Lebensraum*, but even this couldn't dampen Marta's spirits. When she exited the cinema it was as if no time had passed, and at the same time as if a new era had begun. She could hardly speak. It had been, she realized, so long since she'd felt pleasure. Anneliese looked at Marta and Pepik and clapped her hands. "I told you you'd like the city," she said. "Didn't I tell you?"

She too had a big smile plastered across her face, her tension with Pavel momentarily forgotten.

Pepik was hopping from foot to foot. "Dopey!" he shouted. "Sneezy!" And he began to make sneezing noises in the direction of his mother.

On the way back to the Vinohrady they passed the Havlíčkovy sady. Two German Jewish peddlers were sitting on a park bench selling pencils. It was a reminder of the hard times they were living in — but Marta didn't want to be reminded. For now, even momentarily, the hard times seemed abstract. They had been shucked off like a pair of dirty trousers and dropped in a heap in the corner. The people, the automobiles, the vibrant pulse of the city: Marta felt she might as well be living in the fairy tale herself. In a place where *war* was a word never spoken. She climbed the hill home with lights in her eyes.

The following day, though, Karel Čapek died. The radio carried a tribute, noting among his literary achievements the coining of the word *robot*.

"Five years from now nobody will use *robot*," Anneliese said. "*One* year from now." She massaged the nape of her neck with her knuckles.

"You never know," Pavel said testily. Marta saw that the death of his favourite writer depressed him. The radio broadcast had given the impression that Čapek had not even been sick, that he had lost his will to live now that his country was carved into pieces and Hitler was making doe-eyes at the capital.

For the next while Pavel was preoccupied with his new position, leaving the house before the rest of them were up and dashing out to meetings late at night. He avoided his wife, who was out all day anyway, at luncheons with Mathilde or getting a marcel wave with hot irons at the Salon Petra Měchurová. Marta wondered if they would celebrate Christmas, after the baptism incident. Though it was spoken of less frequently, Pavel was, she knew, still angry. On the other hand, Christmas for the Bauers wasn't *Christian*; it was tradition, plain and simple. When Anneliese told her to go ahead, Marta threw herself into the preparations. The kitchen in Max and Alžběta's flat was equipped with something called a blender — she had no idea what it was for — and an electric kettle with an automatic shut-off. Marta made *vánočka*, the traditional holiday bread, and slivered almonds and meringue macaroons with strings baked into them. She put Pepik to work on chains of coloured paper. She was worried that a tree might not appear on which to hang all their decorations, but finally, on the twenty-third of December, Pavel returned home with a scrawny fir. Where had he found it in a city as covered with concrete as Prague? He set it up in the corner of the parlour; the large room made the tree look small, like a naked child shivering after his bath.

"What do you say?" Marta asked Pepik. "We'd better put some clothes on him!" Usually the decorated tree would be presented to Pepik as a surprise, but the Bauers didn't have time for that this year, and Marta was glad to be able to give her charge a project. The Walt Disney film had lifted his spirits temporarily, but he had now fallen into a sullen funk. He reminded Marta of a tiny field marshal, his lead soldiers spread around him like casualties.

On the morning of the twenty-fourth Marta got up early and peeled the potatoes and the parsnips and took the carp out of the icebox. She rolled out some dough for *vanilkové rohlíčky*, and soon the kitchen was filled with the sweet smell of vanilla crescents baking. What else did Sophie usually make? Fish soup, which was served before the carp: it would have to simmer for several hours. Marta made a list as Sophie used to do, and wondered idly where the girl was now. "You shouldn't go," she remembered Sophie saying. "There's a man who is very angry about Mr. Bauer being hired in his place . . ."

Marta went down her list of tasks one by one, ticking off each thing. Finally, at quarter after five, Anneliese came home. "The carp," she said. "Is it sweet-and-sour?" When she knew that was how they had it every year.

At half past six Pavel rang the little Christmas bell. Pepik had been lying on his top bunk staring at the ceiling, but he could not pretend he wasn't excited by the holiday; he dropped to the floor and bounded down the hall to the parlour. Marta stood behind him, holding his shoulders, as they took in the beautiful room. Pavel had dimmed the lights and lit a fire in the hearth and all of the tiny candles in the tree's branches. The flames leapt up and were reflected in the mirrors on the front wall of the parlour and in the big glass chandelier; it looked as if the room were alight with fireflies.

Pepik went straight for the lowest branch, took off a macaroon, and bit it in half.

The presents were laid out on a table by the breakfront. Marta got a big box of chocolates from the Lindt chocolatier shop in Prague. It was a much more expensive gift than the Bauers usually gave her. "No . . . really —" she started, but Pavel shushed her. "We're grateful," he said, "for all your extra work."

His gift for Anneliese was in a small blue box: diamond drop earrings to match the sparkly watch. She held the earrings up to her ears; they were shaped like two perfect tears.

Anneliese's gift for her husband was in a small creamy envelope with his name written on the front in fountain pen. Pavel peeled back the wax seal. Marta watched his eyes move back and forth as he read. She couldn't tell from his facial expression the nature of the message from his wife. Had they worked things out, or was it just a temporary truce?

Marta, for her part, had picked a book about two Czech boys going to the market for Pepik; for the Bauers she had chosen a picture frame in which she had placed a photo of their son sitting on the front steps of the house in their old town. When Pavel saw it, his eyes filled with tears. "What a very thoughtful gift," he said.

Even Anneliese seemed touched. Her fingers fluttered at her throat. "Marta," she said, "you really should not have. This frame must have cost your whole —" But she stopped herself and said graciously, "Thank you very much, Marta." She held the photo up and peered at it again. "It seems a long time ago," she said, a peculiar look on her face. "Doesn't it? If you think of everything that's happened?" Marta knew Anneliese was thinking of Max. She had hoped he might join them for Christmas, but there was still no word from either him or Alžběta.

When the presents had all been opened, Pavel wanted to light the menorah. In the past when Chanukah fell at the same time as Christmas, the Jewish holiday was the one that got forgotten, but this year Pavel was determined.

"Aren't we already . . . how many days —" Anneliese started.

Pavel brushed her away. He wasn't sure, but they would light all eight candles to be safe. He also wanted to say the blessing, which was something that to Marta's knowledge the Bauers had never done before.

Marta watched Pavel, with his eyes closed, chanting the Hebrew prayer. She was flabbergasted that he knew it by heart. Perhaps it had been taught to him as a boy? He threw in something he called the Shema — the Jewish prayer of God's oneness, he said — for good measure. When he was finished he placed the menorah in the window. It was a mitzvah to do so, he said, but Marta saw Anneliese wince. She wouldn't dare criticize her husband, not after what had happened, but then Pavel seemed to reconsider and moved the candle-holder back to the credenza, out of sight of people passing on the street. The lights from the Christmas tree, reflected in the wall of mirrors, filled the room to overflowing with brilliance. By contrast, the menorah seemed small and incidental. It flickered in the corner unnoticed.

~@~

Anneliese was behind closed doors, getting ready for the festivities. They were going to ring in the New Year at the home of Mathilde, her oldest friend from the *gymnasium*. Mathilde and her husband, Vaclav, who owned margarine factories, were having several couples over to celebrate. "Hitler or no Hitler," Pavel said.

Anneliese finally emerged from her room, her face powdered and her hair piled on top of her head. A telegram arrived just as the Bauers were putting on their coats. Although it was sealed inside the usual envelope, Marta had a distinct impression that the delivery boy knew its contents. He furrowed his brow as he handed it over, as if he hated to be the bearer of bad news. Or perhaps it was just that every telegram these days contained bad news.

Pavel took the envelope from the boy.

"Is it Max?" Anneliese asked. She was wearing a clingy red dress Marta hadn't seen before.

"Or Alžběta?"

"Pass me my . . ." Pavel nodded at his scarf, his eyes still on the telegram.

"Pavel. I'm speaking to you."

"It's your man."

"I wish you would —"

"Your man Wilhelm."

Anneliese froze with Pavel's scarf in her hand. "The priest?"

"He's been arrested."

"Arrested? Why?"

"Forget the scarf," Pavel said. "It isn't even snowing."

Anneliese glared at her husband. "Why was he arrested?"

"For baptizing Jews. Why else?" Pavel buttoned his coat quickly. "We're late," he said, without looking at Anneliese. They took turns kissing the top of their son's head and went out the door.

Marta put Pepik to bed. There was a small fuss when he wanted to stay up until midnight, but she remained firm, and by the time she tucked him in he was so exhausted he fell asleep without even a story. She went into the kitchen and cleaned up the dishes, and then she listened to the president's New Year's address on the radio. It was easy to tell by Hácha's voice that he was dreadfully sad. Despite everything that had happened, he said — despite the terrible events of the year — the people of Czechoslovakia still stood on their own land. But would they still be able to say so this time next year?

Marta made herself a cup of linden tea and sat down beside the Christmas tree, thinking about Father Wilhelm. *Arrested*, Pavel had said. For giving out baptismal certificates. She could picture the priest as though he stood before her, the bald patch in the shape of a kippah, the bony fingers interlaced as though in prayer. He'd been so kind to them, she thought, offering to help not only little Pepik but his mother as well. How many others were out there for whom he'd done the same?

Would the authorities now come looking for Pepik? It was certainly possible; an illegal baptism was sure to have reper-cussions. She shivered, wondering what exactly they might be. She lifted her cup to her lips, but the tea had cooled and the

leaves tasted musty, too sweet. People, she knew, were just disappearing these days; it wasn't unheard of for someone to be
present one evening and gone by the break of the new day.
Taken. But could it happen to a child? To Pepik?

And where was Max? He'd promised to be in touch.

Marta pushed her teacup aside. A sick feeling rose in her
stomach: too much carp and *vánočka*. She glanced down at
Pepik's train where it wound between the legs of the table.
Pepik had incorporated some of the lanterns from the
Christmas tree into the scene; they stood in for lampposts in
the little nameless town where his clothespin civilians went
about their lives. One of the lead soldiers had fallen on its
back and was staring up at her. Its mouth frozen open. It
looked as if it were shouting something. As if it were trying
to give a warning.

Max's letter did not arrive until March. Pavel held it close to his
face and read it aloud to his wife: "I trust you enjoy your books
as usual. The one before *The Castle* is excellent."

"Whatever does he mean?" Anneliese asked. "He's talking
about books? Now?"

"It was posted six weeks ago, in January."

"Was it?"

"He seems to be writing in code."

"*The Castle*. By Kafka?"

"That must be the one."

"And what comes before it . . . *Amerika*."

"That was after."

"*The Trial*," Anneliese said.

"*The Trial*. What's the plot?"

She looked up at the ceiling, trying to remember. "The narrator is arrested for a crime that isn't named."

"For no crime."

"Exactly."

"I think we know what's happened to Max."

Anneliese was thrown into a panic. "What should we do?"

Marta was in a corner of the room, dusting the buffet. She saw Pavel spread his hands out in front of him: *Don't ask me.*

The Bauers were sitting at opposite ends of the heavy Victorian sofa; the wall of mirrors doubled them. Everything the Bauers did in the new flat was copied by their doppelgangers: When the Bauers ate, their twins did the same. When they spoke, when they argued, so did the twins. It was as if someone had thought to make a copy of each of them in case something should happen to the originals.

"We should at least tell Alžběta," Anneliese said to Pavel.

"But how can we tell her if we don't know where she is?"

Anneliese reached for her Chanel purse and lit a cigarette.

"We could call Ernst," Pavel said, "to ask what he thinks."

Marta lowered her eyes, intent on her feather duster, but Anneliese was at the phone immediately, her cigarette left smoking in the ashtray. She spoke into the black horn in the middle of the wooden box on the wall and then covered the mouthpiece with her hand. "The operator says there's a line through Frankfurt," she said to Pavel.

"Our calls don't go through Frankfurt. Doesn't she know that?"

Anneliese put the earpiece back in its cradle and went over to the small fire in the hearth. She picked up the bellows and pumped vigorously.

"I had lunch with Mathilde." She turned around to look at her husband.

"And what did the Queen of Sheba have to say for herself?"

"Eight thousand crowns will buy passage to Uruguay."

"'Oh, gazelle, her eyes have captured my heart'!" Pavel sang a line of the popular song.

"They're thinking of going. She and Vaclav."

"Are there margarine factories in Uruguay?"

"Maybe they'll open one. It isn't the point. The point is to get out." Anneliese pumped the bellows for emphasis.

Marta moved a chiselled glass candy dish aside, along with a china bell — the kind used to summon a maid — and dusted beneath them. She had noticed over the past weeks that Anneliese's infatuation with Prague was wearing off, like the novelty of a younger lover. And why wouldn't it? The beautiful opera house had been closed. Almost nobody wanted to meet her for cakes at the Louvre Café: everyone had left or else was busy trying to. And now this news about Max. Arrested. For no reason. Where was he being held?

Pavel stayed seated, his elbows on his knees and his fingers steepled in front of him. "I did hear . . ." he said to his wife. "There's something I heard."

Anneliese put the bellows down. She smoothed down her skirt.

"There's a man," Pavel said. "A stockbroker. British."

"Winton?"

"Poor bugger. The markets can't be good."

"I mentioned him months ago. Don't you remember? Vaclav and Mathilde got their girls on his list."

"What about Uruguay?"

Anneliese sighed. "They're exploring every option, Pavel. That's what people are doing."

"I was thinking of contacting him. Winton," Pavel said, his forehead resting on the heels of his hands. "To see if we can't put Pepik on the list as well."

Marta set the bell back down on the buffet; it made a tinkling sound. "It might be a good idea," she said without thinking. Where she had got the notion that her opinion mattered she didn't know, but it felt almost natural, somehow, to voice it. Pepik was her responsibility, after all. Shouldn't she have some say in the decision? "It might be a good idea to put Pepik on the list," she said again.

Pavel was looking at her, surprised, Marta thought, but not disapproving. In fact, if she wasn't mistaken, he seemed almost impressed.

"Do you think?" he asked. His eyebrows were lifted, his face relaxed. But Anneliese had turned away from both of them, frowning out the window as though she'd noticed something unfolding below that required her full attention, and Marta grew suddenly self-conscious. She nodded once at Pavel, and moved back to the buffet to dust beneath Alžběta's houseplants.

Anneliese fished her cigarette out of the ashtray and took a slow pull. "Why don't we go together?" she asked Pavel, as though Marta hadn't spoken.

Pavel turned back to his wife, the muscles along his jawline tightening discernably. "It's not so simple, Liesel," he said.

"You need an exit visa. You need proof of citizenship. The line-ups at the embassies are from here to Vienna. You need an entry permit for another country." His eyes darted briefly back to Marta.

"Not for Britain," Anneliese said. "Not until the first of April." And she was right, Marta knew. In the wake of the Munich Agreement, legislation had been passed that allowed entrance into England without a permit. A little window; an apology for the betrayal.

You still needed an exit permit from Czechoslovakia, however.

The Bauers talked this over quietly. Pavel thought he could get hold of one.

"With a bribe?" Anneliese asked.

Pavel touched the sofa. "This needs to be reupholstered."

"Not to be crass."

"With money," he said. "Yes."

"Even without the *Ariernachweis*?"

"That's hard for anyone these days. So many families have a grandmother born out of wedlock."

In the mirror over the buffet Marta saw Pavel get up. He took his pipe and tobacco pouch from the credenza and hunched over the table, filling the little bowl and tamping it down. When the pipe was lit, he went back towards the phone to give it another try. The operator said there was a line through České Budějovice, the famous beer town, right away. The earpiece was at the end of a long cord, and Pavel fidgeted with it, waiting. He was put through and explained to Ernst immediately about the letter from his brother-in-law Max. There was a long pause while he listened to Ernst speak.

"Trieste?" Pavel said finally. "Hostage?" He held his pipe away from his face. There was another long pause. Marta could well imagine the voice Ernst would be using — patient, as though speaking to a child.

"You really think I could be taken hostage?" Pavel asked.

He waited for his friend's response. After a few moments he tapped at the receiver on the wooden box. "*Ahoj*?" he said. "Ernst?"

But the line was broken.

The following morning Pavel surveyed his family around the breakfast table, each of them in front of a setting of silver. "How about a trip to the country?" he asked.

Anneliese looked up from her porridge.

"It's March seventh," Pavel said. "The anniversary of Masaryk's birthday. Let's make a pilgrimage to Lány."

"What about the factory?" Anneliese asked.

But at the mention of an expedition Pepik had straightened in his chair and plunged his spoon back into his cereal bowl. "I want to go in the automobile," he said forcefully. He was between schools, and lonely at home. There had been a call from the principal to say his Czech wasn't good enough and perhaps he'd fit in better at the Jewish school. Pavel was furious — Czech was his son's first language — but what could they do? Even he saw that to protest would worsen their case. You didn't want to make a single unnecessary enemy.

"Well?" Pavel said.

"Sounds fine to me," Marta said. "I'll make some *chlebíčky*."

She looked over at Anneliese for confirmation, but Anneliese had pushed back her chair and risen from the table. "Have a nice time," she snapped at the three of them, the circles of pink on her cheeks growing brighter.

"Liesel —" Pavel started, tenderly, but Anneliese interrupted him. "I'm not going. We're on the brink of war and all you can think about is Masaryk. News flash! Tomáš Masaryk is dead!" She was refusing to meet her husband's eye. Furious with him for broaching the subject without asking her first. Or furious about some other transgression Marta wasn't aware of.

She knew that in another lifetime Pavel would have tried to convince his wife, but in the wake of Pepik's baptism and everything else that had happened he seemed unable to summon the energy. "Nobody wants to go without you," he said half-heartedly. He turned to Pepik. "It won't be any fun without Mamenka, right, buster?" But Pepik's nod was uncertain; he couldn't make sense of what was going on between his parents.

"The automobile," he said.

"I'm not going," Anneliese repeated.

Marta groped around for a way to extract herself as well. "Why don't you two gentlemen go together? The King and the Crown Prince." But it was too late. Pavel had given Anneliese a chance and now he hardened against her. It had become a contest of wills. "Nonsense," Pavel said. "There's no reason for you to miss out, Marta. Go and pack those sandwiches. And a Thermos of cocoa for Pepik."

She had no choice but to do what she was told.

Marta was relieved when they finally got in the car and left Anneliese's fuming behind. She felt bad about Anneliese — she felt she should feel bad — but she couldn't deny her excitement at the chance to ride in the front seat. Pavel was freshly shaven and had combed pomade through his hair. He was wearing field corduroys and a pair of cowhide gloves. He turned left at Milady Horákové, left again at Patočkova, and slowly made his way out to the main stretch of road. He was telling her about the Nuremberg Laws — the moment the occupation was a *fait accompli* the Germans had started drafting similar legislation for the Sudetenland — but he seemed for the moment to be discussing a problem he knew himself capable of solving. Pavel believed in himself, Marta thought. He weighed his options, made a decision, and then acted. What else did she know about him? Ordinary things, she thought, but the kinds of things that counted, that made people themselves. She began to list them in her head: He read the business articles first. His drink of choice was slivovitz. He'd begun to carry his Star of David in his pocket . . .

When they drove up the long gravel road to Lány, Marta saw they weren't the only ones with the idea of honouring Masaryk on his birthday. There must have been a thousand people who had shown up at the dead president's country residence to pay their respects. She hoped she would not be called upon to give any political opinions, but the atmosphere outside the estate was more conducive to a carnival than a debate. There were children on their fathers' shoulders, boys in suspenders tossing a bright red ball between them, elderly men leaning on wooden canes. Pavel looked at her across the gearshift; seeing the outpouring of nationalism had bolstered his mood further. "Remarkable," he said to Marta, "isn't it?" His eyes shining.

Marta nodded: *Yes, remarkable.*

They got out of the car and were met with a wall of sound.

Everyone was talking excitedly, it seemed, in families, in little groups of three and four. Marta heard a man in a general's uniform — the Czech colours in his buttonhole — quoting Hitler: "The Czechs are a miserable little race of pygmies."

"He said that?" another man asked.

"Prague will be occupied. There's no getting out of it."

"It's a done deal in his mind," the general answered. "He's already moved on to Danzig."

"Do you know what else he says about us Czechs? That we're like bicycle racers: we bow from the waist but down below we never stop kicking."

"That's true," said a man with skin like crumpled tissue paper. "It was true in the Great War."

"The Brits modelled their Bren guns on our ZGB 33. The ones made in Brno."

"Really?"

"Sure. Bren — *Br*no and *En*field," the general said proudly.

"If only we'd had the chance to use them!"

The men were like little boys with their hands tied behind their backs, Marta thought, denied the chance to stand up to the schoolyard bully. They longed to fight the Germans, longed desperately, and she knew Pavel thought it still might happen. He believed there was still a chance, however remote, that France and England would come to their senses.

Pepik's face was pressed into Marta's hip. He tugged at her arm and she lifted him up, then thought better of it and put him back down. He couldn't depend on her forever. "Why don't you go play with those children?" she said, pointing to a group of boys racing around the perimeter of the field. But Pepik just whimpered and pulled at her arm again.

"You're too big," she said. But she let him rest against her and kept a hand lightly on the top of his head.

They waited in line for their turn to pay respects at the grave. Then they ate the ham-and-swiss *chlebíčky*. Pepik fell asleep in the car on the way home, a line of cocoa dried above his lip. Marta thought that he looked a little like the Führer himself — the small moustache, the thin shoulders — but she figured it was best not to point this out to Pavel. The automobile sped through the countryside. A short gust of snow turned to sleet — later she would think it had been a sign of things to come — and Pavel turned on the car's single wiper. They rode for a while in silence with the steady *thwack* of it like a heartbeat, just there in front of them. Marta leaned her head back, letting her eyes close, luxuriating in the time with nothing to do but be carried along. The road whizzed past beneath them, the tires making a rhythmic thumping. She had almost dozed off when Pavel looked over at her and said, "I know very little about you."

Marta's eyes snapped open. There was a slight tone of accusation in his voice: how could she have worked for him for so long and managed to stay opaque?

"There's nothing to tell," she said. For some reason she felt herself flushing.

Pavel was looking at her, smiling. "A woman of mystery," he said.

She looked back at him, at both his hands on the wheel.

"No, it's just . . ." She faltered. Why *did* she want to keep quiet? It was not quite true that she had nothing to hide, but suddenly she felt that she might tell him anything at all. "What do you want to know?" she asked.

Pavel nodded, satisfied she'd acquiesced. "What do I want to know. Let's see. You were born in Moravia?"

"Ostrava."

"A textile town. Did your father work at the factory?"

She shook her head. "Farm."

He raised his eyebrows. "Your father owned a farm?"

"No. He was the farmhand."

He nodded, understanding.

"We slept in the . . . there was a loft over the stable."

Pavel made a face as if he'd just bitten down on something distasteful, or maybe, she thought, he did not want to think of her there.

"Sisters? Brothers?" he asked.

"One sister." Marta paused. "She died."

Pavel cocked his head to one side. "Oh?" he said. "I'm sorry." He seemed to be considering. "So you and Pepik have something in common," he said finally.

Marta hadn't thought of it in this way before. "We also both love trains," she said, and was surprised by the confession, by the fact that she kept confessing. It was true. She took Pepik to the train station for her own pleasure as well as his. A train meant escape. The possibility of leaving. That forlorn sound that the whistle unspooled, as it drifted out across the dark countryside, seemed so lonesome, and yet so right. It was the exact sound of the emptiness in the centre of her being, like waking up and crying out in the middle of the night and hearing another sadness call back.

"Close family?" Pavel asked. He looked to her for confirmation and she shook her head almost imperceptibly: *No.* Something in the gesture must have told him not to push any further. "What about boyfriends? A pretty girl like you." There was a sly look on his face, the start of a grin, and she saw he was teasing her, that she could get away without answering. But instead she said, "No. I've never . . ."

"*Never.* Really," Pavel said mildly. He squinted, his eyes on the road.

They were quiet for a while, Marta reassuring herself: certainly Ernst didn't count as a *boyfriend*. So it wasn't a lie she'd told. Not exactly.

The countryside receded and buildings reappeared, first just a few and then many. The city was coated in a soft blanket of snow. When they got to the flat Pavel hopped out and opened the gate. He got back in and rode the clutch into the garage. He pulled the hand brake and punched the button that turned the lights off. But he made no move to get out of the car.

In the back little Pepik was still soundly asleep, his head bent back at an odd angle against the seat.

Pavel turned to Marta. He gave her a piercing look, his brow furrowed. "I'm sorry about Mrs. Bauer," he said.

"Sir?"

"The way she behaved this morning."

Something inside Marta tightened, like the lid on a Mason jar. It had been such a lovely day; why did he have to go and tarnish it like this? She was enjoying the chance to talk with Pavel — one on one, two adults — but the only way she could allow herself the intimacy was to put Anneliese out of her mind entirely. "I'm sure I don't know what you mean," she said.

He looked at her tenderly, or at least with an expression she took for tenderness. "And that," he said, "is why we adore you."

Marta's breath quickened; she could not force herself to meet his eyes. But Pavel continued, as though he were speaking not to her but to himself. "You're loyal," he said. "Which is —" He paused, nodding. "— not something to be taken for granted."

"Thank you, Mr. Bauer," she said, but she was confused by the remark. She had the sense that he was referring not to her character but some other event she wasn't aware of.

"I don't take your loyalty for granted," he said again, meeting her eye. "I appreciate . . . many things about you."

The space in the car seemed to have shrunk; Marta was aware of the proximity of her body to Pavel's, of the musky smell of the leather blanket in the back seat, and of Pavel's hand resting lightly on the gearshift just an inch or two away. She looked down at it, and his gaze followed hers. They were still for a moment, both of them looking at the hand. Then she watched — it really was like something from a dream — she watched him lift it and place it, ever so lightly, on her leg.

Marta couldn't speak; then she realized she wouldn't need to. Pavel had opened his mouth first. "I wanted —" he said. But he stopped, and she saw he was looking at her face — she could see his eyes circling her forehead, studying her nose, her dimple — and then he leaned forward and kissed her.

She was so taken aback that it was a moment before her body registered the sensation. His mouth was warm and his lips felt full and hot. The slight taste of cocoa. There was a glimmer of his tongue and she felt a pang low in her belly, a sharp tug like nothing she had felt there before. She waited to feel herself stiffen and pull back, but she felt a different sensation instead — she wanted, she realized, for him to continue.

But Pavel drew away. He looked at her again with that same tenderness and tucked a strand of hair back behind her ear. Then he leaned in one more time. A short, firm finish to the kiss. It was as if he had come to a decision, she thought, and this was his way to seal it.

After that, Marta would think later, everything was ruined.

The following morning Max's foreman, Hans, arrived at the flat. Together he and Pavel were running the show in Max's absence. Marta took his overcoat and said, "Welcome, Mr. Novak."

He *tsk*ed. "Call me Hans."

"Yes, Mr. Novak," she said.

He was a man with a large stomach, and jowls that made her think of a hound-dog. The sort of man, Marta thought, about whom women would say *He's got such a nice smile*, or *He's got beautiful eyes*, but only because they liked him and it did not seem fair that someone so kind should be so unpleasant to look at.

Marta showed him into the parlour, where Pavel had lit a fire in the hearth. The men took off their leather shoes and stretched their legs towards the heat, Hans with his hands folded over his enormous belly. Marta served café au lait from the silver service while they sucked on their pipes. Her trolley was covered with a white linen cloth. "A whore's breakfast," Hans joked. "Coffee and tobacco."

Pavel smiled.

"There are pastries too," Marta said, smiling. She had bought tiny plum donuts, dusted with confectioner's sugar, and two little Linzer tortes from the beautiful patisserie in the Vinohrady. Pavel liked Czech pastries, but served in the French way. He liked to peruse them with the silver tongs in hand.

Marta moved towards Pavel to let him have his pick but found she could not look him in the face. The memory of their kiss was like an ailment spreading throughout her body, making its presence known in her chest, then on her cheeks, then in that unfamiliar tug low in her belly. It had been so unexpected, so out of the blue. And yet she felt, somehow, that she'd loved him all along. The mess with Ernst lifted from her mind like a ribbon of grey cigarette smoke. This is what it was like to be kissed by a decent man, a man who respected you. And she realized it was true — Pavel did respect her, without a doubt. The situation was complicated, compromised, but his feelings about her were pure.

For his part, Pavel acted breezy, at ease. As if nothing unusual had happened. He selected a pastry without looking at Marta. "Intermarium," he said to Hans. "What do you make of it?" He set the donut on his plate and held the tongs out in front of him.

"A pact between Poland, Romania, and the Hungarians."

"But what about us?" The tongs snapped closed.

"We're lost already."

"I went down to the Swiss embassy to try to get entry permits," Pavel said. "I put a small envelope on the edge of the diplomat's desk. He waited until the end of my appeal and then he threw it back in my face."

Marta registered this new piece of information: so Pavel had tried to bribe the Swiss for entry. He too wanted to leave Czechoslovakia. But had he changed his mind too late?

"We're stuck here," he said, as if answering her thought.

His voice seemed strangely loud, Marta noticed. Perhaps he wanted her to leave, to give them some privacy. She moved her trolley into the corner of the room but one of the wheels was sticking; she had to stop and kneel to adjust it.

Hans carefully set down his cup on the china saucer, the dainty gesture comical in contrast to his size. He took on a businesslike tone with Pavel. "You'll get a little reprieve before the Wehrmacht arrives," he said. "I've received word that you're needed to go to the Hungerland factory. On a flax-buying mission."

"Received word from who? *Max?*"

But Hans ignored the question. "We will need to be prepared," he said. "The borders will close. We need stock in order to stay relevant."

Marta thought she caught an unspoken criticism of the way Pavel had handled things in their old town. If he had been prepared, Hans seemed to imply, he might have avoided the factory's occupation. But Pavel didn't pick up on it or else chose not to indulge the foreman. "I see," he said. "To Paris?"

"No, not to Paris. To Zürich." Hans enunciated the city's name clearly. "You are requested to buy as much flax as possible. And meet with the son, Emil. No, not Emil; sorry, he's the one . . ." Hans circled his forefinger beside his temple to show the man was crazy.

"If only we could really spin flax into gold."

"Emil's brother, Jan. He'll be with Mr. Hungerland Senior. There will be a series of meetings about the matter I told you about earlier. You'll have to go for three days."

Marta watched Hans pop an entire donut into his mouth. He

wiped the powdered sugar from his moustache. "Why don't you take Mrs. Bauer and Pepik with you?" he said to Pavel, chewing, his mouth full. "Let them have a holiday. Marienbad is almost on the way. Perhaps you can join Mrs. Bauer at the spa."

Pavel snorted. "And get covered in mud."

Hans swallowed. "And then hosed down. That's the good part, my friend. To be hosed down by a bunch of little milk-maids . . ."

"It's supposed to be a medieval cure."

"It's *some* kind of cure! I'm not sure I'd say medieval . . ."

The men moved over to the big wooden chairs with hunt-ing scenes carved into their backs, the same kind the Bauers had left behind at the old house. They filled the bowls of their pipes again and began discussing politics. There had been an urgent appeal for people to buy defence bonds to protect the republic, and the Bauers had invested in them heavily. "A lot of good it did," Pavel said.

"I suppose it's too late," Hans agreed.

"If only Masaryk were alive."

Hans said that in Masaryk they had briefly realized Plato's philosopher-king.

Marta rolled her service trolley back into the kitchen. The name of the dead president brought back the pleasure of Lány, of Pavel's kiss. She wanted to know the details of the Bauers' trip, when exactly they would leave and where they would stay. They would be gone for three days.

Pepik.

Pavel.

She wasn't sure, suddenly, if she could bear it.

~~~⊙~~~

That night Marta roasted a goose for dinner. She cooked red cabbage with apples and raisins and put a bottle of plum brandy from Max and Alžběta's wine cellar on the table. Nobody asked what the occasion was. Marta kept thinking about the kiss, the unexpected heat of it. This was something other than what had happened with Ernst — the terrible push/pull of power — and something other than the violence she had suffered from her father. It was the same action, the same motion, but it sprang from a different place altogether. How was it that two entirely opposing emotions could take shape in an identical act?

There was something new here, something newly lit that she had not experienced before. A single bright candle on a birthday cake. She felt guilty about Anneliese but she tried not to think of it; she focused instead on feeling so alive.

At the table the Bauers were digging into their roast goose. "Is it true Hitler will invade?" Marta ventured. It seemed suddenly important to understand exactly what was happening around her.

She reached over and tucked a linen napkin into the neck of Pepik's shirt. Red cabbage stained terribly.

Anneliese put down her monogrammed silver cutlery. "Yes, it's true," she said finally, shooting her husband a look.

Pavel said, "I told you, Liesel, we're staying. Your brother-in-law needs me."

Anneliese touched her napkin to her lips. "Keep your voice down," she said. "Nobody has accused you of anything."

Pavel cleared his throat. "Marta," he said, "I almost forgot to tell you. I have to go to Zürich, on factory business. Mrs. Bauer and the Crown Prince will join me. So you'll have tomorrow off and Wednesday as well."

Marta nodded. He seemed nervous, she thought. She watched him move the knot of his tie below his Adam's apple, and was suddenly hyper-aware of Anneliese there at the table between them. All it would take would be a little slip, a glance that lingered a moment too long, and everything would come crashing down like so much glass on Kristallnacht. But Marta was not afraid of giving anything away. Her job as hired help was to hide her emotions. She was paid for it; she was experienced. And Anneliese seemed oblivious anyway, her thin face bent over her cabbage.

"Are we going in the automobile?" Pepik asked.

"On a train."

"On a train! Can Nanny come?"

Nobody answered.

After the Bauers were finished eating and had placed their knives and forks parallel on their plates, they sat smoking for several minutes beneath the oil portraits of Alžběta and Max. Pepik was excused and ran off to attend to his empire. In the kitchen Marta dreamily scraped congealed goose fat into the metal tin under the sink. She filled a big *hrnec* with water and added two whole onions, two whole heads of peeled garlic, and the heel of the red cabbage. All the while she imagined what would have happened if she hadn't found Anneliese in the bathtub in time. If Mrs. Bauer hadn't . . . made it. Could she — Marta — have been the new Mrs. Bauer? She ripped the one remaining drumstick off the goose and used the carving fork to lower the carcass into the pot. Pepik would accept her as his mother — God knows she loved him as one. But what about Pavel? She was a country bumpkin, unschooled in the ways of the world. It wouldn't do for him to have someone like her for his wife. And yet she could have sworn, when he'd cupped her face in his hands, pulling her mouth towards his . . .

Marta lit the stove and left the pot to simmer. She would come back before bed and skim the fat off the surface. By morning the whole house would be filled with the smell of soup, and the Bauers would be gone on their mission to Zürich. She needed to go upstairs and pack Pepik's bag.

Pavel and Anneliese had disappeared, which meant they must be in the bedroom with the door closed. There were two things they might be doing in there; she chose to assume they were fighting. Sure enough, at the top of the stair their argument came into focus. Something about jewellery, about Anneliese's watch. "I want to bring it," Marta heard Anneliese say.

"And where are you going to wear it?" Pavel asked. "In *Zürich*, where we are going for *only three days?*" He emphasized the brevity of the trip, but there was something else in his voice, some kind of resentment, or reproach.

"In the lining of the coat, then."

"I told you, I was wrong. The market isn't good. We can't risk it."

They wanted to sell the watch? Were things so bad? Pavel, she knew, had Canadian railway stocks, investments in a bauxite mine and in his friend Vaclav's margarine factories. But Marta had caught only the tail end of the discussion, and the silence now meant that Anneliese had started to cry.

Marta moved down the hall to Pepik's room. He was cross-legged on the floor, staring at the train, trying to divine some secret from the boxcars. She had a sudden urge to hold him tightly. "Come here, *miláčku*," she said.

Pepik got up and came to her obediently, like one of Karel Čapek's robots, programmed to do as it was told. He needed a haircut and his fingernails needed to be clipped. He was wearing, she saw, the same shirt he'd worn yesterday. She was overcome with remorse — she had let her mind wander, thinking of the father when the son was the one in need of her devotion.

She couldn't imagine what it would have been like if the other child had lived and she always had to divide her attention. She sat down in the rocking chair and pulled Pepik onto her lap. "*Já amor tebe*," she whispered in his ear.

His expression remained blank.

"Show me your Dopey face," she tried.

It took him a moment to understand what she was asking. "My Dopey face," he said, thinking. Then he rolled his eyes up and scratched his temple.

"Bravo!" Marta clapped. "How about your Happy face?"

He beamed. Just briefly — but it was enough to remind her of simpler times.

He ended with Sleepy, resting his head on her shoulder. Marta held him there, drowsing against her chest. She cradled him as if he were a baby and sang *Hou, hou, krávy dou*, about the cows dragging their heavy udders down to the river. Pepik was almost asleep when Anneliese came into the room, her eyes red. There was a streak of mascara below her left eye. "We're leaving first thing in the morning," she said.

Marta felt Pepik stir and awaken against her. "Up you get," she said, patting his backside. "You're a big boy."

Pepik blinked and rubbed his eyes. "Will you measure me?"

"Not now, darling."

"Why don't you go make yourself a cup of tea," Anneliese said to Marta. "I'll get him packed."

"Measure me," Pepik whined.

"I'm fine, Mrs. Bauer," Marta said. "I was just getting up. I'll pack his suit, and the brown knickerbockers . . ."

Anneliese touched her pearls. "No," she said. "You go on downstairs." She fluttered her hand as though shooing away a stray dog.

Pepik pulled on Marta's arm. She stood up, uncertain. "His nightshirt is in the bottom drawer," she said, unable to restrain herself. Anneliese had never in her life packed a travel bag for Pepik.

Marta almost bumped into the door frame leaving the room. In the hall she passed Anneliese's open valise, a set of silver hairbrushes slipped through the loops. The kitchen was already filling with the gamey smell of simmering soup. She skimmed off the fat and turned the heat up again. Fished out the limp vegetables and got a fresh cabbage to throw in. All the while going over it in her head. Why did Mrs. Bauer want to pack Pepik's overnight bag herself? Had Marta done a bad job last time? When was it? The trip to Paris last winter to see the mechanical Père Noël — there hadn't been any complaints.

And why the fuss about the diamond watch? Why had Anneliese suggested sewing it into the lining of a coat?

Marta turned her back and the cabbage rolled off the counter and thudded onto the floor. She picked it up, brushed it off, and laid it back on the board. Lifted the cleaver and hacked it in half. The pattern inside was intricate, the tight curls like two halves of a brain. Marta put the cleaver down on the cutting board, wiped her hands on her apron. She stood, not moving, next to the soup on the stove.

It began at that very moment to boil.

She knew where to look. There was a silver letter opener on Max Stein's desk, and some creamy stationery with the factory's address running across the top. Pavel's Star of David lying next to the pot of ink. There were telegrams stacked under a paperweight: a round stone painted red with a lady-bug's black dots by Max's daughter. Marta picked it up carefully, as though it might be hot. Under it were telegrams from Ernst and from someone named Rolf Unger. And beneath the telegrams, there they were — passports.

She opened one, saw the picture of Pepik staring out at her, and the exit permit stamped onto the following page. If it was fake, it was remarkably well crafted. Under Pepik's name was a cursive C, for Christian. She let the little passport fold shut in her hands. There were three of them, she saw. One for each of the Bauers.

Marta took a slow breath. She covered her eyes with her hand, as she had once seen Pavel's mother do while blessing the Sabbath candles. She told herself that finding the passports did not mean anything. The Bauers would need them to cross the border into Switzerland to buy flax. But somehow, seeing them there, a certainty made itself known. Pavel was not taking his family to Zürich; they were going somewhere else. She was sure of it. And they were going without her.

The Bauers were up early the following morning, and Marta was up along with them to make their breakfast while Pavel loaded the suitcases into the car. Pepik wanted to bring his Princess Elizabeth engine along, and he said so over and over, getting no response, until finally Anneliese shouted at him to be quiet, they were going on a *real* train, which would be much more dangerous and exciting. She was flitting around the flat, picking up things at random — a tennis racquet strung with catgut, the French translation of Hemingway's *A Farewell to Arms*. She poured enough water into Alžběta's wilted hydrangea that it leaked out the crack in the bottom of the pot and Marta had to go for a sponge.

Marta served the porridge, not taking any for herself, and went upstairs to her rooms in a haze. She would clean the dishes once the Bauers had left.

After a half-hour of shuffling and clattering down below Anneliese called up to her. "Marta?"

Marta didn't answer. She heard Anneliese say, "We should at least go . . . We might not . . ." And Pavel said, "No, it would seem too . . ." He pitched his voice louder and called up. "We're off, Marta! See you Saturday!"

There was a pause while he waited for her reply.

"Have a safe journey!" she called back finally, sounding shrill in her own ears. She had been crying, and she was afraid her cracking voice would betray her. She waited until she heard the door close and the key turn in the lock, then watched the car pull out onto Vinohradská Street. Pepik's little face was pressed to the glass. His eyes blinking up at her in the window. She didn't smile, didn't wave — she couldn't bring herself to. Instead she backed away from the window, a palm pressed over her heart.

Marta waited until the Tatra was gone from sight. She flung herself across her blue quilt and began to sob.

~ⓢ~

It was afternoon when she woke. She came down and set the kettle to boil and made herself a cup of linden tea. She and Pepik had gathered the leaves the previous autumn, had dried them and put them in a glass Mason jar labelled "APRIL 1938." Pepik had drawn a smiling sun on the label beside the date. They had brought the jar along with them from their old town. Marta sat for a long time at the kitchen table watching the steam rise off her tea. Her hands resting, palms down, in front of her.

She looked around, at Pepik's half-finished bowl of porridge, the spoon sticking straight out of it like a Nazi flag claiming yet another territory, and at the wooden mill with coffee grounds spilled beneath it. The pan from last night's goose was still soaking in the sink; a skim of yellow fat had hardened on the surface. There was an ashtray on the table, filled with cigarette butts stained by Anneliese's red lipstick. Marta thought she'd better get cleaning — and then she realized she was in no hurry. No hurry at all.

The Bauers were gone. They weren't coming back.

She left the mess and took her tea into the pantry, where she made a quick inventory of food. The big pot of soup would last several days if she needed it to. And before the Steins had fled, Alžběta had stocked up on those trendy new soup cubes. How, Marta wondered, could something so tiny produce a real soup with hunks of sausage and dumplings or with curled potato peelings? But maybe it was possible. They were able to do the strangest things these days. The Baecks, Anneliese had told her, had a machine to dry their laundry.

Marta lit the stove and scraped the fat off the roasting pan. She was getting angry now, going over the details of her abandonment. The pilgrimage to Lány had obviously been Pavel's last patriotic nod to Masaryk. She'd been dragged along, an oblivious accomplice. And Pavel's advance had not been so different from Ernst's after all: he had taken advantage of her, knowing he would never see her again. Last night's dinner table conversation seemed different too — Pavel's nerves, the way he'd kept moving the knot of his tie back and forth below his Adam's apple. It was not about the kiss after all. He was ashamed to be telling her a bald-faced lie.

The thought of what had happened seemed suddenly unbearable to Marta. She ran downstairs and quickly filled a galvanized pail with water and Helada soap — it was the brand she bought for Pepik's benefit, because of the pictures of locomotives that came in every box. She started to work vigorously on the inlaid hardwood floors. The flat was large and the panels were wide and knotted: it was a big job. Marta worked, not thinking. When the truth of her predicament threatened to crash over her, she held her breath and scrubbed harder, as though she could use the rising flood of pain against itself, to scrub away her own terror. To scrub away the image of Pepik's small face, staring up at her from the automobile's window.

She didn't stop for lunch or even for a cup of tea. When she finished with the floors, she moved on to the silver. It needed polishing; whoever worked for the Steins had been lazy, doing the cutlery but leaving the big, intricate pieces that were used less frequently, like the Passover Seder plate. As Marta polished, some Hebrew script came clear. They were cowards, she thought. All of them. To run away so easily from who they were.

When she was finished, she went down the hall and looked at the empty crib. In the Steins' bedroom — which she had already come to think of as the Bauers' — she rifled through the drawers but found nothing other than some lacy under-garments she hadn't seen before and a half-emptied jewellery box. The diamond watch was gone. She left the drawer open — because she could, because nobody was going to return home and catch her. She went into Pepik's room and looked at his small jackets hanging from the antlers of Max's prize stag. Anneliese had forgotten to pack her son's nightshirt: it was still folded in the bottom drawer.

Marta slept badly that night. The empty flat was full of noise: creakings and a ticking that was too uneven to be the grandfather clock. Around three in the morning she thought she heard a key turning. She crept in her bare feet along the Persian rug that lined the hall, and stood looking at the ornately carved wooden front door. A slow squeak came from the latch. She saw the handle turn, but the door didn't open. She waited a full fifteen minutes, shivering under her nightdress, but nothing else happened. Finally she heard footsteps retreating down the building's corridor. She stood there feeling she should do something, notify someone, but there was nothing she could think of to be done, and so she forced herself to go back to bed. She lay there for a long time though, tossing and turning, unable to fall asleep. She was thinking of a sheet of paper she'd found, crumpled up in

Pavel's wastebasket. A single question typed in the centre: *What if she changes her mind?*

∽⊚◦

The following afternoon the brass cowbell on the yellow cord by the front door rang. Marta was lifting the newly polished Seder plate up to the highest shelf; she froze with her hands in the air, as if she were being held up at a bank. Her heart leapt when she thought it was the Bauers, already back — but it was far too soon, she realized, and besides, they would just use their key.

The cowbell rang again and the handle rattled, someone testing the lock. Should she answer? She'd been moving around the flat with the drapes open and the electric lamps lit. It was already dusk. From the street she would have been clearly visible, so she couldn't very well pretend nobody was home. She looked at the door, wishing she could see through the heavy wood to the other side. The knocking started up again; it went on for a full minute. Whoever was there was going to break down the door.

Marta crossed the room, smoothing her hair with the flat of her hand. She moved quietly, and when she pulled the handle the man on the other side gasped in surprise. "Marta! You scared me!" His hand flew up to his chest.

He knew her name. It was Ernst. He was wearing a day cravat and a black homburg. "May I come in?"

Ernst took off his hat and made to step past her, but Marta blocked the door. Her heart was thudding in her chest. Ernst belonged to the old town, to the old factory, not to this new world of Prague. She'd almost succeeded in banishing the thought of their affair; to see him now was to be reminded of a part of herself she'd prefer to forget. She'd relegated him to that tiny corner of her consciousness where her father's memory was hidden. It was a corner she did not visit often.

But Ernst gave her a look, and she found herself stepping aside in deference. He didn't speak at first but put his homburg down on the settee and crossed the parlour, his hands clasped behind him. He stood in front of the silver-framed family photos on the mantelpiece, gazing at them for quite some time. "So this is Anneliese's brother's place," he said finally.

"Sister's," she answered.

"Alžběta. Right." He peered at a picture of little Eva Stein. "What a beautiful baby," he said, his back still to Marta.

He lifted the heavy menorah in one hand, testing its weight. "Are you here alone, Marta?"

She glanced down at her clothes, the dull tweed skirt and the blouse with a stain on the collar. She felt caught out somehow, as though it was her own fault to find herself without the Bauers' protection at a time when she needed it most. "No," she said, "I'm not."

Ernst turned towards her. She was still surprised to actually see him in the flesh, in front of her. It was a little like seeing a ghost.

"The Bauers will be back on Thursday," she said automatically, picking lightly at a flap of skin by her thumbnail.

Ernst set the menorah back down on the mantel and gazed at her, vaguely amused.

"They'll be back on Thursday," she repeated.

Ernst made a little clucking noise. "Is that what you really think?"

Marta shrugged.

"Lying doesn't become you, *miláčku*."

To hear him speak to her this way — the word *miláčku* soft and surprising after the other, harsh sounds — brought tears to her eyes. She thought for a minute that he was going to try to kiss her, and she took a step backwards. The desire to protect the Bauers rose fiercely inside her. "Mr. Bauer had to go away on business," she heard herself saying.

"*Did* he." Ernst stayed in his place. "And let me guess . . . He had to take the wife and child with him?"

It was unnerving to hear him refer to Anneliese and Pepik in those generic terms — *wife and child*. She brought her thumb to her mouth and tore away the hangnail with her teeth.

He raised his eyebrows at Marta. "Well?" Still she didn't answer.

Ernst pulled a mahogany chair out from the table; it squeaked across her newly washed floorboards. He sat down and folded his hands in front of him and leaned across the table, looking at her intently. "Marta," he said, "listen to me."

He waited.

She was listening.

"I'm sorry for what happened between us. For how I behaved." He paused again, as though he'd rehearsed this speech and was trying to remember his lines. "I'm sorry," he repeated. "But Prague is about to be occupied. It won't be like in the old town. Hitler is going to take it all now. Everything." He gestured around him to include the flat, the city, the whole country.

Marta glared at him. Did he think she was stupid?

"I know that in the past I have said some unkind things about the Bauers," he said. "But I need to speak with Pavel now. It's about . . . the factory. It's very important. I need to contact him — for his own good."

Ernst was lying; that much was clear. Either he'd forgotten how frank he'd been with her in the past, or he really did underestimate her intelligence. She was a means to an end, nothing more. She thought of telling Ernst that he too was a bad liar, but she was afraid that if she opened her mouth she would begin to cry.

"They gave you up," he said softly.

She closed her eyes, the truth overwhelming her. She'd been keeping busy cleaning, avoiding it, but she couldn't deny now that Ernst was right. There was no way around it. She'd been abandoned.

"Where have they gone?" he asked. "To England?"

She could feel the tears rising. She held up a finger to show Ernst she needed a moment.

"Take your time."

The grandfather clock doled out its ticking.

"To Wales?" Ernst suggested gently.

Marta shook her head and closed her eyes again. They were gone. But where? She thought back to Pavel's conversation over coffee with his foreman, Hans.

You're needed to go on a flax-buying mission.

I see. To Paris?

No, not to Paris. To Zürich.

They'd been speaking so loudly, like two deaf old generals. Marta remembered how odd it had seemed at the time, and realized all at once that they'd wanted her to hear. That she had been the intended audience for their little performance.

Pavel had been trying to confuse her.

"You know where they've gone," Ernst said.

She nodded yes. Her jaw was clenched shut. After everything they'd shared — the years of her employment, that beautiful kiss — what did Pavel take her for? Something that could be forsaken along with the silverware and linens? He should have known better, she thought. She'd been taken advantage of too many times already. She would not be made the fool, not again, not this time.

She thought back again to the words Hans had spoken: *No, not to Paris.*

Marta closed her eyes and rubbed them with the back of her hands. She looked up at Ernst. "They're on the train to Paris," she said.

PART THREE

OCCUPATION

12 March 1939

My dear Max,

I am writing from Paris. Anneliese and Pavel were due to meet me yesterday. They never arrived. No wire, nothing. I don't know what to do.

If only you were here to advise me.

Where are you, my darling? It has been more than two months since your last correspondence. I am sick with worry and can neither eat nor sleep.

Shall I mail the envelope now? I'm afraid that our time is drawing short, that if we don't follow through on this option the window will close altogether. My instinct tells me to act.

Still, I will await your instructions.

The day is almost done; you are here next to me in your silver frame, your smile beaming in my direction. How I wish I could kiss you! Thinking about you gives me courage. I have said it before, and I don't want you to think me overly sentimental, but it is simply true. I could not live without you.

Your Al

(FILE UNDER: Stein, Alžběta. Died Auschwitz, 1943)

I WAITED A LONG TIME FOR YOU TO SHOW UP.

Every time the restaurant door opened and the little bell above it jingled, my nerves jingled right along with it. I've become good at identifying people I've never met, based on a few photos of their relatives or a letter about how they loved to play marbles as children. I watched the older Eastern European men come in, the Ashkenazi Jews with their thin grey hair and their pocket watches. None of them were you.

I thought: He probably won't come. Why should he want to talk to an old lady anyhow?

But I had put on lipstick before leaving the house. I placed my Star of David on a silver chain around my neck — the only piece of jewellery I have from my mother. I combed my own thin hair and looked at myself for a long time in the mirror.

My eyes are watery, a problem that has increased with age. I blink and blink but they will not clear.

I must seem perpetually on the verge of tears.

You and I had spoken on the phone.

"I need to tell you something," I said.

Silence.

I made myself speak. "You had . . ." I faltered. "A sibling,"

I said. Careful to say this in the past tense. I waited for your response, for the shock or, at the very least, surprise.

"I know," you said.

"You know?"

"I have a photograph," you said. "My father has a baby in his arms."

I was quiet then, puzzling. I had a hundred questions but I wanted to ask them in person. We made plans to meet at 8 p.m. at Schwartz's, a popular Jewish deli on Saint-Laurent. It was a bit of whimsy on my part, but you didn't argue. Our phone conversation, the few words you spoke in that muddled accent of yours, kept playing over and over in my mind afterwards, like the opening phrase of Dvořák's haunting Prague Cello Concerto — I couldn't sleep that night for the music it was making.

The morning of our meeting I forced myself to sit at my desk, pretending to transcribe an interview with a woman in Montana who had just discovered the "Jewish branch" of her family. In all honesty though, I was unable to work, as full of excitement as a teenager heading off on a first date. I'd been waiting for this for more than — Well, I'd been waiting forever.

I should have known better than to get my hopes up. The one thing you most want will always elude you. That's the rule. And I don't care if you call me a pessimist; I come by it honestly. I am also fretful and fussy, even with the people I study. Especially with the people I study. Truth be told, I think of myself as a kind of a mother hen to them. Which is ironic, given our respective ages.

"Would you like a menu?" The waitress looked fifteen years old max. Her halter top showed the delicate dot of her belly button. An outie.

"No, thank you."

She took a step back. "If you don't want to eat . . ." She gestured around at the busy tables. Two old men in sweater-vests were arguing in Yiddish.

"I'm waiting for someone," I snapped. Which felt like a lie even though it was the truth.

I sat in my booth peeling at the plastic on the menu the teenager had left. Latkes, I saw, and Russian borscht. I told myself I would order as soon as you arrived. I was trying to be hopeful.

There are reasons for optimism. Reasons to have faith in humanity. There were righteous Gentiles whose behaviour during the war exemplified the best of the human spirit. But most people, of course, were not up to the task. And some even made it their purpose to turn Jews over to the authorities. The cases that are the hardest for me to imagine are the ones where the betrayer was known to the family. What could make a person turn against those whose daily lives they understood intimately?

Maybe those betrayers did not understand the full implications of their actions. Maybe they came from a background of betrayal themselves. This is one of the things the social sciences teach, one of the few things about which psychology is abundantly clear: we will re-inflict our own wounds on those in our care. And yet these factors don't quite add up. There remain instances that give pause, that force us to consider the darker side of human nature: what the Jews call, I believe, the *yetzer hara*.

Speaking of which, I sat and waited for you for more than an hour. The deli was closing. People were getting up to leave, the women with their glossy mink coats, the men with their felt hats and spectacles. The couples looked happy, even the older ones, and I was reminded that tomorrow was the Sabbath, the day on which it is *mitzvot* for a couple to make love.

At first I felt angry — furious — that you'd stood me up. But under that was something softer, a tugging. I have to be honest: I was sad you didn't come.

I wanted to have someone to belong to.

FIVE

AT NOON ON MARCH 14, 1939, the grandfather clock sounded, the front door swung open, and in walked the Bauers. They'd been gone only two nights but they looked like a band of Junák scouts back from the Krkonoše Mountains. Marta knew something terrible must have happened for Anneliese to let herself be seen in such a state, her hair loose around her face and not a trace of lipstick on her lips. Anneliese went straight to the parlour table and wept. Marta could see it was a continuation — she had been weeping before, then she had to carry her valise, and now she resumed weeping where she had left off.

Pepik disappeared immediately into his Uncle Max's room, and it was Pavel, finally, who came to tell Marta what had happened. He steered her, a hand at the small of her back, out of the front room and into the kitchen. "A drink?"

"No, I —"

But he'd already brought in two little glasses from the breakfront and had filled his own to the rim.

"Neat?"

Marta looked at him blankly.

Pavel lifted a pitcher and added water to her glass. He squinted at Marta, opened his mouth, and closed it again. There was so much to say, and she could see he didn't know where to begin.

"We got turned back at the border," he said finally. "They saw that our documents were forged." He emptied his glass in one smooth swallow. He was unshaven, and there were dark hollows under his eyes.

"The Gestapo came on the train. They took our passports — mine and Liesel's. We were trying to leave the country. To get into Paris. From there Max had got us tickets to London." He ran a hand over the stubble on his chin. "We've missed our chance now, of course. It's too late."

There was a moment of silence, during which they could hear Anneliese sobbing. Marta leaned her temple against her index and middle fingers. What did Pavel expect? If he was willing to forsake her like so much nothing, this is what he'd get in return. She pushed her untouched drink across the table. She cast around for somewhere to put her eyes and found the little wooden coffee mill. Her arms folded squarely across her chest.

"Marta," Pavel said. But she refused to look up.

Pavel sighed deeply. "I owe you an apology. I'm sorry we had to . . . keep our plans secret from you."

She looked again at the coffee mill; two loose beans were caught under the blade. Her stomach did a flip-flop, as though trying to get her attention. An apology? Had she heard correctly?

"Do you understand?" Pavel scrutinized her.

The hollows beneath his eyes might actually, she thought, have been bruises.

"It was to protect you," Pavel said. "So if anyone came asking after us you wouldn't be compromised. We had to keep it secret," he explained. "From absolutely everybody."

He pinched the bridge of his nose. "We didn't even tell my mother."

He paused and frowned. "Which is why I can't figure out who —" But he shook his head and stopped himself before finishing his sentence. "Regardless," he said, "I want you to know that I planned to send for you. From France. I have your ticket." He patted his breast pocket.

Marta looked up from the coffee mill. A ticket? For her?

"And a passport."

He was bluffing, surely. Something inside her had hardened against him, like the pit at the centre of a piece of summer fruit, and she was not about to let her guard down again, to let herself be fooled a second time. But Pavel took the passport from his jacket pocket along with a green and white Wagons-Litz envelope and laid them in front of her on the table. She felt for a moment that she was going to be sick.

"Go on," he said. "If you don't believe me."

She opened the envelope and saw the unpunched slip of paper. Her own name was there, last and first.

Pavel waited.

Marta picked it up as though to verify its physical presence. She was sweating, but her hands were cold. It seemed still that this must be some sort of trick, a way to secure her loyalty again now that things had not gone as planned. But the ticket was very real in her palm, and it had been purchased, she saw, several weeks earlier. If she had not told Ernst what she had told him, would she now be with the Bauers, in Paris? She had never been to France. It made her think of expensive red wine and those delicious *pains au chocolat*.

If she had not told Ernst what she had told him, would the Bauers now be free?

"We thought it would seem suspicious," Pavel said, "to be crossing with a maid . . ." He cleared his throat and said, "— with a Gentile governess in our employment. So I was going to send for you after."

Marta met his eye finally. "Really?" she asked. Her voice sounded meek in her own ears, the voice of a scared child, but she did not look away. She needed to be certain. And Pavel jumped at the chance to reassure her. "Really," he said. "I promise."

The way he spoke made her remember, suddenly, the fullness of his mouth on hers, how he'd pulled her back into his arms one last time. The glimmer of tongue that had set her stomach quivering.

Pavel pushed a thumb into his forehead, between his eyes, and looked down at the unpunched ticket in her hand. Then he lifted his head and looked at her again, the same piercing expression on his face. "I'm sorry, Marta," he repeated.

Marta could not tell exactly what he was sorry for — the lie, his failure to get his family out, or some combination of the two — but the sincerity of his look absolved him completely. She would have forgiven him, just then, for anything.

The events of the previous days came out slowly. The telling of the story had a ritual quality; the Bauers were telling her, ostensibly, but Marta could see that they needed to recount it for each other, for themselves, to try to make some sense of it.

The conductor had taken their passports, squinted at them, and squinted down at a clipboard he was carrying against his gleaming buttons. "Ah," he said. "Pavel Bauer. Off to buy some flax?"

"We knew right then," Anneliese said, "that someone had betrayed us."

Marta made a discreet gesture to show Mrs. Bauer where her eye makeup had smeared. Anneliese dabbed at her eye with the back of her hand.

"He hauled us off the train immediately," Pavel was saying. "He didn't even look at Pepik's passport. We spent the night in prison."

Anneliese started to cry again. Her cheeks were the bright pink of one of little Vera Stein's china dolls.

"In prison? Why in prison?"

Anneliese looked at Marta, exasperated. "Because they were forged documents. They saw we were trying to get out of the country." She wiped her eyes again. "There was an announcement . . . A man called out as we were leaving that this train would be the last allowed through." She blew her nose on her sister's handkerchief. It was monogrammed with a swirly blue A, Alžběta's first initial, as well as Anneliese's own. "The borders have closed," she said. "We're officially stuck. The country will be occupied."

"The borders have closed? Really?" Marta paused, taking this in. Then, because she could not quite fathom the terrible implications, she asked again, "You spent the night in *prison*?"

Marta waited for Pavel to say "Not in prison exactly," but he only nodded. His simple gesture suggested just the opposite, that the word *prison* was woefully inadequate to conjure the night they had suffered.

"Even Pepik?"

"They took Pepik somewhere else. He won't say where."

"The borders are being patrolled. We're stuck," said Anneliese. But Marta was trying hard not to hear this. She thought instead of her young charge, held against his will. "Why did they keep Pepik? He's just a baby!"

"Things are changing. The world we live in is not fair anymore," said Anneliese.

"All of the Sudeten Jews have been sent to a camp," Pavel added.

"A camp? What do you mean?" asked Marta.

But Pavel knew nothing about the camps beyond the rumours. "I do know that we're lucky to have gotten off so easily," he said. "They could have kept us."

"And they did keep our things. The passports, our money, my jewellery."

Marta wanted to ask about the watch sewn into Mrs. Bauer's coat, but that would betray her clandestine listening.

A feeling came over her then, like when she'd had scarlet fever as a little girl. Vertigo, crawling skin, a sense that the world around her was not quite real. Because it couldn't be so — what they were telling her couldn't be true. Her grievance had melted away entirely, and what was left was love for the Bauers, righteous and pure. Like a mother's love, she thought. She would fight for them, protect them at all costs. But were the borders really closing? Would people really be held inside the country against their wills, like animals in a cage? If this was the case, it was slowly dawning on her, then she had done something terribly, irrevocably wrong.

Marta forced herself to take a deep breath. She rearranged

the unthinkable thought to make the Bauers the ones who were overreacting. They would see: all this was easily fixable. Tomorrow she would go down to the station with her savings and buy them new tickets out.

But when Pavel turned on the radio in the middle of the following afternoon, it was announced that Jozef Tiso had just returned from a conference with Adolf Hitler and had proclaimed a separate Slovak state.

"A separate *what*?" Marta asked. With the Sudetenland already gone there would be nothing left of their country whatsoever.

The Bauers stood by the radio as though it were a dear friend on a deathbed. The Czech foreign minister, František Chvalkovský, and President Hácha, they heard, had been ordered to Berlin. Finally, later in the day, it was reported that the German army had crossed the border and occupied the frontier town of Ostrava. Pavel was translating the radio broadcast, but he added the last detail himself. "Ostrava," he said to Marta. "The town where you were born."

Marta crossed the room to the fireplace and stood facing the ornate mantelpiece. She had always thought of money as the great protector and of the Bauers as all-powerful. In the past she had suffered because she was poor, this was true, and did not have the resources to leave her home when she needed to. But it now seemed that no amount of money could save the Bauers from what was happening around them. Hitler, she realized with a shock, was serious. She'd read *Mein Kampf*, and Ernst had explained to her Hitler's thoughts on the "Jewish peril." Perhaps, she thought, by telling Ernst about Pavel's plans to leave, she really had foiled the Bauers' only chance for escape.

Perhaps, because of her, the course of the Bauers' lives would now change.

But deep down Marta did not believe she had this kind of power; she didn't believe she could alter fate. Fate doled itself out according to action, according to how people behaved. The Bauers had proven themselves to be good after all. So things would work out for them in the end.

When Marta woke, it was snowing. She could feel it without having to look; the air was different, muffled in the silence that only winter brings. She fought the urge to fall back into the thick blankets of sleep; instead she got up and put on her slippers and robe and opened the shutters of the little window in the hall.

It was still dark, the barest hint of light on the horizon. Like a premonition, like the last dream before waking.

She picked a bit of sleep from the corner of her eye and stood in front of the window looking down. Her ankles cold beneath her housecoat. The street below was empty; then there was a bicycle. Afterwards she would think back to this lone rider and imagine he'd worn a cape and carried a sword. The Angel of Death entering the city. But it was an officer's peaked cap, a *Schirmmütze*, that he wore, and *feldgrau* wool tunic with epaulettes and glinting buttons. He seemed to have appeared out of thin air, like a villain from a storybook. Marta closed her eyes to try to make the officer disappear, but when she opened them again he was still there, and behind him the whole street was full of soldiers, the Angel's army streaming up the steep hill from the glimmering city below. The snow was falling heavily, making a fairy tale of Prague. The swirling white against miles of black and grey made it seem as if they had come from the world of an old photograph, a world from which all the colour had been drained. And there was something else that made her think they were part of a dream: they were driving on the wrong side of the road.

Marta turned her back to the window. *The Bauers could have got out*, she said to herself. *And you could have been with them.* She spoke to herself in the third person, as someone separate from her real self. Someone else would now have to cope with the crippling guilt — because there was no way she could manage it.

She went to wake the Bauers but saw there was already a light on in the parlour. It was five in the morning but they were already dressed, Anneliese in a knitted skirt and pearls, Pavel in a charcoal suit, his briefcase open on the table. Inside was a fat stack of American dollars held together by a rubber band. The first thing she heard when she came into the room was the Czech radio station: "German army infantry and aircraft are beginning the occupation of the territory of the republic at six o'clock. The slightest resistance will cause the most unforeseen consequences and lead to the intervention becoming utterly brutal. All commanders have to obey the orders of the occupying army. The various units of the Czech army are being disarmed . . . Prague will be occupied at six-thirty."

She continued to listen: the message was being repeated.

Pavel turned to look at Marta, his face pink, as though the knot on his silk tie had been tied too tight.

"We had a phone call from the police chief."

Marta pulled her robe around her body.

"The chief said that we are responsible for opening the factory as usual."

"Can you believe it?" Anneliese asked.

"Then I got another call, from Hans. Offering to blow the factory up."

"It's the ides of March," Anneliese said.

"Blow it up! Why?" Marta looked at Pavel.

"There has been an ordinance issued to install Czech trustees in Jewish businesses."

"Pardon me, Mr. Bauer?"

"They're taking our companies."

Marta looked away. Ernst had been right. Pavel would lose what was his, one way or another. The unfairness of this washed over her. The indignity.

"Hácha's daughter is married to a Jew," Anneliese was saying. "He's supposed to be a moderate."

Pavel snorted. If he had not been so dignified, Marta thought, he would have spat.

"Did you hear about the conversation between Hitler and Chamberlain?" Marta asked. She wanted suddenly, desperately, to cheer the Bauers up; a joke was the only thing she could think of.

"Tell me." Pavel leaned forward, eager to be entertained, distracted.

"Hitler and Chamberlain met in the street. And Hitler said, 'Chamberlain, give me Czechoslovakia.' And Chamberlain said, 'Okay.'"

Marta paused for effect.

"The next day, Hitler ran into Chamberlain again. And he

said, 'Chamberlain, give me your umbrella.' But Chamberlain said, 'My umbrella?! Why, that belongs to me!'"

The Bauers laughed briefly, but Marta could see she hadn't succeeded in lifting their moods. They turned back towards each other right away, faces solemn.

"Did you try to reach your mother?" Anneliese asked.

"I couldn't," Pavel said.

"It's unbelievable. That Hácha signed that piece of paper."

"If he didn't sign we would have been bombed. Right now we would all be a big pile of smoking ashes."

By the time Pepik woke, Messerschmitts were swooping low over the Vltava River, their shadows skimming across the choppy water. They rose steeply to clear the bridges, then plunged back down like hawks heading for the kill. Pepik, still in his blue flannel nightshirt, began to narrate the aircrafts' movements. "Here it comes, ladies and gentlemen . . . an attack like the world has never known . . ." There was something blasé about his tone, though, as if he were a bored field correspondent, a newsman who had seen what the world had to offer and was no longer easily impressed.

Pavel left shortly after seven to go down to the factory. None of the workers had telephones, he said; someone would have to be sent house to house to tell them to report for work. He opened the door to leave; the wind blew in and lifted the edge of his scarf out sideways, like a child's drawing of a snowman. "I'm late," he said. He looked over at Marta then and held her eye for a moment before closing the door. She had a sudden, forcible feeling she would never see him again.

༄

The following afternoon Marta returned from the greengrocer and saw two pairs of men's leather shoes in the hall. Two
well-tailored overcoats. There was something else too, a kind
of hush in the flat. It was the silence of nothing at all being
said, a silence that had come to signify over the past months
that the opposite was true, that things of great consequence
were being said, only behind locked doors.

She went into the parlour and found Pepik beneath the oak
table, holding *Der Struwwelpeter*. "I'm busy," he said.

She crouched down and kissed his forehead. "What time is
it, *miláčku*?"

"Tick tock," he said.

He wrinkled his brow and pretended to be reading, but he
was, she saw, holding the book upside down. She kissed him
again and turned it right side up. He made a little *humph* and
turned it upside down again.

Stubborn, like his father. She heard Pavel come into the
dining room behind them.

The light bulb of happiness flicked on inside her. She
stood to move towards him, then saw the man behind Pavel.
Ernst. She backed up quickly to behind the wall, out of view.
Crouched down and leaned her cheek against the cool plaster.
She could hear her heart in her ears. What was Ernst doing
here? He had obviously not yet succeeded in getting hold of
all of Pavel's assets; Marta surmised that Ernst knew there was
more money hidden away. He would need to work quickly
now that Prague had been taken. He was doubling his efforts.

Ernst had already visited the Steins' flat, of course, the day
he came to ask Marta where the Bauers had gone. But from
her hiding place she could see he was letting Pavel give him

the tour, show him around as though he'd never seen the place before.

He stood at the mantel and looked at the photo of tiny Eva Stein.

He picked up the heavy silver menorah as though for the first time. There must have been something in its weight he found compelling.

Pavel sat down on a dining room chair, crossed one leg over the other, and got out his pipe and his pouch of tobacco. "Now that we're done our business," he said, "are you on your way to the town square to salute Blaskowitz's honour guard?"

Ernst was reaching for his own pipe. Marta saw lines in his hair where the comb had been pulled through. She shifted on her haunches; her leg was falling asleep, but if she stood, she knew, they would hear her.

"I suppose all the German soldiers will be required to stop and salute," Pavel said. "And Blaskowitz's proclamation — that the Germans are here not as conquerors but to create 'conditions for the peaceful collaboration of the two peoples'! How inane! Does he think we're completely blind?"

Marta recalled the most recent sad radio broadcast by President Hácha. He had defined independence as a short period in Czechoslovakia's national history that had come to an end.

Ernst tapped down his tobacco; the two men sucked their pipes in silence, their cheeks moving in and out like codfish.

"There will be lots of Germans at the ceremony tomorrow," Ernst said mildly.

"Because of von Neurath?"

Baron Konstantin von Neurath, even Marta knew, would

be appointed the new leader of the Protectorate of Bohemia and Moravia.

Ernst nodded. "They're sending in special trains from the Sudetenland to greet him."

"They're worried the new *Reichsprotektor* won't be welcomed by us Czechs?" Pavel's voice was gleeful. "There must be fewer Nazis in our midst than we think."

Quite the contrary, Marta thought as she crouched behind the wall. Ernst kept quiet too, and she understood this was his strategy: let his silence be taken as agreement and he would not have to lie outright.

"And what about you?" Pavel asked his friend again. "The powers that be at the factory have sent you up with the schoolchildren to greet the former foreign minister?" He was trying to keep his voice light but he clearly wanted to know what, exactly, Ernst was doing in Prague.

Ernst had a leg crossed over his knee and was bobbing it slightly, like an old lady. "That's right. I'm here to welcome the *Reichsprotektor*."

It was obvious that Pavel wasn't satisfied, but he could not press the matter any further. Ernst must have sensed his friend's uncertainty though, because he said quickly, "Herrick needed someone to do damage control with our supplier in London, and it's easier from Prague. At least, that's what I told him."

He winked at Pavel — Marta couldn't see it but she felt the gesture inhabiting the moment of silence. "I wonder what Masaryk would think if he could see Hácha," Ernst continued.

"They say he fainted and had to be revived by Hitler's doctor. And I heard he was forced to enter Prague Castle by the servant's entrance."

Ernst turned his head sharply. "Hitler? The servant's entrance?"

"Not Hitler!" Pavel said. "Hácha."

Marta's leg was almost completely numb. She willed herself to forget it, to focus instead on the talk in the next room. But when she shifted on her haunches, she found she could not feel the limb at all. There was no choice but to stand; otherwise she would fall over. She rose as quietly as she could and hobbled forward briefly; it was as though her leg was made of wood. She went to skirt the edge of the room and go up the stairs behind the men's backs, but she was too awkward and unsteady on her feet, too noisy, and they both turned to look at her as she entered.

Ernst stood. He and Marta were frozen, two feet apart, their eyes locked.

Pavel cleared his throat and said, slightly puzzled, "Ernst, you must remember Marta, Pepik's governess?"

"Yes," Ernst said. "Of course I do. Hello again, Marta."

He reached over to kiss the back of her hand. It was a gesture appropriate only for a lady — and therefore there was something mocking in it — but Marta had no choice but to submit. Ernst's lips were dry and cold.

Marta thought: Judas and Jesus. A kiss of betrayal.

Her leg was on fire as the blood rushed back through it.

She and Ernst looked at each other again in a contest of wills. All at once it came to her: she would confess. She would tell Pavel everything — that Ernst was against him, that he was the one who had thwarted their escape. If she implicated herself, so be it — she could not bear to keep the secret for a single second longer. But the grandfather clock ticked loudly in her ear and no sound came from her mouth. She willed herself to speak — it was just a matter of getting started, she knew — but the truth was, she did not have the courage. And Ernst had guessed as much. There was a smirk on his face, subtle but undeniable.

If Ernst was outed, Marta would go down with him. And Marta, they both knew, had more to lose.

The moment passed; Ernst said he really should be going. He had business to attend to, he said, and looked over at Marta and winked.

The two men clapped each other on the back and Pavel thanked Ernst for his offer.

"Do let me know," Ernst said casually, "if you'd like further protection for your investment in the manner we discussed."

Pavel cleared his throat, noncommittal. "Did you hear the one about Hitler's conversation with Chamberlain?"

Ernst said yes, he'd already heard it.

"Marta told me that one," Pavel said, pleased to be able to credit her. And Ernst said lightly, "Did she? I'm not surprised. She's a clever girl, isn't she. Your Marta."

On April 5 Baron Konstantin von Neurath, the new *Reichspro-tektor* of Bohemia and Moravia, arrived in Prague. The powers that be had arranged for sausage vendors and old-fashioned minstrels; from down on the street Marta could hear a big brass band pumping out "Das Lied der Deutschen" and the "Horst-Wessel-Lied," the Nazi anthem. A national holiday had been proclaimed.

"Will we hang the swastika?" Marta asked Anneliese. All citizens had been ordered to do so, but Anneliese looked at her as though she were crazy. "Are you joking?" she asked. "We'll pay the fine."

When Marta leaned out the window into the bright spring morning she saw that the bulk of Czech house-holders obviously felt the same. Despite the supposed celebration, she could count only five flags along Vino-hradská Street. The Nazi Party newspaper, the *Völkischer Beobachter*, had reported that all schools and associations would be sending delegations to greet the German diplo-mat, but the crowd looked thin along the sidewalks, and only a few people followed the brigade as it proceeded down to Václavské náměstí for the military parade. Marta saw a group of adolescent boys with Nazi armbands run-ning alongside the procession, their mouths wide open, screaming their enthusiasm into the roar of the wind. But on the opposite side of the street a woman in a red ker-chief couldn't help but cry, tears streaming down her fat cheeks as she gave the Nazi salute.

Pavel was sitting behind the big oak desk in the study, sharpening pencils to exactly the same length and placing them, tips up, in a Bavarian beer mug. The sharpener made a sound like an automobile out of gear. Marta went into the room, willing herself to speak. She had lost her nerve on the day of Ernst's visit but perhaps it wasn't too late. Perhaps, if she at least revealed Ernst's agenda now, further harm might be prevented. It was gnawing at her, knowing what she knew. It woke her in the middle of the night, her heart racing. The awful dreams of her father had returned.

But now when her father turned to look at her, he wore Ernst's face.

"Mr. Bauer," she started, before she could second-guess herself, but Pavel interrupted.

"I've been suspended," he said.

"Mr. Bauer?"

"Call me Pavel."

Marta looked at him more closely then, and saw how he'd changed. It wasn't just that he looked older — which he did — but also that he'd been worn down in some vague yet undeniable way. He was softer, more humble. He was afraid.

"One of von Neurath's minions arrived at the factory," he was saying, "to tell us that we must have a ninety-two percent Aryan workforce, and no Jews in management or upper-level ownership." Pavel pulled a pencil from the sharpener's blade and blew the graphite dust from the tip. "Of course there is no choice but to comply."

He closed his eyes and shook his head. "Quite frankly," he said, "I don't understand why the factory has not been taken away completely."

Marta was still standing on the opposite side of the room. From outside came the sound of someone shouting: a single high-pitched shriek, then silence. There was a second chair on the opposite side of Max's desk; Pavel motioned with his chin for her to sit down. Now was her chance. She didn't let herself stop to reconsider. "There's something I've been wanting to talk to you about," she said.

Pavel touched the tip of his finger to a newly sharpened pencil lead and brought it away — a small black dent remained in the flesh. "Ninety-two percent," he said. "But he seemed to pull the number from thin air." He ran the back of his hand over the stubble on his cheek and then realized she'd spoken. "Sorry?" he said, looking up.

She finally had his attention. She opened her mouth, prepared to tell Pavel everything.

"Marta?" he said.

She closed her mouth again. He was eyeing her curiously now, but all at once she had changed her mind. What had she been thinking? She could no more reveal herself than she could shoot herself in the head. Pavel had been going over and over their failed attempt at escape, worrying it like a loose tooth. Who had betrayed them? He suspected Kurt Hofstader, Max's first manager, the one who had lost his job to Pavel. But how had he known? Someone from the floor, one of the German workers? He and Anneliese had been so careful. Pavel had never once suggested anyone in their old town, and Marta knew it hadn't crossed his mind that Ernst might have betrayed him — any more than it had crossed his mind that *she* might have. His implicit trust in her sharpened her regret. To confess would mean the end of her life, or at least the end of the life she wanted to live, the one at the centre of the Bauer family.

Pavel cleared his throat and Marta realized she had to say something. "It's Pepik," she said. "He hasn't been himself. He's so withdrawn. I'm terribly concerned about him."

It was odd. As Marta spoke she realized that what she was saying was true. It wasn't what she'd wanted to address with Pavel — at least, it wasn't what she had thought she'd wanted to address — but another part of her, she realized, had been waiting all along for the chance to ask for advice about Pepik.

She couldn't stand her own incompetence with the boy lately, her inability to protect him. She pictured him closed up in his room, staring at his train, his face slack. "The occupation hasn't been good for Pepik," she started, and then chastised herself; it wasn't as if the occupation were something that could be corrected for the sake of the child's well-being. But the truth of what she was saying came over her again, and she forged ahead.

"Do you remember when we arrived, in January?" she asked Pavel. "And you mentioned the man who is sending the Jewish children out of the country?"

Pavel gave a little laugh.

"What's funny?"

"You and I. We think alike."

"Perhaps we should try to get Pepik on one of those trains." Marta looked at Pavel. He had inserted another pencil into the sharpener. She corrected herself: "Perhaps *you* should try to put Pepik on one of those trains."

Pavel turned the crank; there was the terrible grinding. "Yes," he said, without looking up. "I think you're right."

She lifted her eyebrows. "You do?"

"On a Winton transport." He raised his gaze then, evaluating her. He blew some pencil shavings off the pointed tip and placed it in the beer mug next to the others. "It's already done," he said finally. "I just heard from Winton's secretary. Pepik is on the list. It's not safe for him here."

Marta blinked, taking this in. It seemed like too much of a coincidence. All the fighting with Anneliese, all Pavel's resisting — was this all that had been required? For someone to ask him pleasantly?

For her to ask him?

But that was wishful thinking. Pavel had come up with the idea on his own.

She cleared her throat. It was real, then? It seemed impossible, suddenly, and she almost wished she'd never broached the subject. She told herself Pepik was too young to travel, but in truth she was also worried about what it would mean for her.

"When does the train leave, Mr. Bauer?"

"Call me Pavel!" he snapped. But he repented immediately. "I'm sorry, Marta, I didn't mean to raise my voice. It's just that it makes me feel so . . . old." He tapped the side of the beer mug with his finger. "June 5. Soon."

Marta nodded.

"So you think it's the right thing to do?" he asked, suddenly uncertain.

She was still unused to having her opinion solicited and felt caught out, as if a roving white searchlight had zeroed in on her and revealed her to have an inner life after all. But she thought of Mr. Goldstein and the Kristallnacht beatings, and of little Pepik forced to sit in the back of the class in their old town. She thought of his big, bewildered eyes. What kind of person was she to be worrying so much about herself? She did want to protect Pepik. Above all else. "It's the right thing," she said confidently. And then: "Does Mrs. Bauer agree?"

Pavel nodded tersely and then changed the subject. He too couldn't stand the thought of Pepik leaving. "Did you see the parade?"

Marta told him about the woman crying while giving the Nazi salute.

"Were they tears of joy?"

"Sadness."

"Yes," Pavel said.

"But she could have stayed home!"

Pavel shrugged. "People are driven by things they don't understand."

"I suppose that's true . . ."

"It's true," Pavel said. "Do you know your own motives? Why you act the way you do?"

Marta was silent.

"There's something else I want to tell you," Pavel said.

Spring arrived like a peddler selling flowers. The last of the snow melted and the lilacs came out, defiant. Tulips and daffodils were laid on various monuments, gracing first one side of the political spectrum and then the other. On Hitler's fiftieth birthday the citizens of Prague mourned their lost sovereignty by laying lilies on the Jan Hus statue in Old Town Square, alongside a wreath emblazoned with the Czech motto: *Pravda vítězí* — truth shall prevail. And on the fifth of May several bouquets were laid on the monument to Woodrow Wilson outside the train station. The former U.S. president, Pavel told Marta, had helped to create Czechoslovakia after the Great War.

Now that Pavel was home all day he had become a tutor of sorts for Marta. He filled her in on bits of history and geography, on facts she was ashamed to think most children learned in their first years of school. He also told her about the new things he was learning about his religion: the famous rabbi Rashi, born of a pearl thrown into the Seine, and the symbolism of the long beards and sideburns like those of Mr. Goldstein. He told her about the bar mitzvah ritual — which she already knew — and that Pepik would have one even though he himself hadn't. In exchange Marta shared the minutiae of her days, telling him about the *zelná polévka* she planned to cook the following evening, or a joke about von Neurath she'd heard from the boy who delivered the coal. It was hard to believe Pavel could be interested, but Marta saw it distracted him. "They give me pleasure," he said. "Your details."

She was flattered, but beneath that she never stopped feeling anxious: there was only a little time left before Pepik was to be sent away. Before Marta would be sent away from the Bauers as well. What good was a governess without a child? She tried not to think about where she would go. About the fate that was sure to befall her.

Anneliese was barely ever home. Only once that month did she and Pavel go out together, to the National Theatre. They returned to the flat after curfew, cheeks flushed pink with the cold. The Prague Symphony's rendition of Bedřich Smetana's patriotic suite, "Má Vlast," had been followed by a standing ovation, Pavel said, that lasted a full quarter of an hour. His eyes shone as he told Marta about the tears in the audience, the cheers and whistles from the otherwise refined European elite. The applause stopped only when the conductor actually kissed the score and held it above his head, like an Olympic athlete with a medal.

Anneliese, who had been rifling through her purse for her cigarettes, said, "It was amazing, really. To be part of that crowd, to stand up together for one thing." She stamped her high-heeled boots to get rid of the snow.

"An army of symphony-goers," Pavel agreed.

"An illusion, of course," Anneliese said. "That we all stand together."

"How so?" Pavel helped his wife off with her fur coat and passed it to Marta to hang in the wardrobe.

"The fellow in the street afterwards, for just one example."

"He was only a little Nazi urchin."

"And the Meyers won't speak to us."

"Do you think I need to be reminded?"

The telephone rang, a shrill *brrrring* that echoed through the flat. Pavel crossed the parlour in his snowy galoshes, leaving a line of puddles behind him.

"Yes," he said. "Speaking." His face was uncertain. He waited, then said, "He's been on the list for a month."

Marta pressed her face into the cold, smooth fur of Anneliese's coat and inhaled deeply: the smell of snowy winter woods and, beneath it, perfume and cigarettes. She hung the coat up and turned the little key in the wardrobe door.

"We received the letter last week," Pavel was saying into the phone. He waited again, listening, and then said loudly, "No, I assure you he is Jewish. As are both his mother and I."

Marta turned and saw Pavel take the Star of David from his pocket and grip it tightly in his palm. There was another long pause before he said, "Yes, that's correct. But it was just a precaution. My wife thought it might help."

He held the horn to his ear and glared at Anneliese.

"No, no," he said again. "I assure you —" Whoever was on the other end interrupted, talking at length. Pavel's face was pinched with the effort to hold his tongue, to hear the other speaker out. "He's *Jewish*," he said, when it was finally his turn. "If you require documentation I will certainly be able . . . He's —" But the other party had hung up; there was a long silence before Pavel too put down the receiver. His cheeks were bright red. "Well done," he said, without meeting his wife's eye.

Anneliese didn't answer.

"You wanted to protect him? Look what your protection has done. Now he can't get out of the country at all."

Anneliese covered her mouth and spoke into her palm, as though trying to muffle her own words. "Who was it? The secretary?"

"Yes, the secretary. And you can guess what he said."

She lowered her head to her hands. "Perhaps if we speak to Winton directly?"

"No," Pavel said. "He made it very clear. The decision was Winton's, in fact. Because, you see, there are so many Jewish children desperate to get out that it simply doesn't make sense to send those with a Christian baptismal certificate."

He paused. "Does it?"

"Oh Pavel, I'm so . . ." Anneliese shook her head and massaged her scalp with her fingers. "Hitler has started killing the Jews. Killing Jewish children. I heard it but I didn't . . ." She blinked, and a single tear rolled down her left cheek. "He can't go? Really?"

"No."

"Can't we —"

"I told you. It's done."

"It's done?"

"It's over," Pavel said.

Brno, 10 June 1939

Dear Mr. Nicholas Winton,

I am addressing you as the mother of Helga Bruckner, who was supposed to be on your children's transport last week, June 3. We received your secretary's correspondence, and understand, of course, that it was necessary to remove Helga from your list due to unforeseen circumstances. I can only imagine the logistical details you are coping with and am well aware that there are only so many spots for a much larger number of deserving children.

I would like to tell you at this time, however, that our Helga was born with a withered leg. I apologize for not notifying you of this earlier. You see, we are accustomed to people judging her for this flaw, which of course is no fault of her own, and we did not want her condition to hinder her chance of leaving the country. Dear Mr. Winton, I am telling you this now in hopes that you will be able to find room for her on your next train. The truth of the matter is, she is very vulnerable, unable to defend herself, and unable to run should the need arise. She walks only slowly, and with a crutch. I do not need to inform you of the political situation here at the moment — you are obviously acutely aware of it, to have embarked on such a noble project as yours is. So I beg you, please, to help our Helga. She is an only child, and exceptionally kind and gentle, and I know she would make any British family happy.

I thank you a second time for your kindness.
Marianna Bruckner

(FILE UNDER: Bruckner, Marianna. Died Birkenau, 1943)

A T NIGHT I WALK BY THE RIVER and think about everything lost. It's a cliché, sure, but for every decision that gets made, a billion other options are forsaken. This is true even of happy events. Take a wedding — one future chosen and an infinite number of others let go. Or conception: Think of all the sperm! Of all the people who now never will exist.

I wonder if this is how my mother thought of me. If she would have preferred me to arrive at another time. Or perhaps as a different child entirely.

I imagine her as a woman not particularly taken with motherhood. As a woman with other things on her mind.

"Lisa," I tell myself, "don't be so dramatic."

The truth is I'm a little prone to wallowing.

After you stood me up at Schwartz's I closed my file on you. I closed it the way I've tried to close the one on my mother, the one that nevertheless always finds its way to the top of the pile. The Freudians were wrong — about so many things! — but the influence of parents, that part at least they got right. There's a feeling that comes over me, a feeling that has nothing to do with my mother and at the same time equals her absence. If I'm walking late at night through the quiet winter streets and the smell of someone's laundry floats up from the vent in their basement. If there's a light on in a living room, a table lamp or the TV's blue glow. If there are people moving around behind a lace curtain. Their details are obscured; I pretend it could be her. The longing sharpens until I think I might pass out. I find some excuse to lean over, to tie up my bootlace; I catch my breath and straighten back up and crane my neck. Trying to get a glimpse. Once a man came to the front door. Snow boots pulled on over plaid pajama bottoms. He cleared his throat. "Can I help you?" he asked.

I realized I'd been standing there for probably half an hour. "Oh," I said. "I'm sorry. I was just . . ." But I could not think of anything I might have been doing, so I turned away and kept walking.

One step. Two steps.

Hope, unanswered over a life as long as mine, becomes more of a curse than a blessing.

I don't really know what to say about my mother. I wonder who she could have been as part of my adult life. When you don't have something, it's easy to idealize it. I understand that, I really do. Still, I hate to hear people complain about their mothers. I always have to fight back the urge to tell them how lucky they are.

Which, of course, would make me sound like a mother myself.

There's a park I sometimes pass when I'm walking late at night. The playground abandoned, ghostly. Sometimes I'll wedge myself into one of the swings and drag my heels in the sand for a while. Once I happened by the park in the middle of the afternoon and the place was full of women and strollers. It was easy to pick out the parents from the nannies. The parents were the ones who were showing off their children, bragging about math scores and soccer goals, as though intelligence and good behaviour on the part of the child makes the parent herself worthwhile.

The nannies had enough detachment to give the kids room to breathe.

Still, it's flesh and blood I wonder about. It's hard for most people to imagine what it's like to have absolutely nobody. No flesh of my flesh, no blood of my blood. For a while there was a glimmer of hope about my father, but that turned out to be a pipe dream. I go weeks, months, without anyone knowing where I am. Without anyone checking up on me, I mean.

I know what you're thinking. I wonder, of course I do.

Is there a childless woman who doesn't?

But I think it's for the best. No, let me rephrase that. I'm sure it's for the best. To have a child is to open yourself up to the greatest loss. All you have to do is think for two seconds about the camps, about the mothers in line for selection who had their children torn from their arms. About the children who were lured into trucks with the promise of chocolate. Herded like baby lambs into holding pens. Stripped and shorn. That's all there was to it. They were gassed to death and burned. They drifted west, a thin scrap of cloud, from the mouths of the godlike chimneys.

And you too are gone from me now, Joseph. I wonder what would have happened if we had found each other earlier. If things might somehow have been different. If you might have lived a life less full of pain. I wonder if there was something more I could have done to make things better for you in the end.

SIX

PAVEL DID IT WITH A BRIBE.

Nobody said as much, but Marta knew there was no other explanation for the sudden retraction of the secretary's firm decision. Winton could use Pavel's money to further finance his altruism; Pepik was on the list and some other child was off. The Bauers didn't speak of this, or of the finite number of futures that could be secured, or about who might be lost because Pepik had been found. Marta's fate was not mentioned either. There was no time for existential questions; the whole thing was so last-minute that they had to leap immediately into preparations.

A list arrived detailing the harsh British weather conditions, and Marta was sent to the tailor to have some new travelling trousers and an anorak made for Pepik. The sole of her left boot was wearing thin and she had to stop several times along the way to adjust her stocking inside it. When she got back to the flat, Anneliese was bent over her Czech-English dictionary. Marta looked around for Pavel or Pepik, but neither was anywhere to be seen. This was the first time the two women had been alone in quite some time — was Anneliese avoiding her? Anneliese lifted her head but kept her eyes on her dictionary. "I'll have a cup of coffee," she said. She was feigning disinterest, but Marta could tell from her voice that she too was nervous about the two of them being alone together.

Marta took off her boots and rubbed the round blister that had risen under the ill-fitting heel. She put the package from the tailor, wrapped in brown paper, on top of the breakfront and went into the kitchen; then she ground the coffee beans extra fine and cut an apple into thin slices the way she knew Anneliese liked it. Grateful to be able to do something — anything — for her. There was a mass of guilt churning around in Marta's stomach all the time now. She'd prevented the Bauers from leaving; she'd sheltered Ernst's agenda; and now she had this closeness with Pavel. She loved Anneliese. Adored her. Marta had always thought of herself as the passive victim, as the one ruled by the will of a foreign body, but she saw now, all at once, that Anneliese felt threatened. Pavel was a country Marta had occupied. And Anneliese was like the native Czechs. Forsaken.

Marta came back into the parlour and set the coffee down gingerly on the table.

"Do you think it's good that Pepik is going?" she asked. Trying to make conversation. And Anneliese looked unsure how to answer. Whether to address Marta as her help or as her equal.

"It's just for a while," she finally said. "Just until all of this blows over."

"Do you think the Allies might still come to our rescue?"

"Just until all this *Jewish* business blows over." Anneliese ran a finger around the rim of her china cup.

"He's such a little boy," Marta said. But then she thought

this might seem unworldly and provincial. "Did you travel as a child, Mrs. Bauer?"

"Certainly I travelled," Anneliese said. "With my parents, as a family. As a five-year-old? Alone? Of course not!" She spoke harshly but Marta knew it was out of worry and she chose not to correct Anneliese, not to remind her that her son had recently turned six. "How will you tell him?" she asked instead.

Anneliese leaned her head on her hand and then lifted it again: she had been to the salon and was trying not to ruin her finger wave. She looked up at Marta, an odd mixture of vulnerability and defiance on her face. "I hadn't thought about telling Pepik," she said. She paused. "Perhaps you could do it."

Marta should have expected as much. The difficult tasks were always left to her, and in a way it pleased her to be given the responsibility. Still, something about it seemed not quite right. She touched her dimple. "Of course, Mrs. Bauer," she said. "I'd be happy to. But I wonder if he shouldn't be told by . . ."

The words *his mother* hung in the air between the women.

Anneliese nodded yes. "But you introduce the idea. Warm him to it." She blew on her coffee.

"Certainly, Mrs. Bauer."

"But don't actually tell him. Leave that part to me."

"To his mother," she added.

As though the idea had been hers in the first place.

Evening had fallen while the two women spoke, and Marta imagined how they would look from the street, silhouettes in a small pool of lamplight, sisters perhaps, confiding in each other. Twenty-three and maybe twenty-six years old, their whole lives ahead of them. She liked to think of her life as a story, of herself as the heroine: a bad start, some stumbling blocks, but she'd make good on her natural promise. She owed that much to Anneliese. She owed it to herself.

"There's something else," Mrs. Bauer said. Her cup rattled when she set it on the saucer. "Would you stay on as cook? Once Pepik is gone?"

"Of course!"

Marta spoke quickly and then hesitated, smoothed down the front of her dress.

"That is, if you'll have me."

How, she wondered, could Anneliese be so gracious? It was the perfect excuse for her to let Marta go, no explanation required, and yet she was choosing not to. Perhaps, Marta thought, it was because everything was topsy-turvy with the occupation. Things were shifting and dissolving, reconfiguring. Who did Anneliese have to lean on?

Marta got up to clear the coffee. "Would you like anything else, Mrs. Bauer?"

"I suppose there is one other thing . . ." Anneliese touched her dictionary with a perfectly shaped scarlet nail. "The English word for *betrayal*. I can't find it in here."

Marta flushed. "That one I can't help you with."

Anneliese shook her head sadly. "I didn't think so," she said.

Marta made her way down the long corridor. The hardwood floor smelled of wax. There was no sound from Pepik's room, and when she opened the door, she saw he had fallen asleep in the middle of the carpet, the loop of his train track surrounding him. His suspenders had been pushed off and several lead soldiers lay scattered around his shoulders. Marta put the package from the tailor on the dresser and looked down at him. His head was thrown back and there was a slight film of perspiration on his brow. He looked as if he was following some epic battle, his eyes moving back and forth rapidly under his lids. She crouched down and tried to pick him up without waking him, but he stirred and opened his eyes.

"I'm sorry, *miláčku*," she whispered.

Pepik squinted and rubbed his face; it was pink and creased with sleep. She pulled back the patchwork quilt on the bottom bunk, propped him up against the feather pillow, and bent down to unbuckle his shoes.

"I don't want to," Pepik said.

"I'm sorry, my darling, but it's already past your bedtime."

"No," he mumbled; he was still half asleep. "I don't want to go on the train."

Marta looked up from his shoes. "You don't want to play with it?"

"I don't want to go on it."

His eyes had fallen shut again, his lashes dark against his face. Marta shook his leg gently. "On this train?" she said, pointing to the Hornby cars stalled on their short loop of track. "That's good, because you're such a big boy you'd never fit in it!"

Pepik kicked his foot away from her. "I don't want to go on a *real* train," he said. There was a waver in his voice; he was caught between throwing a tantrum and falling back into oblivion. How did he know? Had he heard them talking? He couldn't have . . .

Marta lifted his limp arms one at a time and pulled off his

little sweater. There were patches on the elbows she herself had sewn. She buttoned up his nightshirt quickly so the draft wouldn't further wake him. He had almost drifted off completely when Anneliese came into the room. "Good night, Pepik," she said, her voice bright, and Pepik's eyes flew back open.

"I don't want to go on a train!" he shouted.

Anneliese shot Marta a questioning look, not angry so much as hurt that Marta would act so explicitly against her wishes. Later that night Marta tried to explain that Pepik had somehow divined what they were planning, that she hadn't told him anything. She could see that Anneliese didn't believe her though. A second, auxiliary betrayal. Which worked against them both in the end.

A letter arrived from the family that was taking Pepik.

Scottish, it turned out, not British. The note was brief but generous, introducing themselves and saying they were looking forward to meeting Pepik. They had a son just around his age, a son named Arthur, who was bedridden. They hoped Pepik's presence would help in Arthur's recovery. This worried Marta but the Bauers didn't mention it, so she didn't either. The letter closed by saying that the fifty pounds was a sacrifice but they were firm believers in doing Christ's good work. Pavel had been reading out loud; he stopped here and looked at his wife accusingly. "I'd like to have the rabbi come and bless Pepik," he said. "Before he travels." He pulled unconsciously at the skin under his chin, as though evoking a long beard.

"Of course, darling," Anneliese said. Marta waited for her to qualify her remark, but nothing else came, and it was she who asked finally, cautiously, "What about the baptism?"

The Bauers turned towards her, one mind with two faces. Their shared expression told her to drop it.

Marta realized suddenly that there were many things she did not know about the Bauers' relationship, things she didn't understand and never would.

The packing for Pepik's trip was now taken up in earnest. Anneliese had brought out his valise and measured it; finding it two centimetres smaller than the allotted size, she had sent Marta down to the Sborowitz department store to buy a larger one. It was red, with a beige plaid lining, and several centimetres *bigger* than what was permitted, but Anneliese said she was willing to take the risk. There would be more important things to be done on the platform than measuring children's suitcases.

Anneliese began to tick off the items on the packing list. She replaced the short pants with longer wool trousers and substituted his well-worn buckled sandals with a pair of tiny galoshes. The tailor was at work on a jacket that could be worn over short sleeves in the summer and over a sweater in winter.

Anneliese said to Marta, "Of course, he'll be back before the snow comes."

In addition to clothes there was the matter of what the packing list referred to as "sentimental items." In a small envelope in the valise's side pocket Anneliese placed a photograph. It was the family portrait taken after the baby girl's birth: Marta behind Pepik, touching his shoulders, Anneliese off to the side, her sunglasses lowered, and Pavel holding the bundle in his arms. Marta was surprised that this was the photo Anneliese had chosen to send. She thought it would be confusing for Pepik, who didn't remember his sister. "It's just for posterity," Anneliese said, and Marta wondered what she meant. Anneliese kept repeating that the separation would be temporary and brief, but she was packing as though she expected never to see her son again. She attended to the suitcase as if it were a matter of life or death: it was like a body open on the operating table, the internal organs being removed and replaced at will. It was the second time Anneliese had packed a suitcase for Pepik in two short months, and Marta saw that this time she was determined to get it right; it was as if she thought that if she could only choose the right contents they would somehow ensure her son's safe passage.

Pepik observed the packing and unpacking of the suitcase as if he were witnessing a complicated surgery: equal parts curiosity and repulsion. Marta had taken Anneliese at her word, that she would tell Pepik what was happening — children, after all, need to know what to expect — but five days before the departure date Marta found him peering into the depths of the suitcase. "Is Mamenka leaving?" He paused. "Are *you* leaving?" His earlier premonition had vanished from his mind like a nightmare forgotten on waking.

Marta swept him into her arms: his wonderful weight. The buckle on his suspender dug into her side, and she shifted him on her hip, took him into the bedroom, and pulled him onto her lap in the rocking chair. Before she could second-guess herself, she said, "I've got a big surprise. You, *miláčku*, are going on a trip!"

The little smile that had appeared when she picked Pepik up began to drain from his face.

Marta forged ahead: "You've seen all the soldiers in the street? The bad Nazis? You get to *fight* them. From Scotland. You'll march away and help protect the good guys." Pepik's bottom lip was trembling but she blundered on. "You'll stay with a wonderful family named the Millings. In a beautiful house! By the ocean." The lies spilled from her mouth now as if someone else was speaking. "They have a dog!" she heard herself say — where that had come from she had no idea whatsoever. "And a boy just your age named Arthur. So you'll have someone to play soldiers with."

"Another little boy?" Pepik's face brightened. It had been so long since he'd had a playmate of any kind.

"Yes," she said, "but." She stopped and held up a forefinger, about to reveal a top-secret piece of intelligence. "Arthur is sick. He can't leave his bed. So you have a very important job. You'll be responsible for helping him get better."

"That's my job?"

"It's your duty. Can you do it?"

He nodded solemnly. "I promise."

She thought later that she should not have taken this approach. She had not meant to unnecessarily burden little Pepik. But, by the time she realized, it was too late.

Pepik was dead. Marta was sure of it.

She went into his room in the morning and opened the wooden venetian blinds; slats of sun slapped on the floor. She said his name once and then said it again, louder. She crouched down and blew softly on his forehead, which usually woke him laughing, but he didn't stir. Finally she had to take hold of his face and almost yell directly into his ear; he opened his eyes and looked at her, confused, his cheeks flushed.

He didn't recognize her.

She held the back of her palm to his forehead. He was burning up.

Marta assumed he must be upset about their conversation the previous night, and that if she could just take his mind off his impending departure he would be fine, but as soon as he was able to stand, which he could do only clutching her elbow, he leaned over and threw up into his slippers.

"Oh," Marta said. "You're a sick bunny."

Pepik's knees buckled and he collapsed on the bed, banging his temple against the ladder between the bunks.

He slept for the rest of the morning. It was as though hearing about bedridden Arthur had given Pepik ideas of his own. Marta spent the day in the rocking chair next to Pepik, watching him drift in and out, a loose piece of driftwood by the shore. She felt terribly responsible, as though he would not have fallen ill had she done a better job telling him about Scotland. He was soaking through nightshirts faster than she could change them. In the end she decided to leave him naked, with cold cloths on his forehead and neck and just above his tiny, circumcised penis. His sleep was punctuated with little grunts and moans. He woke around midnight and looked at her blankly and asked for a rope ladder. Marta didn't know how to respond and said nothing, thinking he would slip back into unconsciousness, but he furrowed his forehead and repeated the request with force, adding the name *Vera* at the end. "My rope ladder! *Vera!*"

He fell back onto the pillow but the moaning got louder. Was he referring to his little cousin Vera, whom he'd not seen for ages? And a rope ladder! Where had he come up with it?

By the second day the fever showed no signs of letting up. Pavel came in to check on the two of them; he crossed the room and stood very close to Marta. She could smell his aftershave. Something sharp and sugary, like cedars in the sun. "Is he any better?"

"Maybe a little."

"I wanted to teach him some English before he goes."

"*Hello*?" Marta had recently learned the word.

"*Good morning.*"

"And *Where is the toilet?*"

"Good one."

"*I'm hungry.*"

"And what about *I love you*?"

Pavel turned away from her, averting his eyes.

Pepik's sick stomach had reasserted itself and Pavel wanted to prop his son up to be sure he didn't choke on his own vomit. Pepik's body was difficult to manipulate, as if its owner had vacated and left a heavy lead dummy in his place. It took Pavel and Marta several minutes to arrange him, leaning him sideways against the oversized pillows. Their hands touched twice during the operation, sending little sparks up Marta's arm.

The fever burned between them.

"Should we call the pediatrician?" Marta asked.

"We already did."

Marta waited.

"The summons was ignored."

It was the Jewish thing. Pavel didn't say so, but Marta knew.

There was still no improvement by the third night, and the whole family gathered round Pepik's bed. He was flat on his back with the thermometer sticking out of his mouth at a ninety-degree angle, as though from a pork roast. His fever had reached 103 degrees, and Marta had a feeling that they were gathered around a campfire, something hot and dangerous, crackling and spitting. Pepik seemed to sense their presence: his hallucinations came fast and strong as if he were up on stage before them, an actor charged with holding a vast audience's attention. He spat out the thermometer and pulled at the flesh on his cheeks and puffed them out. He began to recite *Der Struwwelpeter* in a high, whiny voice. He pushed back his sheets and made to stand up on the bed, and when Pavel tried to move him back under the covers, he bit his father's hand.

Time had seemed elastic to Marta during the worst of the illness, but with only two days left until Pepik's departure it snapped firmly back into place. Anneliese had to settle on the final contents of the suitcase — she would send the winter pajamas with the feet attached but leave the suspendered bathing costume and cap. She also slipped her diamond watch down into the side pocket of the valise. Marta saw the note: *For my boy who knows how to tell the time.* A lovely gesture. Still, she thought, it was a large gift for such a small child. Perhaps Anneliese had other reasons for wanting to be rid of it.

Marta was responsible for putting a picnic into Pepik's rucksack: two crabapples, some sausage, a small loaf of dark Czech bread. She taped a note to a bottle of Aspirin with instructions that Pepik should take one every three hours. The note was addressed to nobody in particular, and there would be nobody on the train to administer it, but it seemed to comfort Anneliese to include it, and Marta had to admit she felt the same way. Maybe there would be some older girl who would see that Pepik was sick and take him under her wing. It was like putting a message in a bottle: they had no idea if it would arrive.

"Marta." Anneliese drew the strings on the rucksack. "There's something I think I should tell you."

"Those Aspirin have expired?"

Anneliese paused, leaned in closer. Marta saw new wrinkles in the corners of her eyes. "It's just that —" Anneliese started, but stopped when Pavel came in with the suitcase. He fiddled with its lock for several minutes before laying it on the parlour table. It stayed there overnight, like a body before burial.

It was Marta who spent the last evening with Pepik, up in the room that had belonged to his Uncle Max. In the pantry she found a white tray patterned with blue windmills and brought him up a bowl of chicken soup and a little dish of cherry preserves for dessert. "Are you hungry, darling?" she asked.

She didn't wait for him to answer. "You're leaving in the morning! What a lucky boy," she said. "And we will come and meet you in Scotland."

Pepik nodded gravely. His eyes had cleared and he was eating the soup quickly, like a starving man.

"You'll meet me?" he asked, the spoon halfway to his mouth.

"Your mamenka and tata will come as quickly as they can."

"And you too?"

"And me too," she promised. "And me too, *miláčku*." She didn't want to think about the fact that Pepik was leaving — leaving for real — but nor did she want to miss her chance to say goodbye. In the morning there would be parents and crowds of children and train crew. As much as she didn't want it to be true, she knew that this might be their last time together, just the two of them, for quite some time. For weeks, most certainly. Possibly for months.

"Show me your Sneezy face," she said.

Pepik put down his soup spoon, his bowl empty. He made four rapid *achoo*'s into his elbow. Marta clapped her hands together under her chin. "Well done!" she said. "Goodbye, Sneezy."

She thought for a minute. "Your Bashful face."

Pepik fluttered his eyelids shyly. He covered his face with his hands and peeked out at her from between them. She kissed his forehead and both of his ears and said, "Goodbye, Bashful. Travel safely!"

She asked for his Dopey face and his Happy face and his Grumpy face and kissed them all at length.

When the ritual was complete, Pepik lay back on the big feather pillow. He looked pale and sweaty and Marta felt badly for exciting him. She touched his brow: he was still running a fever.

She sat beside him for a while, stroking his hair and wondering what to tell him. It wasn't clear how much he understood about what was happening, and she didn't want to upset him further. She looked down at his soft, round face; his little eyelids fluttered shut. She bent down to his level. "I love you very much," she whispered into the curl of his ear. But somehow this didn't seem enough. There was something else, she thought, something else she should say. "Open your eyes, *miláčku.*"

Tears were running down Marta's face now. She blinked, trying to hide them from Pepik, but they came hot and fast. He looked at her, searching, and lifted a little hand to touch her cheek. "My darling," she whispered, "may you live to be a wise old man."

As soon as she'd spoken she wished to take the words back — she would see him very soon, after all, and she'd not meant to alarm him. But he pushed his head into her chest now, clinging to her tightly, and then he lifted his eyes and nodded. He'd understood her wish for him: a long and happy life. And it seemed — although she might have been imagining it — it seemed he was wishing the same for her.

In the car on the way to the station Anneliese looked out the window, hands in her lap, tearing the packing list into smaller and smaller pieces. It was a short drive, but Pepik put his head in Marta's lap and fell asleep as soon as the car started moving. He woke when they arrived, looked around weakly, and vomited his porridge onto the floor of the automobile. Anneliese pretended she hadn't seen it. It was left to Marta to wipe up the mess with her handkerchief.

Pavel applied the parking brake and turned the key to turn off the car. He had pulled up beside the Hlavní nádraží with its

stained glass windows and the carved faces of women repre-
senting Prague as the Mother of Cities. There was already lots
of activity on the platform: a long queue of adults in front of
a table, and children racing around the entrance to the public
toilets. Pavel leaned sideways against the car door so he could
see his wife in the seat beside him and Marta behind them. He
was grouping them together, corralling them. "Let's make a
plan," he said to the women.

"What do you mean?" Anneliese asked. She was dressed
in a little velvet Greta Garbo hat, a new jacket with shoulder
pads, and leather gloves.

"How will we do this?" asked Pavel.

"Oh, it's revolting." Anneliese rolled down her window
against the smell of vomit.

Pavel nodded towards Pepik, who had fallen immediately
back to sleep in Marta's lap. "Should we carry him?"

"Of course not. If they know he's sick they'll never let
him on."

"I'll get the suitcase."

"He can walk," Anneliese said.

Pavel scoffed. "The Crown Prince doesn't look in great
shape for walking." Marta could feel Pepik breathing against
her, the low heat from his head like a flanker.

There was an hour left before departure but already the train
had pulled into the station. It stood on the track in the morning
sunlight, steaming, a mirage. Pavel got out of the front seat and
Marta heard the trunk door slam and the sound of the suitcase
falling over on the pavement. Pepik sat up, his eyes glassy. "Are
you ready for your big adventure?" Marta asked him.

He clutched at his stomach and hiccupped loudly.

He was indeed able to walk on his own, though, steadied between his parents. Marta was relegated to picking up the rear. This was how it always was, she thought: she dressed, prepared, and comforted in the wings and then passed the child off to his mother before their grand entrance. The Bauers entered the full frenzy of the station with their son wedged firmly between them. "Your tie is crooked," she heard Anneliese say to Pavel. And she watched as he obediently straightened it.

The first thing Marta thought when they entered the station was that all of their worrying had been for nothing. Pepik could have been covered with a bloody, oozing rash and nobody would have noticed. The platform was crammed with families immersed in their own version of what the Bauers were going through; nobody was paying the least bit of attention to anyone else. In every corner there were women weeping into hankies, fathers crouched down before their children, handing out last-minute advice, trying to make up for years of absence. One of the porters had started to stack some of the suitcases and a group of boys was racing around the pile at top speed, like puppies chasing each other's tails. The shouting and crying and counselling combined to form a uniform din out of which only the occasional sentence could be discerned: from behind her Marta heard someone say, "We'll see you again in a free Czechoslovakia!"

But the voice was hushed; there were Gestapo on the platform.

Marta had a sudden flash that there was something they'd forgotten. But she couldn't think what it might be.

Three rough lines were forming at the doorways to the train. A whistle screamed through the morning sunlight. There was a pause in the bedlam, everyone united. The moment drew itself in, solidified, a glass sphere that hung suspended above them throwing off rainbows and sparkles of light, and then it shattered onto the station floor. The crying started up again, and the rapid instructions, and the shrill sound of women's voices feigning cheer. Above it all now the conductors' voices could be heard as they tried to herd the children into the passenger cars. The lines began to move forward slowly.

At the front of each queue someone was ticking off a list and hanging a number around each small neck. There were plenty of children too young to know their own names.

Marta had a sudden inkling of what it meant to give up a child you had birthed. She wanted very badly to touch Pepik. She wanted very badly to touch Pavel.

Over the clamour she heard someone say, "I can't believe everything we used to take for granted." She saw Anneliese smile demurely at a uniformed soldier.

They were being swept forward now, by circumstance and time, by the great push of people moving towards the train. There was a commotion at the front of the line; Marta craned her neck, looking over the heads of a group of grey-haired ladies, and saw the Bauers' friend Vaclav Baeck. He had put his two daughters, Magda and Clara, onto the train, but now it seemed he'd changed his mind. He was speaking rapidly to whomever was in charge, a young man who was shaking his head, *No*.

Vaclav tried to push past the conductor but was restrained. He tried a different tactic, walking several metres down the platform and speaking to a girl hanging out of the train window. There was some more jostling and Marta's view was blocked by a tall man with a high black hat. When she looked again, both of Vaclav's girls were at the window, Clara holding her baby sister Magda awkwardly in her arms. She passed the baby out the window to their father: Vaclav reached up and accepted his daughter as if he were accepting the gift of the rest of his life.

He stood with his wife, blowing kisses at their older daughter, Clara, who would now make her journey alone.

The Bauers too had seen Vaclav's decision, and now Pavel bent down and took Pepik by the arm. "Do you want to go?" he asked, his voice calm. "To Scotland?"

Anneliese's cheeks flushed. "Pavel! That isn't fair." She reached inside her jacket to adjust one of her shoulder pads.

"I didn't have time to teach him any English. How will he manage?"

"The Millings will help him."

But Pavel's eyes were fixed on his son's face as though he were trying to read the future from a cup of muddy tea leaves. "*Miláčku*," he said, "tell me. Do you want to go? Or do you want to stay here with Mamenka and Tata?"

Pepik looked bewildered: the train was shiny and alluring; he was hot and wet with fever.

"Stop it," Anneliese said again, her voice rising. She grasped her husband's shoulder but he shook her off roughly. "I want to know," Pavel said. "I want to do the right thing, the thing that *he* wants."

"Pavel, he's a child. He has no idea what he wants."

Pepik's eyes were darting, panicked. There was shoving behind the Bauers and several people pushed ahead. They were holding things up: the line began to flow past them. Suitcases banged against each other and children hopped back and

forth in excitement. But Pepik would not be going: Pavel had
changed his mind.

There was a loud hiss from the train, the release of a long-
held breath.

Marta had been silent throughout the conversation, a slow
wall of unease rising inside her. Now she snapped into action.
"Pavel," she said. It was the first time she had called him by his
first name out loud, but nobody seemed to notice. "Mrs. Bauer
is right. We've told Pepik he's going. We should put him on the
train."

She was thinking now of her earlier transgression: she had
prevented Pavel and Anneliese from getting out of the country. But could redeem herself still, with their child.

Anneliese folded her arms across her chest. "Exactly," she
said.

Pavel looked not at his wife but at Marta. He was still
uncertain, but her confidence settled it.

"If you're sure," he said. He looked down at his son, whose
chin had fallen down on his chest. "You'll go, *miláčku?*"

Marta could see Pepik was not following what was being
said, but he nodded weakly, and that was enough.

The Bauers re-entered the line and were pushed quickly
forward. Everyone was crying; the organizers had assigned a
woman whose job it was to physically remove each child from
the parents' arms. It was like asking them to chop off their
own limb: you couldn't expect them to do it themselves. Pepik
was gone from them before they realized what was happening.
His little back was swallowed up by the train. Marta and the
Bauers shoved their way down the platform, through the dense
crowd of bodies, trying to follow from outside his progress

through the cars. Marta could smell the rank body odour of an elderly man behind her; he shifted and she was elbowed in the ribs. She angled her body away, trying to see Pepik, but there were so many parents with their faces pushed up against the window that she couldn't get close to him. "Where is he?" Anneliese asked, desperate. "You'll see him soon," Marta consoled her. "He'll be back before we know it."

The train gave a low moan; it began to move slowly down the tracks. The crowd shuffled along next to it; the air filled suddenly with a hundred white handkerchiefs.

It was Marta who spotted Pepik finally — he'd made his way quite far down the train and was hanging out the window, calling to them. His little cheeks pink with effort, or with fever. She suddenly remembered what it was they had forgotten: the blessing from the rabbi, for safe travels.

Pepik looked as if he'd just realized the same thing. Someone must have jostled him or pushed him from behind, because his expression changed, as if he had looked into the future, as if he had suddenly remembered something that he desperately needed to tell them.

This was the last thing — the thing Marta would remember: his little mouth wide open, that O of surprise.

PART FOUR

KINDERTRANSPORT

SEVEN

THE TRAIN WAS LONG AND BLACK, and entering it was like being swallowed by a snake. The snake had dislocated its jaw to take Pepik in, and now he was being worked down into its body, deep, to the tip of its tail. Pepik made a little slithering motion; he put his hands on his stomach and imagined the way the snake felt, all the little bodies tumbling down inside it. There were so many children. His eyelashes were wet but he blinked and swallowed, swallowing himself, letting himself be swallowed.

The snake was getting full. Soon it would slither off through the grass.

The last car of the train was crammed full of children. Two sisters clung to each other, crying. The older girl had skin the colour of flour and hair like a Brillo pad. Every minute or so she would take a deep breath, wipe her cheeks, and say brightly, "We'll get to go to the seaside!" or "The Fairweathers have kittens!" and then immediately dissolve back into sobs. Behind her was a little boy, barely old enough to stand, clutching a bottle of milk in the centre of the aisle. Someone bumped into him; he rocked back and forth on his heels like an inflatable clown and toppled in slow motion onto his bottom. The milk spilled down his front. The boy's mouth opened, wider and wider, like a pupil dilating; it hit the end of its reach and he started to howl. An adolescent girl who had been put in charge of the carriage jumped to her feet. "Oh shoot," she said. "You little rascals! Everyone into their seats!" She clapped her hands together. She picked the milk-soaked toddler up, struggling under his weight and trying to console him, but seemed at a loss when faced with the wet vest. A moment later she had put the crying child back on the floor and was flipping through a *Film Fun* magazine.

Pepik took a seat next to a fat boy whose cheeks looked like apples. The train had not yet started to move but the other boy had already taken out his lunch bag, had unfolded the news-paper wrapping, and was scarfing down *chlebíčky*. The girl in charge of the carriage had her face buried in her leather bag and was taking out its contents item by item. A comb, a bar of dark chocolate. She unfolded a pair of tortoiseshell spectacles, placed them on her nose, and turned towards the window — looking not at her parents on the platform but at her own reflection in the glass.

Pepik wanted to take his sweater off — he was so hot — but it got tangled in the leather strap of his rucksack and he struggled, sweat pouring off him. His arm was stuck behind his back, and he twisted his torso and thought hard about the snake that could wiggle its way out of anything. His arm came free. When he turned back to sit down, the boy with the fat cheeks had taken his seat. "What's in your lunch?"

"Nothing," Pepik said. He drew his own brown paper bag protectively towards his stomach. The boy made a lunge for it; Pepik turned quickly, and his head reeled. The sound of his heart beating behind his eyes was the sound of a thousand stallions galloping through the Black Forest at night. He needed to get off

the train. It came over him suddenly and urgently. It was as if his
father's words were water behind a blockage in a pipe: they burst
through all at once. *You don't have to go if you don't want to.*

He didn't want to!

He put his rucksack down on the floor and the fat boy
stuck his hand in and came out with one of the crabapples.
Pepik didn't stop. He pushed his way past two older boys who
were making fart jokes in German and squiggled up under a
wall of girls. When he came up, he was right in front of the
window. The platform was packed with crying faces but he
saw Marta immediately, her long, dark curls and dimple. She
didn't even need to smile: the dimple was always there. Pepik's
eyes locked on her like the clasp on his valise.

Marta was scanning the length of the train, looking for
him too.

Pepik started screaming. It was a wordless scream, a blast
of pure sound, and only after several seconds did the individual
words begin to assert themselves, flinging out in every direction like silver balls in a pinball machine. "No! I don't want
to! I don't want to go!" he shouted. "Tata, I don't want to go,
come and get me, I don't want to, I don't want to goooooo!"
The words flew through the air, over the crowd, and pinged on
the station floor unnoticed. His parents still couldn't see him.
Behind Pepik came an adult voice telling the children to move
away from the windows and sit down so the train could start
moving. Pepik had wedged himself halfway out of the train:
the edge of the sill was digging into his stomach. The words
kept coming, one after another: "Mamenka! Tata! I want to
stay here with you! I want to, I want, Tata . . ." And then Marta
caught his eye. A little look of surprise popped up on her face

and she squeezed his father's elbow and pointed to where
Pepik was.

Pepik drew a big breath. He clung onto his nanny with his
eyes, with all his might. She had seen him. She would take him
off the train.

The adult voice behind him was getting louder. Children
were being pulled away from the window, peeled off like
leeches from sunburned skin. The train began to move. It
lurched slowly, the sea of parents and grandparents lumber-
ing awkwardly along with it. They couldn't keep up. Pepik had
to turn sideways to keep his family in view. Sweat was pouring down his back. He opened his mouth to scream again and
felt a hand on his collar. A strong tug pulled him backwards
into the train. "I don't want to go!" he shouted. "I want to
stay with Tata Nanny I don't want I want —" But the adult,
a woman with sturdy shoes and a pointed face like a beagle's,
had already moved on. She was making her way purposefully down the length of the car, plucking the children from
the glass and snapping the windows closed and locking them.
Pepik had fallen against an armrest and it took him a moment
to straighten. By the time he did there were too many bodies;
it was impossible to see over everyone's heads. He ducked
down and tried to crawl through the other children's legs but
got kicked in the jaw. He finally made it to the clear pane of
glass, but the train was already gone from the station. Looking
back he saw fields, soft and green in the June afternoon, and in
the far distance the last few white handkerchiefs, rising up like
fluttering doves.

⟍ⓔ⟋

The rocking of the train put Pepik to sleep. When he woke, the sun was going down. It was a dot of fire on the edge of the horizon and it burned a line towards him. It lit a small fire between his eyes.

He felt his lashes catching, the little lick of flame rising up into his brain.

There was a baby asleep in a bureau drawer balanced on the seat across from him; the drawer rocked precariously each time the train hit a bump, but nobody came to move it. Pepik leaned forward and vomited onto the floor beside it. Darkness fell like a suffocating blanket; it was hot in his head and tears slid down his face. Nobody came to put a cold cloth on the back of his neck. Sweat dripped off his face. The fat boy with the pink cheeks was asleep with his chin on his chest. Identical twin girls with blond pigtails pointed at Pepik and whispered. Their voices were like twigs snapping in a fire or snapping beneath his feet, he couldn't tell which. When he looked down, though, he saw he was walking. He and the other children were being herded up a gangplank towards a big boat. The train had disappeared — a magician's trick — along with everything that came before it. His mamenka and tata, his nanny. Pepik let himself be jostled forward. He was instantly devoted to the boat, its shiny silver propeller, the enormous hull that would shoulder its way through the rough waves of the English Channel. All those hours under the dining room table with his train might never have happened. The boat was his new love.

A bunch of boys were throwing a ball of socks back and forth in the air. When Pepik looked more closely, the socks sprouted wings and flapped off into the morning.

The next time he woke he was shivering. The edges of his vision were hazy but a clear spot had opened in front of him, as though someone had breathed hotly on a pane of frost-covered glass. He saw two boys, knees drawn up to their chests, sleeping beneath a single wool jacket. And when he rolled over he saw that there was another boy curled up behind him, every inch of his face covered in freckles. He had a tag around his neck with a number on it. Pepik felt his own neck and realized he was wearing a tag as well. He tugged at the string, trying to pull it off, but the boy told him he must keep it. "For your family," he whispered in Czech, as though conveying something top secret. "So they can meet you."

"Today?"

The boy nodded.

"And Nanny?" He wanted them, immediately. His tata and mamenka. He wanted Marta to come and change him — he had wet himself in the night — and he started to whimper.

"It's okay," the freckled boy soothed, in the voice of a practised big brother. "They'll be there to meet you."

The children were herded onto the deck to eat sugar sandwiches while the sun rose. The bread was white and fluffy and tasted like cake. Pepik thought of the German soldiers, with their appetites for Czech desserts. He remembered Tata saying that only once every larder was bare would the Nazis go back where they came from. After the snack he and the others were herded down another gangplank and into a big glass-domed station, where a crowd of adults came down on them like an avalanche. There were mothers pushing prams and men in steel-toed workboots and couples with white hair leaning on canes. The freckled boy was whisked away by a woman with one arm in a sling. Pepik waved but his new friend didn't see him, his face already buried in an ice-cream cone. Men were still unloading suitcases from the belly of the ship and heaping them in a big pile. A group of older boys were climbing on them; one made it all the way to the top and stood there, teetering dangerously, shouting, "Take that, Blaskowitz!" as he fired his imaginary rifle into the crowd.

A young woman arrived, in elbow-length gloves and a wide hat; she lifted the infant and left the empty drawer on the floor. She was smiling as though she'd won the lottery.

The station slowly emptied. Children went home with their new families. A slower trickle of adults was arriving now, more elderly people, a woman in a wasp-waisted bouffant dress and a garden-party hat, apologizing for being late. These adults squinted at the remaining boys and girls, trying to see which was theirs to take home. Pepik sat against the wall, wrapping the string of his rucksack around the tip of his finger, tighter and tighter, until the finger turned a violent red. He kept his eyes fixed on the station door. When it opened, he stood up, expectant. He was going to see his tata! And his mamenka! And Nanny.

Where were they?

Nobody came.

Pepik sat back down again.

There was an older girl who had not been fetched either. "I'm Inga," she said.

Pepik looked at her blankly. She was the girl, he saw, with the *Film Fun* magazine, the one put in charge of the train carriage who'd been so excited to set off on such an adult journey.

"It's Norse," she said. "My name. I am guarded by Ing, the god of fertility and peace."

She looked at Pepik, waiting for a reaction. She sat down beside him and started to cry into her hands.

～⊚～

It was a man with a briefcase, finally, who came over from a faraway table to where Pepik and Inga were sitting. He had droopy brown eyes and bushy sideburns. "What are your names?" he asked. Pepik didn't understand the words. The man shook his head slowly, as though he had done something he was very sorry for. He had a long, thin loaf of the fluffy white bread in his hand, and he broke it in two and gave them each a piece. Inga stopped crying for just long enough to cram her portion into her mouth. The man motioned for them to get up and follow him; Inga smoothed down her green checked skirt, still chewing. She wiped her face and picked up her purse, digging in it for her tortoiseshell glasses.

The man led them out the station door and across a stretch of hot tarmac. He waddled a little, their two cases banging against his legs. His car was different from Tata's, with two windshield wipers instead of one. A horse blanket covered the worn-out upholstery. Inside it was stifling hot, and the man leaned over and rolled down Inga's window and then leaned into the back seat and rolled down Pepik's. There was the sound of the engine turning over.

Pepik fell asleep the minute they started moving.

When he woke, Inga was looking over at him warily. "*Kam jdeš?*" she asked.

Pepik rubbed his eyes. "I'm going with you."

Inga glared at him. "Now you are. But after. Where are you going?"

Pepik shrugged.

"I'm going to the Gillfords in the countryside," Inga said. "I'm going to learn to ride a pony!" She fixed her gaze in the middle distance as though a pony had materialized in front of her and she could climb onto its back and ride away into the future. "There will be two other girls there," she continued. "Sisters. They'll be almost the same as my real sister, Hanna," Inga said, but Pepik thought she sounded uncertain.

"We're in Scotland," he said, because he needed to say something.

"No we're not. Don't you know anything? This is Liverpool. We're in England!" She looked down her snub nose at Pepik. "How old are you anyway? Six?"

Pepik nodded.

Inga looked surprised. "Well, that explains things."

The car continued past open fields, through little towns with outdoor cafés and wrought-iron tables set up in the sun. The man looked over his shoulder and spoke to them and Pepik was surprised to hear Inga reply. Just a few halting words, but her ability to speak the funny language made her immediately desirable in his eyes. "I want Nanny," Pepik whimpered.

Inga didn't reply.

"Where are we going?" he tried again.

"To London," Inga snapped, but the uncertainty had returned to her face. She turned away from Pepik and looked out the car window. "My father is a specialist in internal medicine. My *real* father. In Prague."

From her shaking shoulders Pepik saw she had started to cry.

They drove for what seemed like days, past factories and warehouses, and finally the man pulled over and stopped in front of a long brick building. It was divided into many smaller houses attached side by side. They stood at attention like a row of lead soldiers. Pepik put his hand into his rucksack and felt around, first touching a sausage he had forgotten to eat and then landing on his own soldier, cool in his hand, readying both of them for battle. *"Pow!"* he muttered under his breath. They had arrived. The fight against the bad guys could begin.

Inside, the house was dark. The entire front room was filled with a big oak desk, but it didn't have carved lion's feet like his Uncle Max's in Prague. It wasn't as neatly organized either. There were stacks of notebooks and open folders piled on top of each other; in the centre of the desk was a big sheet of cardboard covered with photos of children's faces, each one with writing underneath. Inga moved some books aside and sat down daintily on the edge of the sofa. She pursed her lips and took out a lipstick; she made several attempts before making contact with her mouth.

Where was Arthur?

There was a door at the back of the room, open just a crack; maybe Arthur was in there, sleeping.

The man sat down behind the massive desk with the brief-case open in front of him. He began writing things down, checking off a list. Lifting stacks of paper and peering underneath them. Inga had moved on from her lips and was taking down her hair — the length of it was surprising to Pepik. She tipped her head to one side and began braiding, her fingers working swiftly.

"Where's Artoor?" Pepik asked.

Inga looked cross. "Who's Artoor?"

"The sick little boy."

"The only sick boy here is you."

She crossed her legs and started braiding the other side of her head.

"The other boy, with . . ." Pepik started, but he faltered. He needed to fight back. He clutched the little soldier in his fist.

Inga wrinkled her nose in his direction. She concentrated harder on her hair, her fingers whizzing.

Several minutes later the doorbell rang.

"Come in!" the man called, but the door was locked. He fumbled with a bundle of keys. More English adults appeared; there was more babbling. Inga stood up as though she understood the conversation, which turned out to be true: she was leaving. "*Čekat!*" Pepik said. "Wait for me!"

But it was too late. Inga was gone. She didn't turn around to say goodbye.

~ c ~

When Pepik woke, there was light streaming in the window. He was in a big feather bed. The man with the briefcase was moving around the main room like Tata, in a clean suit and tie. Pepik crawled out from under the covers and padded over to him. "*Činit ne dovoleno,*" he said.

He grabbed onto the man's trouser leg and clung there. The man laughed and lifted Pepik up, making a groaning noise to show what a big boy he was. He pretended he was about to throw Pepik onto the couch, and Pepik squealed. The man repeated the motion, swinging Pepik into the air again and again and then finally letting him fall into a big pile of laundry. It was warm and smelled like soap. Pepik wondered if the man's soap came with the same pictures of steam engines as theirs did at home.

Home.

Sunlight knifed through the window and made him squint and close his eyes. He would stay here with this man. Sleep in the big bed and eat the fluffy white bread, and Nanny and Mamenka would come to meet him.

Today would be the day.

The man with the briefcase had gone back behind the desk and was rustling his papers again. Every now and then he would peer over at Pepik and speak to him with the funny words. Pepik let them wash over him like bubbles in a bath. He let himself drift. A feeling of moistness was gathering in him, rising up from his toes, through his legs, a gush of heat that rushed through his stomach to his throat and his mouth.

He turned and threw up onto the floor.

The man looked up sharply from his folders. He sighed heavily and let his chin fall to his chest. When he looked up, there was an expression on his face that Pepik recognized, one he had seen on the faces of adults so frequently over the past months. Disapproval? Disappointment. Something to do with water on his forehead. The thing he had accepted that had ended in his being sent away. What was it? He couldn't quite remember.

But he knew it was his own fault that he was here.

The sun piercing the windowpane had sharpened to a point, all its heat focused on Pepik's head. He was a little bug under a magnifying glass, about to catch fire. He wriggled, trying to move away from the glare, but his body was too heavy. The man came over to pick him up and he went limp at the adult touch.

He felt soft, like chocolate left out in the sun. But he would be safe here. This man would love him and keep him.

When he opened his eyes next, though, he was back on a train.

❧

There was a woman waiting on the platform, and Pepik loved her at first sight. Her eyes were soft and warm like melted caramel. She crouched down in front of him — he could see the glint of hairpins in her hair. This was Mrs. Milling, this beautiful woman the same age as Nanny who would take him home and help him fight the Germans.

"*Jsem hladový*," Pepik said. He clung to her with his eyes.

The woman put a hand over her heart, as though taking an oath. "Look at you," she said. "Precious thing. I wonder what you're saying."

Pepik leaned his head on her shoulder. The woman laughed. "What's this?" She pointed to his chest.

Pepik looked down and saw a number pinned there. From upside down he could make out a two and two fives.

"*Jsem hladový*," he repeated. Something in him was reaching up towards her — not his arms but something in his chest. Something small in the very centre of him was straining up towards her. Mrs. Milling's eyes were full of tears.

"Who do you belong to, I wonder? What's that language you speak?"

She smelled of talcum and of roses left to dry in the sun. Pepik waited for Mrs. Milling to pick him up, but she didn't. The porter had placed Pepik's red suitcase on the platform and he tried to drag it towards her so she could take him home. He was tired and hungry; he wanted a bowl of kashi sprinkled with chocolate, the way Nanny made it. His suitcase made an awful sound, like a prison door scraping open. It reminded him of something that he pushed to the bottom of his mind. Of a night he did not want to remember. Why was Mrs. Milling just sitting there? Perhaps he hadn't been polite enough. Hadn't Tata taught him to introduce himself properly? "Pepik," he said, and extended his small hand. But someone gripped his shoulder from behind, and he turned to see a round man shaped very much like an egg, with skinny limbs sticking out from his body. The man's arms and legs made Pepik think of Tata's pipe cleaners.

Mrs. Milling stood up from her crouch. A blond wave had fallen from her hairpin; she tucked it behind her ear. "Is this your son?" she asked. "What a darling little —" But the man had a task to accomplish. He spoke to Pepik in the funny language and tried to pick him up. Pepik squirmed away and managed to drag his suitcase a few more feet towards Mrs. Milling.

He was going with *her*; she would feed him sweets for dinner and teach him to read, once and for all.

"Excuse me," Mrs. Milling said. "I didn't mean to intrude."

The egg-shaped man lifted Pepik's suitcase. He put it under one arm and lifted Pepik up under the other, gripping him firmly so his little legs were sticking out sideways and his face was looking down at the ground. Pepik's stomach lurched. He craned his neck, looking for Mrs. Milling. Where had she gone?

"Mamenka!" he shouted.

The man kept walking, carrying Pepik like a bundle of wood. He climbed some stairs up to a tram and set Pepik

down in the seat beside him. The man didn't speak to Pepik
for the next forty minutes.

They arrived at a house and a woman came out to greet
them and usher them in. She was older and greyer than Mrs.
Milling. A face like a slice of bloody roast beef.

"So here you are."

"*Jsem hladový*," Pepik said. He sat down on the floor cross-
legged.

The egg man shrugged at the woman. "Blimey." It was the
first word Pepik had heard from his mouth.

The woman bent down and inspected Pepik as if he were
a cabbage at the grocer's, picking through his hair, looking
behind his ears for dirt. The procedure continued for several
minutes; she seemed to be finding him deficient. Her voice
was kind though, and for a moment the little songbird stirred
inside Pepik's chest, the one that had sung for Mrs. Milling.
But the woman stood back up and crossed over to the kitchen.
There was a black line of soot running up the wall from the
stove to the ceiling. She took a cloth and rubbed at it vigorously. Then she looked back at the round man, as though surprised to still find him there. "Go on," she said.

She motioned with her chin in the direction of a set of
stairs. The man picked up the suitcase in one arm and Pepik in
the other as though he were a pile of lumber. Pepik went limp
and submitted.

The room at the top of the stairs had wallpaper that was
dotted with red and blue sailboats. The floorboards were blue,
like the sea. Two beds that smelled of mothballs were pushed
up against opposite walls: Pepik would sleep by the window.
The man plopped his suitcase down and looked at the second

bed, uncertain. There was someone in it, someone so small that he barely made a bump beneath the covers. Pepik tiptoed over and peered into the other boy's face. He had pale sandy hair and a light dusting of freckles across his nose. Clear, almost translucent skin. As though the little stove inside him that kept him alive was having trouble reaching all the way up to the surface.

"Artoor?"

The boy was still as stone.

"*Halò?*"

The boy gave a low moan. If this was Arthur, then the people downstairs were the Millings. It was Arthur's noise of pain that welcomed Pepik, that told him he'd reached his new home.

Several hours later Mrs. Milling — the real Mrs. Milling — came upstairs. She opened the gold clasps on Pepik's red suitcase. "*Pro boha, co je tohle?*" he said.

He had not seen its contents since leaving Prague; it was like a box of trinkets or magical charms, each one possessing a secret power.

The beautiful diamond watch could transport him back in time. And the little galoshes were for walking on water. He would cross the ocean on foot if he had to.

But he would not have to. His family would come and meet him. Nanny Marta had promised.

Mrs. Milling dug through the suitcase. She lifted the newly sewn little dress pants. "Well, aren't you the posh one," she said. "You come from money? Do you?"

She held up his nightshirt, which she changed him into quickly and efficiently, despite the fact that he was a big boy and able to do this by himself. Pepik realized he was not going to be made to brush his teeth. The sheets looked smooth but were rough to the touch, and he felt very high off the ground after sleeping for months in the bottom bunk in Prague. Mrs. Milling tucked him in tightly, so he could barely move his limbs. He felt like a letter sealed into an envelope.

"Chci napsat dopis," he said. *"Pani. Potřebuji pero. Můžeš mi podat pero, prosím?"*

Mrs. Milling looked at Pepik. Her face was a blank sheet of paper.

There was no bedtime story. Mrs. Milling left the room briefly and came back with a thermometer. Pepik opened wide and stuck out his tongue, but it was her son Arthur's temperature she was interested in. She gave the thermometer a vigorous shake after pulling it from Arthur's mouth, as though she hoped to change the number she saw there. Then she flicked off the light and the room was plunged into blackness.

"Sladký sen," Pepik said to nobody, and nobody answered him back.

He leaned back on his pillow. He could see out the window from his bed: the sky was slowly ticking down into a cool cobalt blue. There were a few stars out, messengers arrived too early. Down the length of the block there were long rows of brick houses, and warehouses with their gates closed and locked. The front windows were lit, small squares of yellow against the blackness, so that the street looked like a filmstrip. He thought of Snow White, of the Happy dwarf and his own Happy face, but he didn't feel happy; he felt terribly alone. If he crushed his head up against the wall he could see all the way down the street. He needed to keep watch for his family walking up the long road towards him.

Tata would be in the middle, with Mamenka and Nanny on each of his arms.

Pepik had smuggled his lead soldier into bed with him, and as his eyes adjusted he pushed the covers back and set the soldier on the windowsill. He sat up and crossed his legs, watching. He and his soldier standing guard together. How impressed Tata would be to see him up so late, defending the house, his gun at the ready.

"At ease," he commanded the soldier, roughly.

He didn't want anyone getting shot by mistake.

Across the room Arthur's breathing was raspy and irregular, like someone tuning a radio, stations coming in and out of range. There were long stretches between breaths. Only now, in the darkness, did Nanny's words come back: it was Pepik's job to help Arthur get better.

"Artoor?" he whispered.

There was phlegmy gasping from the other bed. Finally Arthur spoke. "I need help. Call my mother."

It was like hearing a dead body come suddenly back to life. Pepik imagined Arthur reaching out a clammy hand to touch him.

He didn't understand Arthur's words, and didn't answer.

∽๏∾

Morning was a needle plunged into his arm. He woke to a chill draft of air. The covers had been pulled back and Mrs. Milling was standing over him. Her eyes were small and black and her lips were pressed into a perfectly straight line. Pepik tried to pull his knees up to cover himself, but it was too late. He'd wet the bed. She had seen.

"*Zarmoucený*," Pepik said.

Mrs. Milling held her breath.

She worked quickly, matter-of-factly, pulling off Pepik's nightshirt and underpants. She managed to strip the sheets without moving him from the bed, manoeuvring his body into different positions and cradling his head under her arm. She bundled the offending sheets into her arms and left him there, naked and uncovered.

Pepik was cold, and the skin of his bottom was red and sore. The pain in his stomach reasserted itself, and he turned his head to the side and threw up on the blue floorboards.

Two minutes later Mrs. Milling returned carrying a pile of clean sheets. She was humming under her breath, but when she saw the vomit she stopped, her song breaking off mid-note. "What . . ." She leaned down and sniffed at the little pile of regurgitation, the white jelly of last night's boiled cauli-flower flecked with yellow. Then she shouted something in the direction of the hall; the round man emerged eventually at the top of the stairs, out of breath, a bottle of tomato ketchup in his hand.

"Look, Frank! He's ill!" Mrs. Milling motioned her husband over and showed him the vomit. "More germs for . . . Doctor Travers said . . ." She was talking quickly and gesturing at her son; she sounded like she might burst into tears.

Pepik rolled over and cradled his head in his hands. It dawned on him suddenly that morning had arrived. He'd fallen asleep at his post. Nanny hadn't come in the night, and Arthur was still sick. He had failed them. He had failed all of them.

By mid-morning Pepik was feeling a little better and half expected Mrs. Milling would make him go outside to play, but she preferred to treat him as a second sick son, bringing glasses of flat ginger ale to both boys, sterilizing the thermometer between uses. Later in the afternoon she came in to finish unpacking Pepik's suitcase, and found the unsealed envelope containing the photo. She took out the family portrait and looked at it closely, taking her time.

Mrs. Milling looked up at Pepik. "You poor darling," she said softly, as though she had just now realized that Pepik, too, had a family that loved him desperately. She pulled him against her in a kind of awkward squeeze.

When she went to put the picture back in the envelope, she paused, thinking better of it, and propped it up on Pepik's bedside table instead. There was Mamenka, looking off to the side; Nanny was behind Pepik, her hands on his shoulders, her eyes cast down at him, proud.

Mrs. Milling pointed to Nanny. "Mother," she said, enunciating clearly.

Pepik looked at her blankly; she said it a second time.

He repeated it back to her, one syllable and then the second. "Mo-ther."

Marta. *Mo-ther.*

His first English word.

Mother.

When Mrs. Milling was gone, Pepik picked up the photo. His head felt funny when he looked at Nanny's face. He rested his hot cheek against the cool plaster of the wall. Then he propped up the photo beside the lead soldier and placed the beautiful diamond watch beside that. It was like a row of three charms. The soldier stood for Tata with his Winchester rifle, and the watch for Mamenka, dressed up for a night on the town. The photo was Nanny: *mother*. He arranged them in one way and then shifted them around, as though he believed that if he stumbled on the correct order, he might evoke their flesh-and-blood equivalents.

Five nights had passed. They still hadn't arrived.

Pepik lay back. He let the three charms stand guard in his place.

He woke again a little later and opened one eye. Mrs. Milling was standing at the window, her grey hair straight to her shoulders. She held Pepik's diamond watch in one hand. She was looking at it closely, running her finger over the stones, as though wondering if it could possibly be real. He saw her hesitate for a minute. He saw her slip the watch into her pocket.

Pepik had crawled into Arthur's bed. He was so lonely; the other child's presence helped him sleep. It had been hours, though, since he'd felt Arthur move. Mrs. Milling crossed the floorboards towards the two boys and Pepik closed his eyes tightly, as though to make himself disappear. She touched his shoulder and began to talk crossly, starting up a stream of

English scolding. It was the third time this had happened, and she did not want Pepik giving Arthur any more germs.

Mrs. Milling lifted the covers briskly, like a waiter lifting a silver dome from a plate of food. Pepik saw her fingernails, bitten to the quick. She leaned forward to feel her son's forehead, and paused with her palm an inch from his skin.

"Arthur?"

She said it like a question and waited for a reply. When none was forthcoming she said it again, sharply this time — *Arthur* — and a third time, and a fourth. She held his chin in her hand and moved his head from side to side, grasped his little shoulders and squeezed. She was repeating his name, her voice gaining strength like a siren.

Pepik saw the first tear appear, like the first star on a late summer evening.

It trembled in the bottom corner of her eye, hanging there for what seemed like an eternity. It grew and swelled and finally slipped off her bottom lashes, missing the bedspread and landing on the blue floorboards.

Pepik imagined he heard a little splash.

More tears followed, pouring from Mrs. Milling's eyes. Pepik was pushed from the bed and went into the corner of the room and curled in a ball and covered his ears. Mrs. Milling was screaming. She was shouting for her husband and shaking Arthur's body, her face bright red, her eyes wide. She collapsed over the bed, pressing her face into her son's chest, her wide shoulders heaving. She shook Arthur again and again, as though she couldn't believe it, as though if she shook him hard enough his pale eyelids would flutter open.

Arthur was still and white, his features carved out of wax.

Mrs. Milling screamed as if she were being torn to pieces. She pawed at her face and pulled at her hair, sobbing.

Hearing Mrs. Milling opened something in Pepik, punctured a raft made of twigs and balloons. Water rushed in. It covered his legs — he wet himself almost immediately, the urine seeping out around him in a circle on the floor — and rose past his chest, and then his shoulders. It filled his mouth and he choked and gagged; he put his hand to his face and found it soaking. He was crying so hard he could not get his breath. He doubled over, vomiting. Everything from the past year that he had managed to bury inside him was being pulled up through his body, ripped out of his mouth. The sharks were below him, his legs in their jaws. He let go. He was quickly pulled under.

Pepik was sent to a home full of boys. An orphanage run by the Catholic Church. At night the big room fell silent. It was a silence that filled up with deep breathing, the creak of springs as someone turned over, a fart followed by laughter. The boys fell asleep one by one, like candles being blown out on a birthday cake.

Pepik lay still, eyes wide open, picturing his hunger. He was an empty shell alone on a beach in the moonlight. The waves came and went; he was filled and then emptied. Emptied, and then emptied again.

He knew he had just arrived, but where had he come from? Arthur was hazy and vague around the edges. Pepik thought back to that long, quiet street. To the hours and days he had spent watching by the window.

For whom had he been waiting? The people in his photo? Whoever they were, they would never find him now.

They would come from the east, looking for a ghost. Dragging their shadows behind them.

PART FIVE

PAVEL AND ANNELIESE

June 1939

Dear Pepik,

Mamenka and I send you a hug and a snuggle. We look at your photograph every day and pray to God for your safekeeping. But why have you not written, miláčku? How we long to hear from you. To hear any news from you at all.

Your Nanny Marta sends you many kisses as well.

I hope you have been receiving our letters, that Mrs. Milling has been able to find someone to translate them into Czech for you. I am sorry we did not have time to help you learn more English before you left. I know the Millings will teach you the language and will help you answer our requests.

Please tell us what you are doing every day, and what you are eating. And about your new friend Arthur. We know you will be very kind to him and help him get better.

The house is so quiet without you. We miss your train tearing around its track. I am almost inclined to set it back up.

A train will always remind me of you.

I will sign off for now, but I promise to write again soon. And you do the same. We will all be most happy to receive some news from our darling big boy.

With love and kisses,
Tata

(FILE UNDER: Bauer, Pavel. Died Auschwitz, 1944)

I KNEW AS SOON AS I HEARD THE DOORBELL RING.

I had not given you my address, but deep down I'd been expecting you. A slight man with sloped shoulders and bushy grey eyebrows. Dandruff on your jacket. You were leaning on a cane. You wore that dour expression I've come to recognize, the resignation that is almost a kind of play-acting: choosing to go through the motions of living for the benefit of the outside world.

It's a show badly acted, a small child's charade.

And it's true that, although you were in your seventies, there was still something of a child in your eyes.

"I'm Lisa," I said.

You held out a hand: hair on the knuckles. "Joseph."

Name changes are common, and translations into English. I didn't miss a beat. "I know who you are."

You looked almost as though you recognized me too — squinting, trying to place a vaguely familiar face.

When of course you didn't know me from Adam. Or Eve.

"Will you come in for tea?"

I could see you taking in the dirty casserole dish in the sink, the towering stacks of periodicals against the walls. There was nothing I could offer you to eat: the fridge was empty save for some Chinese takeout mouldering in a Styrofoam container. From the way you looked around my apartment I gleaned you were the fastidious type, that your own small house was perfectly neat and organized. But instead of feeling self-conscious I experienced a kind of relief, the relief of being seen for myself, for who I really am. You made yourself at home, looking for somewhere to hang your coat.

"I'll take it," I said.

Our fingers touched as you passed the coat to me, and I felt a rush: here was the child from the letter I'd been carrying. Here, in front of me. In the flesh. The most important Jewish prayer — the first one I learned — ran through my head: *Shema Yisrael Adonai Eloheinu Adonai Echad.*

Hear, O Israel: the Lord is our God, the Lord is One.

When I looked up, you were moving a pile of blankets off the end of the sofa. You patted the space. "Come and sit." I was jerked out of my spiritual reveries, irked that you thought the hospitality was yours to offer. But then I saw this was just your way of getting down to business.

People become nervous when they learn new things about their past.

"Tell me everything," you said, before I could even sit down.

I thought to myself, *If only.* Because, of course, there is so little I know. And so much more that's been lost.

"I'm Lisa," I said again, and launched into my shtick, explaining my tenure in the Holocaust Studies department, the oral histories I've been taking from the Kindertransport children. You were nodding rapidly — this was all information I'd left on your answering machine — but I was reciting it mostly for myself, to ground myself in the facts of my own existence. Because I too feel displaced and uprooted. I too have very little to cling onto.

"You found . . . what? A letter?" you asked.

"Some letters. From your mother and father."

"To me?"

"Just a minute."

I went into the study and brought out the thick file. Written on the cover in blue magic marker were the words: "BAUER, PEPIK (PAVEL AND ANNELIESE)." An address followed. The sevens had dashes through them in the old-fashioned European style.

I could see you were unprepared. "I thought that nobody wrote to me," you said, your eyes on the names.

"Yes," I said. "I gathered that."

I was ready to tell you the whole chain of events — the visit to the archive that had turned these up along with several other files from the area — but I saw then that the details would only muddle things. I looked at you, my gaze steady.

"I thought I had no parents," you said.

"Everyone has parents."

"You know what I mean."

"What about the photo of your family? The one you told me about on the phone?"

"But I had no reason to believe they tried to contact me."

"Shall I get our tea?" I asked.

But you weren't interested in tea. "I thought —" you said. "What happened to them?"

I didn't answer right away. About either what I knew or what I didn't know. "You're Jewish," I said finally, thinking this would give you a clue.

You looked at me blankly. "I go to church," was all you said.

So there it was. Someone else lost.

"Of course you do," I said. "Of course."

There was a look on your face that was almost but not quite indifference, as though we were talking about something with nothing whatsoever to do with you, something at a great remove. But I've learned not to be fooled by an apparent lack of interest. It is almost always the legacy of dashed hopes.

"So those are letters from my parents?" You raised your eyebrows at the thick file.

"Didn't I already —?"

"From both of them?"

"And from your nanny."

A look crossed your face then that I've not quite seen before. It was as if you had been slapped unexpectedly by someone you knew and trusted. "A nanny?" you asked. "I didn't — I had no —" But you did remember; it was coming back into your body, sluicing through you like a tidal wave, complete and overpowering. "Her name was . . . ?"

"Marta," I said.

You nodded, eyes upward. "Yes."

What would it be like to know nothing of your origins, to spend decades craving and wondering, and then, at the end of your life, to be delivered an answer? To realize that all your misery was for nothing, that you'd been wanted after all.

Wasn't that what I was hoping for too?

"Where did they come from?"

"Your family?"

"The letters."

"From the estate of a family named Milling. Where you were placed, very briefly, before . . ."

I paused here, not wanting to name what had happened after that.

Your eyes bugged out a little and you looked as though you were drowning. "I have no recollection of anyone named Milling," you said stiffly. But you were holding your temples in the palms of your hands and your eyes were darting from side to side.

"Why don't I give you a moment."

You nodded, grateful, and I headed for the door. When I reached the threshold, I looked back. You were still holding your head in your hands.

The distance you'd travelled was hard to imagine. The train trips, the boat rides. Later, the airplanes. And those, of course, were only the geographical trips. I don't have to mention the other kinds of displacements, the other leaps you'd made. When I looked at you that day, you seemed so overwhelmed, a jet-lagged, bedraggled voyageur.

I left you alone to read your family's letters. Went into my office and checked my email. I politely but firmly declined a request from a doctoral student looking for a supervisor in the field. Perhaps I was not polite. I was certainly firm. I could see you through the open door: you had leaned your cane against the wall, its handle stooped like your own shoulders. You sat down in front of the letters. "And so," you said. When you finally flipped the file open, the action was fast and decisive, like ripping off a Band-Aid.

I forced my gaze back to the computer, where I read a notice about a department meeting three times, not registering anything. I don't know why the secretary — Marsha? Melinda? — still sends me these things. She knows I've retired. When I looked back up, I saw two letters on the table in front of you, laid out one beside the other. I'd had the letters translated, and I could tell you were suspicious, lining the English up against the Czech, as if some mistake might be revealed in the space between. I called out, "Pepik!" You didn't lift your head. "Joseph," I said, remembering. "Are you . . . okay in there?"

You waved your hand in the air without looking up, as if you were shooing away a dog.

It pleased me a little, this offhand gesture, as though you knew me well, had known me forever.

When I came in half an hour later, your cheeks were wet with tears. I pretended not to notice.

"You can keep the file if you want," I said. I was surprised to hear myself offer this; usually I just give out photocopies.

"Yes," you said. "Please." And then, "I have so many questions."

"Shoot," I said. But you only sat there with the thick manila file in your hands. You took a deep breath and exhaled slowly. "These are just —" You looked up at me weakly.

"Heartbreaking?"

"Yes."

I lifted my hand to brush a hair off your jacket but lowered it again, not wanting to seem patronizing.

"They loved me," you said.

"Yes."

"And they ended up . . ." Your voice trailed off. You gripped your cane as though it could support you even from your seated position. "What happened to the baby?" you asked. "The one from my photo."

I hesitated, hating to be the bearer of more bad news.

"I don't know for certain."

You nodded. "Okay."

We looked at each other for a long moment.

"You think she . . . ?" you began.

"I think —" But again I lost my nerve. I've had this conversation many times, but the cliché is true: it doesn't get easier.

"Lisa," you said. My head snapped up at my name. You were looking at me steadily, as though to reassure me — to reassure both of us — that whatever I had to say could not be that bad. "That baby — Is she you?"

"She isn't," I said. "I'm not."

"What happened to her then?" you asked again.

There was no choice but to tell you the truth.

I answered. "That baby was killed."

Most often they come looking for me.

Everyone has a story to tell, and the children of the Diaspora are no different. They want to be heard, like everyone else. Heard and understood. Even more so.

Years ago I was invited to be a keynote speaker at the second official Kindertransport reunion. At the opening banquet I gave my usual spiel, and when I got down from the podium I was practically mobbed. At a certain age we all become aware of our mortality, and suffice it to say that these people were already well past that age. Blue hair and dentures. Sour breath.

I know, I know — who am I to talk?

I booked enough interviews that weekend to fill my entire next book. It would be relatively easy to write — a summary of the transcriptions, a qualitative analysis using variables of selfhood and self-concept. And yet, as I gathered names and email addresses — or phone numbers, because many of my would-be subjects didn't have email — I was aware that something was missing, that the most important piece of the puzzle had not yet fallen into place.

I began to fear I'd been on the wrong path. That I should have been writing something else altogether.

And so it was that I showed up at your place seven days after our first meeting. Your home was a bungalow in the west end of Notre-Dame-de-Grâce, red brick with a wire fence enclosing the small backyard. Inside, the house was organized and clean, sparsely furnished. Cream-coloured carpet covered every square inch of the floor, kitchen included. I thought this was odd. Perhaps you didn't want your feet ever to get cold.

You had spent the entire intervening week reading and rereading the letters from your parents and Marta. I don't know how I knew this, since you didn't mention it and the letters were stacked neatly in the folder, which was itself placed neatly in the centre of the dining room table. But I got a flash, as if in a horror movie, of the table's gleaming surface scattered with the papers and you, late at night, half mad, with your head in your hands.

You looked at me directly, composed. You were wearing a worn grey sweater with leather patches on the elbows. There was a pot in a tea cozy and a plate of store-bought cookies, the variety pack: rectangular chocolate, round vanilla with cherry jelly in the centre. Despite the table's being set for tea I saw you were not interested in small talk. "How long have you had these?" you asked, pointing at the folder of letters.

I needed a moment to compose myself. I pulled back a chair and sat down. Then I nodded at the cups and saucers. "Shall we?"

"How long?" you repeated.

"Six months."

You were still standing, your knuckles gnarled against the handle of your cane. "Then why didn't you —" But you stopped, remembering that it was you who had stood me up at the deli and not the other way around. "I don't know what I was expecting," you said at last. "Something else. Not this." And you spread your free hand in front of you, as though presenting me with the letters yourself. I recognized the helplessness inherent in the gesture.

"So," I said, "tell me what you thought."

I've learned to ask open-ended questions, and I thought this would get you started, but you just shook your head and walked over to the kitchen counter. You stood by the window over the sink, looking out at the tiny fenced-in yard. There was one letter you had removed from the file, a letter you had singled out from the others. With your back towards me you picked it up from the counter and began to read. Your voice was steady, with a kind of restraint in it, as if you were a tightrope walker and each word in front of you a step.

You had to focus very hard not to fall off.

"'Dear Pepik,'" you read. "'Mamenka and I send you a hug and a snuggle. We look at your photograph every day and pray to God for your safekeeping. But why have you not written, *miláčku*? We are desperate to hear from you. To hear any news from you at all.'"

It was the letter, of course, that I was intimately familiar with. But hearing it read by the grown child to whom it had been addressed . . . When you finished reading I tried to but could not look you in the face. It was too bare, too personal. I had never in my life felt so close to someone and at the same time so impossibly far away.

I didn't meet your gaze, afraid of what would be revealed if I looked up.

"I want to thank you, Lisa," you said finally, in that half-Czech, half-Scottish lilt of yours. "For getting in touch. You have changed — I don't know how —"

You cleared your throat and looked down at the letter held loosely in your hand, the letter that had arrived so improbably across an ocean of time and grief. The file folder was still in the middle of the table, and you opened it and found the place where the letter belonged chronologically. You put it back in, closed the folder, and patted it just once. A gesture that said *There now, that's finished*.

Then you got up and went over to a small desk in the corner of the room. "Now it's my turn," you said. "I have something to show you."

You came back and placed a photograph in front of me on the table, the one you had told me about. It was obviously old, with a yellowing border and a big crease down the centre where it had been folded. There were two women in the photograph. One must have been Anneliese Bauer. The other I knew to be Marta.

There was also a man with a baby in his arms. Here was the sibling you'd always known about. She was swaddled in a blanket, her tiny face obscured. But it was the baby's father who captured my attention. Pavel Bauer. I stared at his features, drinking him in. He was maybe five feet eight inches — nine maximum — with slight shoulders. But sure of himself. Even through the photograph I could feel his steady presence. And I wasn't just seeing what I wanted to see.

I could have stared at him for hours, the dark hair and sloping brow, but you pointed to the fifth person, the boy in the picture. It was easy to see, even across the vast stretch of time, that the child was you. The same bright eyes, the stubborn jaw. Small, like your father. A scrawny child.

I refrained from saying this aloud.

You pointed next to Marta, who was standing behind you in a cardigan and a simple housedress. Her dark curls were pinned at the nape of her neck. She was just behind your right shoulder, holding herself a little stiffly for the camera.

"That's my mother," you said. You were proud, but trying to conceal it. You cleared your throat and pointed at her face again.

We stayed like that for a minute, looking down at the photo together.

When I finally spoke, it was as if someone else were animating me: the words seemed to come of their own free will. I turned towards you.

"Joseph," I said — Joseph or Pepik: I never knew which to call you. "That wasn't your mother," I said.

You looked at me as if I'd given you two weeks to live. That same gape, the incomprehension.

"That's my mother," you said forcefully. This was the one thing you knew, the thing you remembered to be true, and you weren't about to let me take it away so easily. You pointed again to Marta. Your finger covered her face. "Don't you recognize me?" you said.

"Yes. The little boy is you. But the other woman" — I pointed at Anneliese — "she was your mother."

In the photograph Anneliese was looking uneasily in the opposite direction. You flicked your eyes over her.

"That one?"

"Anneliese. Pavel's wife."

You tapped your fingernail on Marta. "What about her? The one touching my shoulder."

"She wasn't your mother."

"Who was she?"

"Your nanny."

"She was my mother?"

"No. She was mine."

～⊗～

Anneliese Bauer disappeared entirely. It's hard to make sense of this: someone exists and then doesn't. Her diamond watch is all that's left of her. I couldn't believe it had survived all this time, something so valuable: the archivist who gave it to me said she'd found it after the Millings died. She knew by the inscription that it had not belonged to them, and figured the rest out via the letters in the safety deposit box. The watch had stopped, of course. I had it repaired. Time took up its post again, resumed the heavy lifting. Memory is a stone that is difficult to budge. Especially as it applies to family. To Pepik's and mine.

We were half-siblings, you see. We shared a father. Pavel. In some ways we shared a mother too. Marta was — must have been — extremely close to Pepik. I was her only biological child, however. There's part of her that only I can claim.

Pepik's cancer had spread throughout his body by the time of our first meeting. I didn't know it the day I visited him, but already nothing could be done. He was well enough at first though, and for the next few months I visited him regularly. I would take the bus across Montreal and we would walk on the mountain in the evenings. We imagined that the city spread out below us was Prague, the last city where our parents were alive. We wondered aloud about our father, Pavel Bauer. Did he ever stroll with Pepik's mother, Anneliese, in the long hot summer of 1939? Did he stroll with Marta — with *my* mother? We were like gossipy teenagers, Pepik and I. We did everything together. Once I even went to church with him, although it pained me a little to rub up so closely against his loss of faith. I myself do not believe in god, so it isn't the Jewish religion that I grieve but the culture embedded in it.

Or maybe it is the other way around.

Either way, when I think of the human potential stolen, of the millions of little lights snuffed out, I can't help but wish for a kind of redemption. I can't help but wish that the living, at least, would embrace what was taken from the dead.

Not that I am one to talk.

But then again, since Marta wasn't Jewish, I feel myself not especially welcome. Judaism is passed down on the mother's side, so I don't officially count.

I would, of course, have been Jewish enough for Hitler. I assume that is part of the reason my mother left the Bauers when Pavel got her pregnant. Or perhaps the Bauers sent her away themselves. There was Anneliese to think about. Still, I grieve the Jewish half of myself I grew up not knowing, and I try in my own way to honour it. I have a Star of David that belonged to my father, Pavel — my mother passed it on to me before her death. I wear it under my sweater, next to my heart. I even keep the Sabbath in a manner of speaking. Joseph — Pepik — refused to join me: he said it felt unnatural. So I would eat by myself, fumble my way through the blessings over the bread and wine. I still do this most Friday nights. I could seek out other people, but I have no real desire. It's the time of the week I feel most acutely alone. And I feel a kind of perverse enjoyment in it.

I did, as I've said, once have a lover — a woman, yes — but that was so long ago now.

The list of those lost grows.

"Was I right about your baby sister? She was killed?" I asked Pepik that day when I first visited his home. We had gone out into the small fenced-in yard. The clouds were low and grey. "Your full sister," I clarified.

He turned his face towards me. "Why do you ask me?"

"I thought you might have done some research."

And it turned out he had. In the week since I'd delivered the letters he'd put the other pieces in place.

"Yes, you were right," he said. "Theresienstadt. Auschwitz." The rubber tip of his cane was sinking into the dark earth. "I thought it was you. The baby in my photo."

I told him again that it couldn't have been. The date on the back of the photo said 1937, and I didn't come along until several years later. Until Pepik had already been sent away to Scotland. So the baby in the picture was a second sibling he'd never known.

It was also hard at first to make him believe that Marta wasn't his mother. I pointed repeatedly at Anneliese: he spent a long time looking at her face.

Yes, he said, he did remember something. Yes, there was a flicker.

But when he looked at Marta, her hand on his young shoulder, the word *mother* flashed across his mind.

I can see what he was thinking. In the photo, Anneliese is holding herself slightly apart and her eyes are to the side, as though something else has caught her attention, something slightly fearsome that is moving towards her. Marta is the one who is leaning into Pepik, whose gaze is cast down in his direction. If I had to pick the mother of the pair I would pick Marta too. There's a tenderness to her, a warmth that makes me know I was lucky to be her child, even for the short time we lived together on this earth. There was also a particular naïveté about her, something close to childlike. She didn't know what was coming.

My mother, Marta, died in a DP camp in 1946. She had nobody left to help her. She got sick, and she perished.

What did you expect? A happy ending?

Sometimes I am envious of the Kindertransport children I study, who often have no memory of their childhoods. This oblivion seems to have passed me by. There are things from my childhood I remember in near-perfect detail, from the years both before and after my mother's death. Things that haven't helped me live a happy life. Oh no, quite the opposite has been true.

Meeting Pepik was a bit of goodness, though. We had a small window of time in which to enjoy the gift we'd found. We'd been alone all our lives, and suddenly we each had family. When he grew too feeble to walk on the mountain, we would go to the parkette across from the depanneur, sit on the cold bench, and watch the pigeons pick potato-chip bags off the sidewalk. There was not joy, exactly, in finding each other — we were too old, too set in our ways — but our pain was dulled. What we felt was not quite pleasure, but contentment. We had each finished our searching.

The truth is I know almost nothing about what happened in the Bauer household in the fall of 1938 and the spring and summer of 1939. The events I have put down here seem as likely as any others — that's all. It was my hope, in the last year of my half-brother's life, to construct some kind of narrative, a story for him to hang on to. In the final months he reminded me so very much of a child, lost under the sheets of his sick-bed. Like a small boy waiting for a bedtime story, as though he had been waiting all his long life for someone to come and tuck him in.

And so I did. I wrote during the days: the story of Pavel and Anneliese Bauer, the story of their child's governess, Marta. Then, in the evenings, I went to Pepik's house and relieved the home-care nurse I'd hired. I sat by Pepik's bedside and read him the story, one chapter at a time, as I wrote it. I used the letters in my possession to cobble together a version of events, arranging disparate pieces into something that seemed whole.

Pepik would comment when his gut told him something had been different, and I made notes in the margins and typed in the changes at my desk the following day. A few things we put down with a high degree of certainty. The rest we made up, taking scraps from our dreams, setting them on paper to make them make sense.

As I said before, though, this isn't a story with a happy ending.

They're all dead now.

Pavel, my father.

Marta, my mother.

Pepik's mother, Anneliese.

Pepik himself died a year and four months after I met him. The cancer was everywhere; he was in so much pain that I couldn't fault him for refusing treatment at the end. My only regret is that he died before I could finish writing the story. I wanted so much for him to have some sense of completion, some resolution — even imagined — to the tragedy that opened his life.

Instead I was left to write the final chapter as a tribute. I've put it down here in memoriam. For Pepik.

EIGHT

SUMMER SOLSTICE ARRIVED LIKE A slap across the face. The Jews were officially expelled from the economic life of Prague. The whole Protectorate of Bohemia and Moravia would be *Aryanized*: this was the word the Nazis were using. The singing of "Má Vlast," the patriotic song that had caused such an uproar at the National Theatre the previous winter, was banned in pubs and cafés. It was against the law to boo during German newsreels. Cutting German telephone lines was punishable by death. And Reichsprotektor von Neurath could now make laws on his own. No confirmation needed from the courts; his whims would become part of the Czech criminal code, just like that.

Karl Frank had given a speech: "Where once the swastika flies, there it will fly forever."

By law — as Ernst had predicted to Marta — the Bauers were forced to register all their assets.

"I'm a respectable citizen," Pavel said sadly as he sat in the dining room one evening. "A factory owner. Kind to my workers." He held a paper clip in his hand, bending it into a straight line. "I even supported the land reform," he said. "Which meant giving up land out of principle."

His papers were spread over every piece of furniture. Marta was in the kitchen, chopping onions. She wondered how she was supposed to set the table for their meal when it was covered with carbon paper and pencil shavings. "What if I just don't do it?" Pavel asked. "What if I don't register my assets?"

Marta saw Anneliese look up from the *Prager tagblatt*.

"You'll get us killed," she said evenly. She was wearing a new navy blue dress, her dark curls pinned in two buns on either side of her head.

"But how will they know?" Marta heard Pavel ask. "The company, fine. But the other . . ." He cleared his throat. Marta wasn't sure if he was referring to the Canadian railway bonds or to his mother's villa on the Seine or to various bank accounts he might or might not have opened in other countries. Ernst had got his hands on some of Pavel's money but had been unsuccessful, Marta surmised, at accessing the bulk of his estate. So at least there was that small consolation.

The onions stung her eyes; she wiped away a tear with the back of her arm. Through the open kitchen arch she saw Pavel jab at the paper in front of him with the tip of his pencil. "How do they define a Jewish company?" he asked Anneliese. "What does it mean, 'under the decisive influence of Jews'?" He made quotes in the air with his fingers. "It means nothing. You can't prove that anything is 'under the decisive influence' of anyone at all!"

Anneliese put her newspaper down and crossed the room. She stood with her back to her husband, staring out the window. "They're going to take it all now. Turn everything over to the *Treuhänder*. No exceptions." She lifted a foot, balancing on one ruby heel.

"How are you such an expert all of a sudden?"

"It doesn't take a genius," Anneliese said.

Marta thought Anneliese sounded a little defensive. She wiped her hands on her apron and dumped the onion peels in the bin. She came into the parlour.

"My father," Pavel was saying, "fought for the Germans in the Great War."

"Really?" Marta asked.

"Yes," he said. Surprised she didn't already know. He picked up the paperclip and dug the point into the pad of his thumb. "So they'll come and take the flat. And send us where? On vacation?"

"Just wait a little longer." Anneliese's voice was firm. "Something will happen."

But Pavel loosened his blue silk tie, pulled it off, and threw it down on the table. "What do you mean, 'something will happen'? Something like God sending down an Egyptian plague? Or something more along the lines of our child being sent out into the wild blue yonder never to be heard from again?"

Because this was the heart of it, Marta knew, the thing nobody was saying. It had been almost a month, and still no word from the Millings. Mathilde Baeck had received several letters, two from the foster parents, and a drawing by her Clara of the Hook of Holland, the sun rising over the bow of a big ship on which a herd of stick children were grinning. Marta tried to feel happy for the Baecks, happy that at least some people knew the whereabouts of their child, but despite herself she felt the unfairness of it, and a bitter jealousy. It was not that she begrudged Mrs. Baeck her knowledge of her daughter but that she so wished for something comparable from Pepik. Her longing for news of him was physical; her arms hurt for wanting to hold him. Already she was beginning to forget his voice, the little suckling sounds he made as he was falling asleep. His train was abandoned; the track was dismantled and pushed to the back of the closet. The lead soldiers were buried like casualties in a shoebox beneath the bottom bunk. There was no train under the parlour table now, but a ghost train had replaced the real one, and this at least was vivid in Marta's imagination. She could see it flashing around the silver loop of its track, could hear the little bell singing its departure.

Anneliese was now gone from home almost all the time. She reappeared at odd hours, wearing shoes Marta didn't recognize. Once she came home with a big bouquet of roses — difficult to get under the ruling Nazis — and Marta found a card torn up past legibility in the wastebasket. Not that she was snooping, of course. It was her *job* to take out the garbage.

She went into Max's study to empty the bin there and found Pavel sitting behind the desk. The room smelled musty, like dust and ink. Darkness had fallen; Marta crossed the room and switched on the lamp. The little pool of light lit up Pavel's face from below; he was wearing an expression of perfect sadness, his mouth turned down at the corners.

Pepik's Sad face.

"Are you busy?" Marta asked.

There was a piece of paper in front of Pavel, a sheet of Bauer and Sons stationery. He was holding a fountain pen in his hand. "No, not busy," he said. But he was casually trying to cover the letter with his elbow.

"I can just . . ." she said, nodding at the door. "If you're in the middle of something."

"No," Pavel said. "Please." He motioned to the straight-backed chair across from him. She wished he would come out from behind the desk and sit with her, as he sometimes did, in the velvet armchairs by the window — she felt like a client in a law office with the huge expanse of wood between them. But he stayed where he was and Marta made herself as comfortable as she could. Pavel, she saw, had pushed his paper under an atlas.

"I had a hopeful letter yesterday, from the embassy in Argentina," he said. "When I followed up today, though, they told me my contact had been terminated."

"I'm sorry to hear that," Marta said. Truthfully, though, it was to be expected. Nobody was able to get out anymore. She was a little surprised that Pavel kept trying.

"Where's the bin?" she asked, remembering what she'd come to do. She bent and looked under the desk.

Pavel ignored the question. "Slivovitz?" he asked. There was a silver tray with a bottle on the desk, and two little shot glasses.

She straightened and nodded. "Thank you," she said. "Then let's write to Pepik."

Pavel uncorked the decanter; it made a loud *pop*. He cleared his throat. "I was just doing that."

"Of course," Marta said; she tried to keep her voice steady. But she lowered her eyes and looked at her hands. She'd thought writing to Pepik was something they shared, a common activity that drew them together. They'd been writing to him for days now: it was like reading to someone in a coma — there was no way to know how much was getting through. Pavel wrote in big block letters, as though his son might be able to read them himself, and Marta didn't remind him otherwise. She felt it excused her own childlike hand. She addressed each envelope, added an AIRMAIL sticker, and affixed the Nazi postage. She sent each letter separately, so there would be more for Pepik to open.

The days went by and they waited. No reply.

"I was writing to the Millings, in fact," Pavel said now, filling their glasses. Marta knew that he wrote frequently to his son's temporary parents, thanking them for the safekeeping of his son. He never forgot to ask after Arthur, he'd told her, and send his best wishes for their son's speedy recovery. He even went so far as to send his prayers.

He stoppered the bottle and looked up at her. "I was asking if the Millings need any work done. You know," he said, speaking quickly, "if they need a handyman. Or someone to drive their car."

Marta squinted, not comprehending.

"If they need me to do any work," Pavel said. He looked at her fiercely, ashamed but defiant, and she saw all at once: he would be a butler, or a chauffeur. Anything to get them out. It was much easier to get the exit papers, she knew, if you had a letter of employment.

Still, this was wrong. It was not the way the world was meant to be. There was an order to things, and Marta did not want to think of Pavel, so kind and upstanding, as a servant in someone else's home. She did not want to imagine him humbled that way. If this could happen to him then nobody was safe; there was no way of protecting oneself after all. A bit of blackness began to creep into her body. It was instantly recognizable, a grey haze at the edge of her vision that made her see things as other than they were. And the weight in her chest, the sense she was drowning . . .

She tried to change the subject. "Who is this Adolf Eichmann exactly?" She'd heard someone in line at the butcher's say that the high-ranking Nazi had arrived in Prague.

Pavel's voice was brisk. "The SS Jewish expert. So-called." He drained his glass in the manner of the Russians: politely, but completely. He raised his hand. "Another?"

But Marta's drink was untouched.

"Eichmann heads the Zentralstelle für jüdische Auswanderung," Pavel said. "The SS department in charge of robbing and expelling the Jews. They set up shop in Vienna last year." He paused, and she knew he was thinking of his brother Misha, forced to scrub the streets and then drink his pail of dirty water. Where was he now? And his son, Tomáš, and his young wife, Lore?

Pavel tipped his head back and swallowed again: two short bobs of his Adam's apple. The room had gone from dusky to dark. The light from the lamp barely touched it. Marta expected this would be the end of the conversation, but Pavel said, "I saw him last week. Eichmann. Passing in the street. He looked . . ." He gave a half-smile. "He looked like a dog."

"Eichmann? You saw him?"

Pavel nodded and she tried to imagine the man: small black eyes like messengers of death. Just then the doorbell rang. Marta put down her glass and ran a hand over her curls, stood up and straightened her skirt. She went into the front hall, Pavel following, both of them expecting a boy with a telegram. But it was as if Pavel's description had conjured Eichmann out of thin air, and there he was in front of them.

"*Guten tag,*" he said. "I'm sorry to bother you." His jaw was vaguely canine, it was true, but he was cleanly shaven, his hair cut very short, and so polite that Marta felt the Nazi uniform must be a mistake: he must be heading out to some sort of costume party or masquerade.

Behind her she felt Pavel freeze. He was taking in the stylized swastika, the military decorations. She could tell his instinct was to turn and run, but faced with this man, this paragon of good behaviour, the gentleman in Pavel rose to the surface to meet him. "Please come in," he said, his German perfect. One man of the world recognizing another.

The man introduced himself: "*Ich bin?* Werner Axmann."

So, not Adolf Eichmann after all. But a Nazi on your doorstep could mean only one thing.

And yet, Marta thought, the man was behaving strangely. He did not seem about to drag them off and throw them in prison. He hesitated, like a shy boy summoned to the front of the classroom to give a speech. Like Pepik, she thought for a moment, but the comparison was unseemly and she pushed it quickly from her mind. In front of her the officer stood waiting for inspiration, waiting for something to materialize from within the flat to guide him. A moment of silence passed. He looked down into his folded hands as though trying to read crib notes hidden there. "I'm sorry to disturb you, Mr. Bauer," he said again, "but is your wife at home?"

The question was met by Pavel's blank stare. "*Sicherlich,*" he said, but he made no move to fetch Anneliese.

The officer's square jaw was set. He had green eyes, Marta

saw, that looked almost like chips of emerald. He cleared his throat and shifted from one foot to the other. Somebody had to do something, Marta thought. She turned to get Anneliese and saw that Mrs. Bauer had already come into the room behind them. Her red lipstick was fresh, her eyes wide with fear. Marta said, "Mrs. Bauer, there's somebody here to —" And then she looked at Anneliese again and saw surprise of a different kind on her face. Mrs. Bauer already knew this young officer. All at once it was clear to Marta that Anneliese was not about to be hauled off to Dachau. That the German was paying her a different kind of visit.

Anneliese stared at the man. "What are you doing here?" She closed her eyes and shook her head almost imperceptibly. "You promised me you wouldn't . . ."

Marta looked over at Pavel. His cheeks were burning red. He too was starting to understand.

"I told you never to —" Anneliese said, but she couldn't finish. Her eyes were full of tears. She looked from the young man to Pavel and back, two parts of her life colliding. The officer took a step into the hallway. His boots squeaked on the floorboards. He was younger than Pavel, bashful but emboldened. There was nothing Pavel could do to hurt him.

It was Pavel who spoke first. "If you have business to attend to with my wife," he said stiffly, "I would ask that you attend to it elsewhere." He did not look at Anneliese.

The younger man acquiesced, apologetic. "It will take only a moment." He said to Anneliese, "I'm very sorry to disturb you, Mrs. Bauer." He spoke formally, Marta thought, but his expression betrayed a close familiarity. He raised his eyebrows at her: *Let's get out of here.*

Anneliese had no choice. She crossed the floor and took her hat with the blue ribbon from the stand. She followed her young officer out the door.

It occurred to Marta then that life was inherently unstable. That things were always changing, and just when you thought you'd reached some sort of balance, some kind of understanding, everything would change again. That this, ultimately, was the only thing to count on. She'd thought she knew Anneliese — she did, she supposed, in many ways — but here was the wild card, the blind spot made suddenly clear. And though it was easy to judge what she now saw, she realized also that it wasn't that simple.

The officer, for example: he must actually care deeply for Anneliese. Whatever was going on between them exactly, he was willing to risk his position — and maybe his life — to spend time in her company.

They looked good together, Marta thought. An attractive German couple.

You'd never guess. If you didn't already know.

That evening Marta followed Pavel into the study. They stayed in there with the door closed for quite some time.

They did not speak of what had happened earlier, of the German or the various repercussions of what had been revealed. Instead they wrote Pepik, and then sat in quietness drinking their tea.

"I received an odd telegram from Ernst today," Pavel said. "I wonder about him sometimes."

"You wonder?"

"I just get the feeling — I can't really believe —"

Marta stopped with her teacup halfway between the saucer and her lips. The linden-scented steam. "You can't believe what?"

But Pavel only shook his head. He was too loyal, Marta thought. An optimist. Even with what he'd just learned about his wife, it was still in his nature to give people the benefit of the doubt. Marta admired this, as she admired so much about him.

"I met a man who was in Dachau," Pavel said instead. "The rumours are true."

Marta set her cup down on her saucer. The china made a small tinkling sound.

"Dachau. The camp," Pavel said.

"There's sugar," Marta said, for she'd heard enough about camps in the past weeks to last her a lifetime. Nobody seemed to know exactly what went on in them, and she couldn't help but picture the row of little fishing cabins she'd once seen in a sporting magazine. But she knew that the truth was something more ominous. She wanted to speak about something else, but Pavel wouldn't be dissuaded. "The man I know who was in Dachau. He's a Sudeten Jew." He looked at her. "Like us," he said. He paused. "Like me," he corrected, and looked away.

"What did he say?" Marta asked. "About the camp."

"He wouldn't say anything. Nothing of substance." Pavel scratched his forehead and looked up at the chandelier. "He was released under oath."

"But they let him out?"

"Business reasons, probably. His children are still in there. They know he won't talk. They've got hostages."

"So he wouldn't say anything?"

"Only that he's seen the worst."

They were quiet then. Marta wondered what exactly *the worst* might mean.

Pavel cracked his knuckles. "I was wrong?" he asked. "About all of this? Getting out, being Jewish? Anneliese was right and I was wrong?" He was looking at Marta, wide-eyed. "My life's fallen apart. Should I have seen it coming?" he asked.

Something rose up then in Marta, a fierce desire to protect, not unlike what she'd felt at the train station months earlier, when the Ackerman boy had hit Pepik with the stone.

"You were brave," she said gently. "You did what you thought was best."

Pavel laid his hand palm down on the desk.

"I did," he said forcefully. "I did do what I thought was best. I simply could not have imagined . . ." His words were loud, and then quiet again. "I miss my son," he whispered, his voice hoarse.

Marta looked up at Pavel. She covered his hand with her own.

A rumour was going around that Adolf Hitler was compiling a list of all the Jews. Strange as it was, the image had weight to it in Marta's imagination: a long piece of paper stuck in an Underwood typewriter, unscrolling down the back of a card table, across a polished office floor, and out into the reaches of eternity.

Pavel in the end had registered his assets, so if such a list existed he was on it.

"But what would the Nazis do with that list?" Marta ventured.

Pavel looked up. He didn't answer.

It was August 1939. The only thing anyone talked about was what would happen when the Germans invaded Poland. Marta remembered Anneliese's words: *Just wait a bit longer. Something will happen.* But nothing did. Marta waited for Mrs. Bauer to explain, to reveal the exact way in which officer Axmann would come to the rescue. Anneliese had been promised that her officer would help. If Axmann had been sincere, though, he had obviously come up short. No visas materialized, no affidavits — her man had failed her. There was nothing Anneliese could say, so she didn't defend herself; it was useless. Pavel would never believe her.

Marta understood that Anneliese really had been trying to save them, that a beautiful woman had very few options. She'd been trying in the best way she knew how. But still the Bauers' empire crumbled under Marta's eyes. There would never be peace in their time.

Pavel was cordial with his wife, as though she were a houseguest. In another era, Marta thought, they might have kept up more of a pretense, fooling those around them into thinking that their marriage was still solid. But now, with the country falling to pieces and their only son lost to them, there was no point. The stakes of their life together had been torn up. Anneliese stayed in the bedroom smoking cigarettes and painting her face. Pavel moved his things into the guest room: his cotton nightshirts, his robe. His shirts loose and empty on their hangers like the shirts of men gone to their execution.

One evening he took Marta for a stroll.

"What about the curfew?"

"What about it?" Pavel said.

They avoided Vinohradská Square, sticking to the side streets, the leafy avenues and parks. Marta saw that Pavel had been holding back for the sake of appearances. But now that he knew his wife had strayed, he would permit himself the same.

"It's not as though I've behaved perfectly," Marta said. But Pavel only laughed. "You couldn't be more perfect if you tried."

Pavel still didn't know about the grave mistakes she'd made with Ernst, and Marta pretended that his love equalled forgiveness. She pushed back her unease about Anneliese at home alone, with nobody. Here, finally, was the acceptance Marta had longed for all her life. The love she'd so craved. She let Pavel guide her through the breezy evening under the full moon and told herself she had no choice, told herself she wasn't responsible for whatever had gone on between the Bauers. She knew this wasn't entirely right, but the truth was that something had been torn open inside her and something even more powerful released. Something swift and warm between herself and Pavel that she was helpless to resist.

Marta wanted to lay herself down in it. She had a very strong urge to submerge, to submit. Were there words for this feeling?

"I'm happy," she said.

It seemed improbable in the face of her guilt, in the face of what was happening all around them, but Pavel just squeezed her arm. "I'm glad."

He leaned over and touched her dimple with his nose.

"I'm ready," she said.

He eyed her.

"I'm sure."

He said, "Follow me."

～❧～

Max and Alžběta's flat was on the top floor of the building. Pavel led Marta up the staircase to the roof. She stepped on the heel of his shoe and he winced but didn't let go of her hand. When they got to the top there was a little door, like in a fairy tale: you could squeeze through it and come out in another world entirely.

They stood up on the top of the building; the air smelled like rubber, or asphalt, and the perfume from the magnolia blossoms was almost oppressive. Darkness had fallen; the flowers were huge and pink, like planets orbiting the blackness. From far away came the sound of a siren. The lights of Prague were spread out beneath them, and above them, the sky's fireflies. This was what they had been waiting for, this particular night, this place. Pavel took off his coat and Marta lay down on it without speaking.

There was no talk, no foreplay, and yet he was so gentle. He kneeled down and pulled up her dress; he pulled her stockings down as if he was unwrapping a most precious package. He looked at her lying there, exposed, with a kind of longing on his face that scared her. Then he undid his fly. She saw him for the first time, fully erect, above her. He knelt down with his pants still on and spread her legs and entered her.

It didn't hurt — not like it had with other men — or rather, the brief pain was more like unbearable pleasure. He covered her face in kisses. There had been so much waiting, so much building; he could not move swiftly enough now. He thrust into her again and again, as though he too was trying to absolve himself of something, or push himself into a future he couldn't imagine.

It was as if he'd opened up a part of her she hadn't known existed. Marta heard a low moan and realized the sound had come from her own mouth. Pavel was gathering her in, all the lost pieces, drawing them up to the surface of her skin. Every bit of her tingled; when she opened her eyes, it was as if she were flying through a field full of shimmering stars. They were whizzing past her in all directions, little explosions of colour and light, filling her eyes and her face and her mouth until she was full everywhere, until every part of her was glimmer and heat.

Marta herself was the star that Pavel wished on.

And me? I was the answer to their wish.

M Y NAME, AS I'VE TOLD YOU, IS ANNELIESE.
I didn't tell you?

Just Lisa, for short.

I don't know why my mother, Marta, chose to name me after Anneliese Bauer. After the woman who must have been, in some ways at least, her competition. Perhaps she felt guilty for the sins she'd committed against her. Or perhaps it was a gesture of love and respect towards someone who had just been deported to the east.

I have no reason to think that my mother was a betrayer, except for a slight tendency in that direction I have noted in myself.

I've taken some leaps in writing this tale. I've been fanciful, sure, as a writer is allowed to be. As she must be. And Pepik was a very generous collaborator. It was his idea for me to tell the story from Marta's perspective. To have Pavel choose Marta over Anneliese, letting our father's final love be for my mother, not his own. We were both aware that the opposite could have been true: that Pavel's affair with Marta might have been a one-time, meaningless tryst, a mere distraction in the midst of encroaching desperation.

After all, the Bauers had had two children together. The

infant from the photo, whom Pepik didn't remember, went to
the gas chambers too. There must not have been room left
for her on the children's transports, or else her parents did not
want to send such a young baby. I gave her a different death. It
was just wishful thinking.

Pepik's cousin Tomáš got out from Vienna but died in the
bombings in London.

Here are the few other things I do know for certain:

Pavel and Anneliese Bauer lived in a small town in Bohemia. Just after the Münich Agreement they relocated to
Prague. There was a cook in their employ whom they left
behind. They chose for some reason to bring the governess —
my mother — along with them.

There are documents showing that the Bauer family tried
to leave the country prior to the Ides of March, just before
the Nazis entered Prague. I don't know what exactly happened
that day, only that they did not make it out.

Pavel and Marta had sex at least once. The proof — what is
it they say? — is in the pudding.

The next, and final, trace of my father Pavel's existence is
the date he was deported to Auschwitz.

Ernst Anselm was a real man about whom a biography
has been written. He lived in Moravia and had a wife and two
teenaged daughters. A gentle man known especially for his
love of animals, he was personally responsible for the betrayal
of more than forty Jewish families. He seems to have made a
sport of it: befriending them, engendering trust, and then, at
the eleventh hour, turning them in. It's a wonderful book, a
perceptive study of the darker side of human nature — with
which, in what are supposed to be my "golden years," I am

admittedly somewhat preoccupied. Ernst Anselm lived hours away from the Bauers, so it is unlikely that he knew them personally. He's included here only to further expose him. It's my own small way of holding him accountable.

As for me, I've told you what I set out to tell you. My mother, Marta, died when I was very young, and the intervening time, between that terrible event and my arrival as a young adult in Canada, is nobody else's business. You might think it strange, given that I've spent my entire professional life hearing and recording other people's stories, that I have chosen to withhold the bulk of my own. Well, I've observed that there is healing in the telling, but there is also something that gets lost. The past is gone, and we cannot get it back. In setting it down in one particular way, the other versions slip through the cracks. All the possibilities lost to the sands of time.

One thing I remember vividly: when I gave Pepik his mother's diamond watch, he got a particular look in his eye. It was as though time had begun again, as though for *him* it was not too late.

I don't know much about Pepik's childhood. He himself remembered very little about his life in Prague or about the journey that brought him from Scotland to here. By the time I found the letters in the archive in Glasgow, both of the Millings were dead. There is no official record of their ever having a son of their own; it was common enough for a childless couple to sign up to be foster parents. But there is still the question of the letter from Pavel, of the Arthur referred to within.

Another thing we never figured out is why Pepik was moved to the orphanage. This again, unfortunately, was far from uncommon. It was wartime, money was scarce, people were displaced for all sorts of reasons. The memories Pepik had of the orphanage were few and far between, but they were clear, he said, even vivid. It is to protect his privacy that I have not included them here.

What I'm telling you — haltingly, I realize — is that this is just one way it might have happened. Nothing is certain, save what meets us at the end. After Pepik died I learned the Mourner's Kaddish, the prayer for the dead. It doesn't mention death but praises God and gives thanks. I marvel at this, at the faith woven into its words. I'm an old woman now and I can't help but wonder. Who will pray for me when I'm gone?

I have tried, all these years, to see their faces. Not the images frozen in photos but their *faces*, their gestures, who they were. I would give almost anything — I *would* give anything — for a single memory of my father. The way he held a pen, the backs of his hands. To summon the sound of his voice. And my mother — the smell of her hair, damp after her bath; the weight of her arms pulling me in. In the end, though, all I have is a list of names and dates. And so I inscribe them here, the family I never knew. It might seem morose to end with the dead, but I am thinking of posterity. I don't have to tell you the reason for this. Soon there'll be nobody left to remember.

Rosa (Berman) Bauer 1885 – 1943
Pavel Bauer 1907 – 1943
Marta Meuller 1915 – 1946
Anneliese (Bondy) Bauer 1912 – 1943
Eliza Bauer 1939 – 1942
Alžběta (Bondy) Stein 1914 – 1943
Max Stein 1890 – 1943
Eva Stein 1937 – 1943
Vera Stein 1934 – 1943
Misha Bauer 1905 – 1943
Lore (Leverton) Bauer 1910 – 1943
Tomáš Bauer 1935 – 1941

⁓◉⁓

Joseph (Pepik) Bauer 1933 – 2008
Anneliese (Meuller) Bauer 1940 –

THE TRAIN OF MEMORY SLEEPS ON ITS TRACKS. At night, in the station, the shadows gather around it, reaching out to touch its cool black sides. The train stretches back, far out of eyesight. Where it comes from is anyone's guess.

At dawn the ghosts retreat, take their place as shadows in the corners of the lofty-domed station. The train sighs on its tracks, a traveller hoisting very heavy bags. We roll over in our beds; we cough, stretch a little; the train of memory starts to move forward. Slowly at first, but gathering speed. The landscape drifts by like the last wisps of a dream. In the early morning hours the train begins to move into the opposite of memory. Into a future time when someone will look back at us now, wondering what our days were like and why we did the things we did. Or why we did not act, as the case might equally be.

Someone will be unable to make our lives make sense.

The train has no answers, only forward momentum. We open our eyes; it is moving very quickly now. Moving always ahead. It never arrives.

ACKNOWLEDGEMENTS

Many thanks to:

The Canada Council for the Arts
The Ontario Arts Council
The Toronto Arts Council
The Hadassah–Brandeis Institute

The EU's Culture Programme and the Odyssey Program 2007
Le Réseau Européen des Centres Culturels de Rencontre
IMEC's Abbaye d'Ardenne in Normandy, France
Schloss Bröllin in Pasewalk, Germany
The Milkwood Artist Residence in Cesky Krumlov, Czech Republic

Michael Crummey
Steven Heighton
Lucy Pick
Hanna Spencer

Sarah MacLachlan and everyone at House of Anansi Press
Mary-Anne Harrington at Headline in the UK
Claire Wachtel at HarperCollins in the US

Jacqueline Smit at Orlando / AW Bruna in the Netherlands
Ornella Robbiati at Frassinelli / Sperling & Kupfer in Italy
Zoë Waldie at Rogers, Coleridge, and White
Anne McDermid, Martha Magor Webb, and Monica Pacheco
The New Quarterly

I read extensively on the Kindertransport and on the lives of the
Czech Jews around the time of the Munich agreement. While
my sources in their entirety are too numerous to mention here,
I would like to acknowledge the following: *The Jews of Bohemia
& Moravia: A Historical Reader*, edited by Wilma Iggers; *Letters
from Prague 1939–1941*, edited by Raya Czerner Shapiro and
Helga Czerner Weinberg; *Hanna's Diary 1938–1941* by Hanna
Spencer; *Pearls of Childhood* by Vera Gissing; and *Into the Arms
of Strangers: Stories of the Kindertransport* by Mark Jonathan
Harris and Deborah Oppenheimer.

Tommy Berman, one of the original Kindertransport children,
shared with me his memoirs, as well as the letters written from
his birth parents in Czechoslovakia to his adoptive parents
in Scotland. While the story here is not his, he provided the
inspiration.

Many thanks, as always, to Thomas, Margot, and Emily Pick.
I would also, and most especially, like to thank my partner
Degan Davis, whose help on every level was invaluable, and
my wonderful editor Lynn Henry, who I had the pleasure of
working with for the third time. I couldn't be more grateful.

ABOUT THE AUTHOR

ALISON PICK was the 2002 Bronwen Wallace Award winner for the most promising writer under thirty-five in Canada. She has published two acclaimed volumes of poetry, and her writing has appeared widely in magazines, including *The Walrus*, *enRoute*, and *Toronto Life*. Her 2005 novel, *The Sweet Edge*, was a *Globe and Mail* Top 100 Book and was optioned for film. Currently on faculty at the Banff Centre for the Arts Wired Writing Studio, Alison Pick lives in Toronto with her family.